Helen Dickson was born and still lives in South Yorkshire, with her retired farm manager husband. Having moved out of the busy farmhouse where she raised their two sons, she now has more time to indulge in her favourite pastimes. She enjoys being outdoors, travelling, reading and music. An incurable romantic, she writes for pleasure. It was a love of history that drove her to writing historical fiction.

PENNILESS UNTIL THE EARL'S PROPOSAL

Helen Dickson

MILLS & BOON

First published in Great Britain 2024
by Mills & Boon, an imprint of HarperCollins*Publishers* Ltd,
1 London Bridge Street, London, SE1 9GF

www.harpercollins.co.uk

HarperCollins*Publishers*, Macken House, 39/40 Mayor Street Upper,
Dublin 1, D01 C9W8, Ireland

ISBN: 978-0-263-32088-6

09/24

MIX
Paper | Supporting
responsible forestry
FSC
www.fsc.org   FSC™ C007454

This book contains FSC™ certified paper and other controlled sources to ensure responsible forest management.

For more information visit www.harpercollins.co.uk/green.

Printed and Bound in the UK using 100% Renewable Electricity at CPI Group (UK) Ltd, Croydon, CR0 4YY

Chapter One

It was a glorious May day. The sun had risen out of a broad expanse of opal mist, and scraps of cloud floated like spun gauze in the sky. Oak, ash, sycamore, cherry and lilac trees were bursting into full flower, and trumpet-headed daffodils and clusters of primroses were scattered throughout the park that belonged to the Sinclair family of Endcliffe House.

This was the day Lady Juliet Sinclair first set eyes on Marcus Cardell, the younger brother of the Earl of Cranswick. Seated in the trap, she slowed her pony to a more sedate trot. The park stretched out in shades of green and brown and grey. Stabs of sunlight between the clouds edged the colours in bright gilding. For those few short minutes as she travelled along, there was just her and her pony—no duties, no expectations, just a wonderful forgetfulness of all the trials and duties that awaited her back at Endcliffe House.

Juliet had set out to take Mrs Ruskin some freshly baked bread. With three children to feed and her husband unable to find employment, Rose Ruskin struggled daily to give them sustenance. A movement to her right caught her attention. She glimpsed a rider and horse galloping with exhilaration some distance away. Halting the pony, she paused to watch with interest the sheer might of the large bay horse and the energy of the claret-jacketed rider, seemingly at one with his mount. Directing her pony beneath some sheltering trees, she continued to watch until he had disappeared from sight.

With a flick of the reins, Juliet continued on her way, having a strong inkling as to the identity of the rider. He belonged to the gentry, that was for sure. She had heard that Marcus Cardell had taken up residence at Mulberry Hall, a property passed on to him by his mother, the dowager Countess of Cranswick. The house had been occupied by the Countess's widowed brother, Lord John Sutherland, the Earl of Ashleigh, who had died when he had taken a tumble from his horse during a hunt two years back. Without offspring, the property had passed to his sister, whose eldest son was to inherit the Cardell ancestral estate in Sussex. The dowager countess handed over Mulberry Hall to her second son, Marcus Cardell, a military man. The title went with it, and Marcus Cardell had become Lord Cardell, the Earl of Ashleigh. Juliet assumed the gentleman she had seen must be him.

Rose Ruskin, a small brown-haired woman in her thirties, welcomed her warmly and invited her inside her spotlessly clean cottage. Juliet placed the basket of bread with the addition of some cold meats on the table, which was immediately scrutinised and exclaimed over by her three young daughters with great excitement.

'Thank you, Lady Juliet,' Rose said, gently shoving her daughters aside. 'I am pleased to see you, and I am always grateful for the food you bring. Things are—difficult just now, with Joe unable to find work.'

'I know that, Rose, and I like to think what I bring alleviates the difficulties you face. When my brother decides to come home, I will try and persuade him to find your husband some kind of employment on the estate.'

'I can't pretend that I won't be pleased if you could do that. Joe's at his wit's end not knowing where to turn next—and now he's been accused of poaching on the Mulberry Hall estate. I fear he is to be arrested at any time.'

'And has he, Rose? Is there any truth in what he is accused of?'

Rose lifted her chin, and her voice when she spoke was adamant. 'No, there is not. My Joe knows the punishment for poaching. He's a proud man and knows it's more than his life is worth to steal from another man's property.'

'That's just as I thought.' Juliet knew Joe Ruskin as a fine, upstanding and honest man, and she could not imagine him doing anything that was against the law. 'Try not to worry, Rose. I will do what I can. I promise.' Stepping outside, she was stopped in her tracks when she came face to face with the gentleman she had seen riding through the park striding across the yard, having tethered his horse to the gatepost. He presented a dark, forbidding figure, his grey breeches moulding to his muscular legs and thighs, his claret coat fitting his physique without a crease. His white shirt was open at his tanned throat, and his hair was as black as a panther's pelt.

'Can I be of help, sir?'

He looked at Juliet with cool disdain, his eyes, as they passed over her, condescending. 'I am here to speak with Mrs Ruskin. It concerns her husband.'

Juliet was unsure whether to take this as information or an instruction to move out of the way. There was an authority and assuredness of his own infallibility in his look and his manner that she did not like. She thought she had never seen such a dark and dangerous face in her life. His eyes were light blue to be almost silver, glittering beneath scowling dark brows. His nose was straight and haughty, and those hooded eyes with their thick lashes were mesmerising. They seemed to glow, seemed to promise future delights. He exuded sensuality and animal magnetism, and she could well imagine that women would vie for his attention.

'Mrs Ruskin is inside. I do so hope you don't bring bad news, sir.'

He glanced at her and looked away again, as if she were a person of no consequence. 'And you are?'

'Juliet Sinclair,' she answered amiably, though it almost choked her to be polite in the face of so much rudeness.

'Well, Miss Sinclair—'

'*Lady* Juliet Sinclair.'

This caught his attention and he looked at her again, one dark brow cocked.'

'My, my,' he remarked with an underlying sarcasm. 'This just gets better and better. You are a relation of Richard Sinclair?'

'He is my brother.'

'Yes, of course he is. I remember meeting him in the long and distant past when I visited my aunt at Mulberry Hall. On the demise of your father, he is now Earl of Endcliffe, I believe.'

'Yes, he is.'

'Of Endcliffe House—although I hear he spends most of his time in London, squandering his time at the card tables, while the running of his estate is left to his steward. His tenants feel at liberty to poach game on my estate—while, it would appear, his sister plays lady bountiful,' he said, eyeing the basket on the table, visible through the open doorway.'

Juliet's face was a mask of indignation, her hands clenched, but when she spoke, she kept her anger in check, knowing she had to placate this insufferably arrogant lord if she was to plead Joe's case and keep him out of the lock-up to await the magistrate's pleasure.

'If that is how you see me, then, yes, that is what I am. I do what I can, Lord Cardell.'

'I do not recall introducing myself, yet you know who I am.'

'You accused Mr Ruskin of poaching game on your estate, sir, so I assume you must be Lord Cardell.'

'How perceptive you are, Lady Juliet.' He looked at her hard for a moment longer before turning his attention to Mrs Ruskin, his gaze resting briefly on the three children standing as stiff as little soldiers in a row, their eyes wide and their mouths agape with fear in the face of this new threat in the shape of the all-powerful Lord Cardell to their young lives.

Juliet felt anger rising inside her on seeing the confusion and fear on the children's young faces. Lord Cardell approached Mrs Ruskin.

'May I speak with you, Mrs Ruskin?'

Rose bobbed an awkward curtsy. 'You may, sir. Please step inside—but if it's Joe you want to speak to, he isn't here just now.'

'That's unfortunate,' he said, stepping over the threshold into the kitchen. 'Have you any idea as to his whereabouts? Apparently, he was seen by one of my keepers running off, having bagged a couple of hares.'

'That would not be possible,' Juliet said, quick to contradict him.

'Oh?' he said, turning his head to look at her once more. 'And you would know that? Why not, pray? You are accusing my keeper of lying, are you, Lady Juliet?'

'I'm afraid I am, Lord Cardell,' she replied, facing him squarely. 'You see, Mr Ruskin lost a leg in the Peninsular War. I imagine it is rather difficult trying to run on a wooden leg, wouldn't you agree? So, either you have a very slow-moving keeper, sir, or he is lying. Which is it to be?'

Lord Cardell's gaze remained fixed on her while he digested this piece of information and then looked back at Mrs Ruskin, clutching her youngest child to her skirts. 'Lost a leg, you say?'

'No, I say,' Juliet countered firmly. 'Mr Ruskin has been unable to find work due to his disability.'

'He is your tenant, Lady Juliet. If, as you say, Mr Ruskin's disability has prevented him finding work—'

'Not prevented, Lord Cardell. He has tried. No one will employ him.'

'Then as an act of generosity, could you not find some employment on your estate to suit his disability?'

Furiously, Juliet found her cheeks turning red. How she would like to tell this arrogant lord to go to the devil and mind his own business, but it would do Joe no good in the long run if she were to lose her temper. One of the girls had picked up on the mood inside the room and started to cry and shrank into the girl next to her.

'Don't cry, Mary,' Juliet said gently. 'Everything will be all right. I'm sure Lord Cardell doesn't mean any harm to come to your father, and that it's all one big misunderstanding.'

'It most certainly is not,' Lord Cardell stated coldly.

Juliet glared at him. 'Do you have to do this in front of the children?' she remarked haughtily. 'Can you not see that your very tone and accusation against their father frightens them?' She saw his shoulders stiffen and his eyes sliced over her. She could almost feel the effort he was exerting to keep his anger under control. The man had a ramrod posture and an aura of exacting discipline as he irritatingly slapped his boots with the crop in his gloved hand. She glanced at it as it tapped out a rhythm. 'And do you have to do that? You act as if you are about to set about us all with your crop for some misdemeanour reported to you by your incompetent keeper without knowing the true facts.'

'Might I remind you that neither do you, Lady Juliet.'

'No, I do not, but unlike you—who was so quick to jump to conclusions and think the worst of Mr Ruskin, I am willing to give both men the benefit of the doubt until I have been made aware of them.'

Lord Cardell returned her gaze steadily, studying her as though she were some strange creature he had just uncovered. At least six feet four inches tall and with amazingly arresting light blue eyes he was a strikingly handsome man. Rugged strength was carved into every feature of his bronzed face, from his straight dark brows and nose to his firm and sensually moulded lips to the square, arrogant jut of his chin. To Juliet at that moment, he was also formidable, every line of his face set with disapproval.

Turning her back on him, Juliet settled her attention on the quietly weeping child. 'Hush now, Mary. Lord Cardell will do you no harm—is that not so, Lord Cardell?' she said, hoping for confirmation without looking at him.

'Of course not. Don't be ridiculous.' Looking at Mrs Ruskin, his expression softened slightly. 'I apologise if my coming here has upset your daughters. That was not my intention. They are children—I have a daughter of my own, and I would not dream of harming her or frightening her in any way.'

'Of course not, Lord Cardell, but they are sensitive souls. Anything that is said against Joe distresses them,' said Rose.

'Precisely,' Juliet said, 'and for that reason alone you should have more control over your temper.'

'Then I will be on my way before I cause more upset.' With a nod to Rose he went outside.

Juliet looked at the weeping child. 'Come, Mary,' she said as Lord Cardell strolled across the yard with a loose, confident stride, looking as though he owned the place. 'Dry your tears. Lord Cardell did not mean to frighten you.'

Her words seemed to calm the child, not because she was able to believe them but because of the unselfish confidence of the lady uttering them. Raising her head, she smiled at Juliet, but her shoulders remained drooped in dejection. Juliet fished a handkerchief out of her pocket and went to the unhappy girl. 'Here, let me wipe your face.' Gently she dabbed at the cheeks of the child, who was looking up at her with solemn brown eyes that reminded Juliet of a wounded puppy.

Rose stepped forward and put her arm about her distressed daughter. 'Don't worry about Mary, Lady Juliet. She cries all the time since Joe came home without a leg. She'll get over it given time.'

Juliet looked at Rose and smiled, wishing she could dispel the unhappiness and the fear she felt for her husband from her eyes. 'I'm sure she will—as sure as I am that everything will work out, Rose. Tell Joe to come and see me when he comes home and we'll see what is to be done about this poaching business. I don't believe it of him for one minute—and I think Lord Cardell will realise his mistake of listening to his keeper without proof of Joe's guilt.'

Without looking in Lord Cardell's direction, where he was trying to calm his restless mount that was pawing at the ground, eager to be on its way, she walked to where she had left her pony and trap, surprised when he followed her, feeling his penetrating eyes on her all the time. She turned to face him.

'Have you had an edifying look at me, Lord Cardell?'

'Not quite. It is to my advantage that I get to know who my neighbours are. I hope this minor issue with your tenant is not going to affect neighbourly relations between us.'

'As to that, we shall have to wait and see,' Juliet replied tightly, finding it difficult to show leniency towards him in light of what had just occurred. 'Where Mrs Ruskin is concerned, having her husband accused of poaching is far from being a minor issue. What are you? Some kind of monster? The Ruskins are gentle people, living their lives and troubling no one. And suddenly you come along and threaten to have Mrs Ruskin's husband and the father of those children arrested, thrown into jail and transported to goodness knows where.'

'Come now, that's a bit extreme, don't you think?'

'No, it is not. That's what happens to anyone caught poaching. How could you do that?'

'I can and I will. I cannot have anyone poaching my game. If he is indeed guilty of the offence and is seen to get away with it, it will send out the wrong message, and I will have all and sundry doing the same. I will not have it.'

'I can see that,' she retorted scathingly. 'You really are the most ill-mannered, inconsiderate man I have ever encountered, Lord Cardell,' Juliet upbraided him coldly. 'My mother always told me that such an outward display of temperamental frustration as you have just shown is regarded as a sign of bad breeding.'

His eyes narrowed and his lips tightened. 'Your mother was probably right, and I daresay I am what you accuse me of being. It goes with the title.'

Juliet was in no mood to be mocked, and she could see by the gleam in his eyes that he was doing exactly that. 'Then with you as an example, I can only hope that you are the last titled Englishman I shall ever meet.'

'As the sister of an earl, I would very much doubt that. And since we are bandying words, Lady Juliet, you really are the most infuriatingly outspoken woman I have ever met.'

Raising her head, she fixed him with a level gaze. 'I agree, I am outspoken—be it a failing or a blessing, I care not one whit. I dare say a lot of things to a man who scares children half to death,' she said, and with good reason, for the terror she had felt as a child locked in a dark cupboard for hours on end by this particular gentleman she had not forgotten—although in his arrogance he would have no recollection of the fact, and she would not humiliate herself by reminding him of the incident. She would not forgive him that act of cruelty. 'I imagine you also terrify each and every one of your servants so they creep about in fear of you, and that your whole house vibrates with tension that springs from you, Lord Cardell. By the look on your face, I would wager I have hit a sore spot. Please don't disappoint me by holding your temper. I would hate to see you explode with the effort.'

'Believe me, Lady Juliet, you would not want to see me explode. I have a temper, I admit it, when I am driven to it. And how I run my household and treat my servants concerns only myself.'

'Be that as it may,' she said with a defiant upward tilt to her chin, her voice edged with high indignation, 'you still have no proof of Joe Ruskin's guilt. Besides, innocent or guilty, you have no standing here. While my brother is absent, I have the authority on this estate.'

Lord Cardell cocked an arrogant brow. 'And you are sure of that are you, Lady Juliet?' Her expression told him that she wasn't. 'We will have to wait and see what the law has to say about that. Now I must be away. I have an appointment to keep and I am already late.'

Turning from her, he mounted his horse with an athletic grace that did not surprise her in the slightest. She would have expected nothing less from this arrogant lord.

'You will find the shortest route back to Mulberry Hall is to ride through the park which belongs to my brother, Lord Cardell. Although if you do so, I must warn you that you could be apprehended for trespassing. But worry not,' she said, when his expression became one of surprise. 'I am sure Richard would show you more tolerance and leniency than you have just shown to Mrs Ruskin.' She switched her attention to his mount pawing its hooves on the ground, clearly impatient to be off. 'You seem to be having difficulty controlling your horse, sir. Is it not time you taught it who is master?'

'I assure you he knows who is his master.' He looked at her closely. 'What a firebrand you are, Lady Juliet Sinclair. It appears to me that you are in need of some mastering yourself. Should your brother fail to do so, I would be honoured to put myself forward. Teaching a lovely young female how to behave like a lady should be—interesting. I would use the same tactics as I would at taming a horse. I would soon have you doing my bidding and swooning at my feet.'

His hollow chuckle held a note of mockery. A flush of anger spread to the delicate tips of her ears. 'Why, you conceited, unmitigated cad…'

'I get the gist,' he said, cutting her short with a low laugh, noting the icy fire that smouldered in her deep amber-coloured eyes.

Suddenly he seemed to relax in the saddle and his lips curved into a smile, taking Juliet by surprise as she stared at him. It was the most engaging smile she had ever seen, the smile of a man who finds the whole world a delightful place to be. It was a smile that lit his eyes and caused her heart to flutter.

'You are arrogant if you believe I would ever swoon at your feet. Thank God I am not afflicted by such weakness.' She stepped away from him and his horse, finding his closeness and the way he towered over her a little intimidating. 'Be on your way, sir.'

Not yet ready to be dismissed, he hesitated. 'At least allow me to escort you to Endcliffe House.'

Her chilled contempt met him face to face. She stepped back. 'I am quite capable of taking myself home. Go away and take that vicious beast with you,' she snapped, glancing irately at the bay stallion that had begun to snort and stamp impatiently, its vigorous temperament reminding her so very much of its master.

'Aren't you taking a risk? You might be set upon by footpads or worse. Anything could happen to a woman travelling alone.'

'It just did, and I am of the opinion that I'm in less danger of being set upon by footpads than I am from you. At least they may have better manners.' Turning her back on him, she hoisted herself up into the trap, taking up the reins.

He sighed, feigning disappointment, slowly shaking his head. 'Such ingratitude.'

'Ingratitude?' she gasped. '*You* call *me* ungrateful after the distress you have caused Mrs Ruskin by accusing her husband of poaching your rabbits?'

His eyes gleamed with amusement. 'Have it your way. You know, Lady Juliet, I cannot believe that here we are crossing swords in this undignified manner, two sensible people arguing about rabbits. If there has been a misunderstanding, then I will apologise to Mrs Ruskin and her husband most sincerely. Rest assured, I shall look into the matter immediately.' He pulled on the reins and turned his restless horse about. 'I sincerely hope that when next we meet, this unpleasant issue will have blown over and we behave as acquaintances should. I am certain that as neighbours, we are going to get on famously.'

'Really? You are sure of yourself, sir—and conceited if nothing else.'

Juliet's voice held a note of reproof that finally penetrated Lord Cardell's intensity. He gave her a startled glance, then a disarming smile and impudent honesty.

'Not always. Only when I see a lovely young woman I would like to know better.'

'I see.' Juliet lifted a disapproving brow. 'And you hope to make a good impression, I presume.'

'It had occurred to me.'

'Then you will be disappointed that you have not, sir.'

'So, am I to understand that calling on your brother is out of the question?'

'That's right—at least not until your manners improve. Good day to you.'

'And good day to you too, Lady Juliet.'

He kicked his horse into motion. His laughter drifted back to her, his mockery infuriating her yet further. Urging her pony on she glared after his retreating figure, muttering all kinds of threats under her breath. She had never met a man who had irritated her as he had just done, and it chafed her sorely to consider his flawless success.

Riding away, Marcus halted his horse and turned and looked back. He watched with a brooding attentiveness in his eyes and not without a good deal of interest as Lady Juliet Sinclair travelled in the opposite direction towards Endcliffe House. Hostility from ladies in her position was not something he had encountered before. Most young ladies were more than eager to be amiable to him—although perhaps she'd had good reason not to be in her defence of Joe Ruskin. He was, after all, one of her brother's tenants and Lady Juliet was convinced of his innocence.

Perhaps she was right and his accusation had perhaps been a little hasty, but having been most put out on receiving a letter from his mother forbidding him to bring Adele, his six-year-old daughter who was a sensitive child, to Mulberry Hall until he was more settled and had put his mind to finding himself a wife and mother for his daughter. Adele would remain with her in London for the time being or at the Cardell estate in Sussex.

Continuing his journey back to Mulberry Hall, he became thoughtful. He'd spent a little time in London before coming to Surrey. As soon as word got round of his return, invitations to social events had rained down on him. Before his marriage, his potent attraction to women had been a topic of much scintillating feminine gossip, but marriage and his military career had taken him out of the public eye. Now he was back, a widower and about to take up residence at the fabulous Mulberry Hall estate—a draw for any aristocratic family with a bevy of unmarried daughters.

But age and his experiences in Spain had changed him. Now he possessed a haughty reserve that was not always inviting and set him apart from others in society. He was always careful to choose a mistress whose company he enjoyed. She had to be intelligent and sophisticated, who would not mistake lovemaking and desire with love, and moreover, she had to be a woman who made no demands and expected no promises.

He missed his military life and his fellow soldiers. Since arriving at the house, he realised he would have to give himself up to the day-to-day running of the estate. He had called in the bailiffs to give an account of their management, accounts gone in to, acres of land ridden over and meetings with his tenant farmers. Alone in his elegant house, he restlessly wandered from room to room, unable to escape the throbbing emptiness and his longing to make it a family home once more.

His mother was right. Now he was home he must put his mind to remarrying, his wife, Elizabeth, having died giving birth to Adele. He had been fond of Elizabeth and had mourned her passing, but he had not loved her in the romantic sense. Desire, he understood. It was a more honest emotion. Passion and desire were easily appeased—fleeting—and easily doused. When he chose a woman to be his wife, he would be careful to choose a woman from a good family, whose company he enjoyed. But the most important thing of all was that she would be a good mother to his daughter. Adele was his priority. This was non-negotiable.

With Mulberry Hall within his sights, Lady Juliet drifted back into his thoughts, and a faint sensual smile quirked his lips. Her features had an aristocratic cast to them, and she had an air of good breeding. She had a face of unforgettable beauty, with high delicately moulded cheekbones, a perfect nose and generous lips. It was a strong face but essentially feminine. She had the kind of looks which few men failed to respond to with interest and some women with envy. She had worn a bonnet, but what he had seen of her hair, it was the colour of burnished gold. She was vibrant, vital and bold, but there was also about her a mysterious, almost sweet and gentle allure. Her form was slender and appealing. He smiled, looking forward to their next meeting, for as close neighbours, it was inevitable that their paths would cross in the future.

As for this matter concerning Joe Ruskin, maybe his keeper had been mistaken after all. He would look into the matter.

As Juliet travelled the well-worn path back to Endcliffe House, she was determined to cast Lord Cardell from her mind. The man was obnoxious, she decided, and not worth thinking about, although he was terribly handsome—she would grant him that. There was also an uncompromising authority in the set of his jaw and an arrogance in the tilt of his head that was not to her liking. But considering the remarks he had made regarding her brother, there was more than a ring of truth in what he had said. She prayed constantly that Richard would exchange the bustle of London for the grace of Endcliffe House. Since the death of their parents, their mother just one year before their father, Juliet had learned not to expect any form of duty from her brother, who was wrapped up in his own self-indulgent world of gambling and all the pleasures London had to offer.

At twenty-one years old Juliet was younger than Richard by three years, but she had always been the sensible, practical one, while he was somewhat reckless and foolhardy and liked to live life to the full and in comfort. She had soon learned that where Richard was concerned, her own wishes were not to be consulted, and she was forced by circumstances to live in genteel poverty, to be the keeper of Endcliffe House and to put all her youthful energies and her loneliness into their home, where she was responsible for all the household matters and the staff—of which only a handful of the old retainers remained.

On Richard's last visit to their home, she had confronted him, begged him, as she had done countless times in the past, to give up his reckless, expensive way of life and return to live in Surrey, for if he did not heed their situation, then ruination would soon be knocking at the door.

Whenever she had broached the subject, Richard was at once defensive and would become angry, finding her persistence to try to reform him extremely irritating. London, with its splendour and corruption, its squalor and excitement, thrilled and entertained him in a way his provincial home in Surrey had never done. His taste for pleasure and his capacity for enjoyment lifted his spirits in the restless, teeming city.

But enough was enough. After his last visit to Endcliffe House, discovering that the only valuables remaining in the house—their mother's jewels—had disappeared, and knowing Richard must have taken them, and knowing exactly what he intended to do with them—that he would sell them in order to pay for his gambling, she knew they could not carry on like this. An inexplicable weariness and pain lay heavy on her heart. If they had to sell her beloved home, it would tear her apart. She would fight tooth and nail to hold on to it.

Ever since their father had died, leaving them in dire straits, with Richard away in London, she had come up against so many obstacles and had almost worn herself out in the bargain. She was to travel to London shortly to attend a prior engagement. It would be the perfect opportunity to confront her brother. She would try again to make him see the error of his ways, but she did not hold out much hope of success.

As she neared Endcliffe House, she thought how different her life would have been had she married Thomas. The image of his handsome laughing face flashed before her. Everything about him had drawn him to her. She'd been young and with the naivety of a girl who'd had a sheltered, loving upbringing, and being a man from a family with great affluence and a proper lineage, Thomas had been the epitome of everything she wanted her future husband to be.

She remembered the first time they had met at a soiree in London. They had spent the entire evening in each other's company. They met on several occasions after that night. Her eyes would light up when he came into a room, and she would hang on his every word with a rapt expression on her face. He told her she was the most beautiful woman he had ever seen and that he had fallen in love with her the first time he'd laid eyes on her. She remembered the rapture she had felt when he had taken her in his arms and kissed her, then the blessed relief when he'd asked her to be his wife. Both families were in favour of the match, and she'd accepted him gladly, but her happiness led to heartache when, as a young commissioned military officer, he departed for the Peninsular with Wellington's army.

He'd left with the sun shining on his hair, standing with one hand on his sword in the attitude of a Greek god, appearing to Juliet unbearably heroic. They would have been married by now had he not been killed at the Battle of Albuera in Spain just a few months ago. She would never forget the day when the tragic news had come to her and all the pain and desolation that had come with it. Never had she believed she could feel such pain, such anguish that went deep—deeper than anything she had ever known.

His death had coincided with the death of her father, and with this, combined with the worry that they might lose the Endcliffe estate that had been in the Sinclair family for generations, she had continued to carry on. Richard had suggested she should seriously consider seeking an affluent man to marry to solve their problems. Even though she had a sense of responsibility towards Richard stronger than it should be, it was there and was an intrinsic part of her. But she was unwilling at this time to be made a sacrifice. It was one of the few times she had lapsed into self-pity. She would rather marry a man she had chosen than one forced on her.

Whatever the outcome, she was determined never

again to feel for any man the way she had for Thomas, that no man could ever take his place. She had hardened her heart, resolved that no man would ever breach it.

Chapter Two

It was a week after her encounter with Lord Cardell that found Juliet riding alone in the lush green water meadows, interlaced by a network of silvery streams off the winding river where moorhens and swans were gliding gracefully between the rushes and reeds. The day was hot and sultry, and on a day such as this, Juliet had only one purpose in mind. The small lake surrounded by trees was her own secret place, a place where, when things were bad, she could escape to. After making sure that she was quite alone, kicking off her shoes and removing her thin cotton day dress, she waded into the lake, the water bathing her flesh beneath her petticoat like a soothing cool balm.

Dipping below the surface of the warm, clear water she began to swim, stretching her body to its full length. It was a simple exercise, requiring little thought, although she was well aware that if she should be observed indulging in such outrageous behaviour, it would be considered unacceptable and her reputation would be in ruins. But now, with the sun on her back and in dire need of respite from the many problems that beset her and having no wish to marry in the foreseeable future, she thrust these thoughts away. Here she could be herself. It was her secret pleasure.

Only the subdued call of birds and the lazy drone of a browsing bee disturbed the silence of the woodland as Marcus rode slowly along the dim chequered path. He came out of the trees and on to the edge of the small lake. It basked in the benign warmth of the sun, and long tendrils of willow brushed the surface. Aware of the seclusion of this place, taking a moment to enjoy his surroundings, dismounting, he tethered his horse to the branch of a stout tree and strolled beside a slow, meandering stream, watching the clear water as it tumbled lazily over its rock bed.

The day was hot and the water looked cool and inviting. Resting his back against the trunk of a sturdy beech, he stood and gazed at the vista before him, beautiful and tranquil in its simplicity and natural state. The lake shone like glass beneath the sun and, momentarily dazzled, he failed to see the bobbing head in the centre of the lake until it came closer to the edge. When his eyes came to focus on it, it took a moment for him to register that someone was out there swimming. And it was a woman at that, for her long hair trailed behind her as she swam with strong, sure strokes.

Marcus continued to watch as she lifted herself effortlessly out of the water and began to wade back to the shore. She was too absorbed in wringing the water from her hair to notice him. That was when he realised the swimmer was none other than his neighbour, Lady Juliet Sinclair. As slender as a wand, her perfectly rounded breasts rose in two delectable white hemispheres above the lace of her petticoat. Saturated, it clung to her, outlining her body, her hips arching from her small waist, and the perfect shape of her legs. Her breathtaking beauty quickened his soul and stirred his mind with imaginings of what further loveliness lay concealed beneath her flimsy attire.

Marcus was riveted. Vibrant and vital, she had a freshness and a delightful simplicity that captured his attention. In those first dazzling moments, he acted as any hot-blooded male would, and all he could do was stare as a thrill of excitement ran through his veins. But Marcus Cardell was no ordinary male and he recovered at once.

Suddenly her back stiffened and she became still, like a young animal that has caught the scent of danger. She spun round and her gaze flew directly to where horse and rider stood. Eyes narrowed, with a proud lift to her head she waded out of the water and moved towards him, seemingly not in the least embarrassed at confronting him in her sodden petticoat. There was indignation in the thrust of her chin and anger in her eyes. Stopping a short distance away, her feet were luminously white on the green grass. How small and slender they were, like a child's, Marcus thought. Her eyes were heavily lashed and tilted, almost feral, a warm shade of amber, and her honey blond hair clung to her shoulders in long silken skeins. Something that had lain dormant for many years stirred inside him. There was something about her, the boldness in her eyes, the tilt of her head, that attracted him.

As immobile as a lizard, Juliet stood in front of her neighbour who was staring at her with an intensity she could feel, and inside her, something started to tremble, a tiny quiver of alarm that somehow managed to make itself felt despite her dislike of this man and the numbness inside her. He seemed to fill the space around her, his presence almost overwhelming. Her nerves vibrated. It was as though she were awaking from a long sleep, and she suddenly felt extremely vulnerable and exposed. She was determined not to let him see how his sudden appearance affected her.

'Lord Cardell! We meet again,' she said in a voice as calm as may be, her manner unwelcoming. 'I was unaware that I was being spied on.'

Lifting her chin haughtily, Juliet met his light blue

eyes that were observing her with frank interest—far too much interest, she thought as he scrutinised her with a thoroughness that made her feel more undressed than she already was. His gaze moved over her unabashedly. She stiffened with indignation. No man—not even Thomas—had looked at her in quite that way before. Her pride had been pricked, and after their disastrous meeting the day before, she was in no mood to forgive this impudent lord for being at hand when she was so scantily clad.

'I trust you've had an edifying look, Lord Cardell. Not satisfied with tracking down poachers, you also ride about the countryside on the lookout for defenceless ladies.'

White teeth gleamed in a reckless smile as Lord Cardell responded. She was like a kitten showing its claws. Again, his gaze slid from her moistened lips, following the line of her throat down to the tantalising orbs of flesh exposed to his view above her clinging wet petticoat.

'You? Defenceless? Now you do exaggerate. Something tells me you are afraid of no one.'

His voice was a lazy drawl, his manner calm, deliberate. His light blue eyes were cool, his wide, beautifully shaped mouth held in a stern line. As on their previous meeting, there was no warmth, no humour to soften those perfectly chiselled features. She sensed he was a hard man and that he could be utterly ruthless if the need arose. The skin was stretched tautly across his high cheekbones, and his rich dark hair was ruffled from his ride. He was wearing brown boots, snug tan breeches, and a thin lawn shirt beneath his dark green jacket.

His sudden appearance only seemed to exacerbate Juliet's temper. 'Have you nothing better to do with your time?' she said, going to where her dress was draped over a bush and beginning to pull it on over her sodden petticoat. Any other day she would have lain on the soft grass to allow her clothes to dry before doing so, but her impatience to be away from her neighbour was paramount to that.

'Since you are only recently ensconced at Mulberry Hall, I would have thought you had better things to do with your time.'

'I suppose I could find something to occupy me,' he replied easily, seemingly amused as she struggled to put on her dress, 'but I can't think of anything more pleasurable just now than looking at you. I was merely out riding. The day is too pleasant to remain indoors.'

'I see. Then it is time you consulted with your steward regarding the boundaries of your land, otherwise you would know that you are trespassing. This is private land.'

A slow appreciative smile worked its way across his face as his eyes raked her from head to toe once more and then came back to her furious eyes. 'I do apologise, but my crime, if that is what it is, was well worth it,' he said smoothly.

'My brother has been known to prosecute trespassers.'

'Is that so?' His eyebrows arched and his eyes gleamed with sardonic amusement, which seemed to infuriate her all the more as she sat on the ground and began pulling on her stockings.

'There are notices.'

'I'm afraid I didn't see them.'

'You would have—had you kept to the paths.'

'Forgive me, but it is not every day I come across a young woman cavorting nearly naked in a lake.'

Unashamed of her behaviour and resenting his inference, she threw back her shoulders and lifted her head haughtily. 'I was not cavorting. I was swimming—which I do quite often when I have the time. Besides, no one ever comes here, so it is quite safe for me to do so.'

'*I* came, Lady Juliet.' Stepping away from her, he gazed at his surroundings. 'These water meadows belong to your brother, is that right?'

'Yes. Why do you ask?'

'No reason.'

She glanced at him sharply. 'They are not for sale.'

'I didn't imagine for one moment that they were. Whenever I came to visit Mulberry Hall with my brother as boys, we used to come to the water meadows. This lake was one of our favourite spots to swim.'

Juliet looked at him and could envision a tall youth with shining black hair wading through the water. She smiled tightly, not feeling too generous towards him just then. She was still put out that he had forgotten all about their meeting when she was a child. Half her hair was damp and hanging limply about her shoulders. Her dress was rumpled and damp from her undergarments. She brushed the damp tendrils from her face and took a deep breath, willing herself to maintain some semblance of calm.

'And what else did you do when you came here?'

'The usual thing boys do—rode through the woods kicking up leaves, took off our boots and followed the stream all the way to where it joins up with the river. But most of all we used to daydream. Of course that was in the days when our families were friends as well as neighbours, and no one would dream of accusing the other of trespassing.'

'No, I don't suppose they would,' Juliet said, having tugged on her boots and impatient to get on home to remove her wet petticoat, which was most uncomfortable beneath her dress. 'However, times change. Nothing remains the same. Now if you will kindly step out of my way, I will leave you. Since you are familiar with the lake, you might like a swim,' she said on a note of sarcasm. 'You have my full permission to do so.'

Lord Cardell raised a sardonic brow at her tone and contemplated her snapping amber eyes. 'Thank you, but I will forgo the opportunity to do so today. That's quite a temper you have there.'

'Yes. It can be quite ferocious when I'm provoked.'

'Now, why would I want to do that?' he said smoothly, an almost lecherous smile tempting his lips. 'I would much rather we progress to something of a more intimate nature.'

Juliet eyed him warily, unconscious of the vision she presented with her clothes clinging to every delectable line of her body. He was far too close for her peace of mind and automatically she took a step back. His eyes mocked her cautious retreat, but he made no comment on it. 'What do you mean?'

'That I wouldn't mind finding out what it is like to kiss those sweet lips, although I have the distinct impression that would be stirring a volcano and that it would erupt in my face.'

All Juliet's wrath came rolling back and she faced him with the molten blaze in her eyes. 'Why, you conceited ass. Kiss you? Why on earth would I want to do that? I'd as soon kiss a mule.'

'I assure you that it wouldn't be nearly as much fun as kissing me,' he chuckled infuriatingly, the sound low and deep in his chest. 'A mule, being a sexless beast, wouldn't kiss you back.'

Juliet stared at his arrogant features, at the mocking light in his enigmatic eyes, realising that he really did want her to take the initiative and kiss him. Silently she cursed herself for being so stupid as to try to get the better of this man, who was way beyond her sphere in both age and experience.

Directing a glance of wry humour at her, Lord Cardell's eyes narrowed and he said, 'Tell me, Lady Juliet. Are you normally hostile to everyone you meet, or is it just me?'

Her chilled contempt met him face to face. 'It's just you.'

'Do you mind if I enquire as to why?'

'You can ask, but I'm not obliged to answer.'

'You have certainly none of your mother's good manners,' he remarked. 'As I recall, she was always a delight to be with.'

Juliet paled at his mention of her mother. He was quite right. Her mother had been goodness and patience personified, and no matter how hard Juliet had tried to model herself on her throughout the years, she had failed miserably. 'Thank you—yes, she was. My mother was quite exceptional. Now please excuse me,' she said, taking hold of her horse. 'I am not noted for my patience—which you will have observed.'

'You also have plenty of cheek, I'll say that,' he chuckled softly.

'Say what you like,' she retorted, her defiant chin elevated to a lofty angle. 'I do not care.'

'Hostile too. I don't usually encounter such hostility from young ladies.' He cocked a dubious brow. 'However, I find it hard to believe that your brother allows his sister to indulge in such wanton abandonment.'

Juliet tossed her head haughtily, stepped onto a log, hoisted herself up into the side-saddle and adjusted her skirts. 'What my brother does or thinks is none of your business. Now please go away. Not only are you a trespasser, you are offensive.'

'I apologise if that's how I seem to you, Lady Juliet,' he said, placing his hand on her horse's neck. 'But I have to say that you are the rudest, most impudent young woman I have ever come across, and I have every sympathy with your brother,' he told her calmly. 'And why your parents didn't take you in hand before their demise, I can't imagine. My father would have had you locked in your room with nothing to eat and drink but bread and water for a week.'

For an incredulous moment Juliet was speechless, then, forgetting her intention to ride away, she glared down into his far too handsome face, with authority and arrogance stamped all over it. That was the moment she decided he was detestable.

'Then I can only thank the Lord that he is not *my* father, who was more civilised. Now, kindly remove your hand from my horse and stop bothering me so that I can be on my way.'

Lord Cardell grinned affably and removed his hand and stepped back. 'I think I like bothering you, Lady Juliet, and I shall enjoy bothering you a good deal more before I'm done.' Inclining his head politely, his eyes doing one last quick sweep of her delectable body, he said, 'Good day,' and turned away to go to where he had left his horse.

Juliet rode back to the house, but suddenly the brightness of the day and the breeze held a bitter chill. What a dreadful, dreadful man their new neighbour was, although she had to admit that her manner towards him had been less than ladylike. Her mother would have been appalled with her for showing such rudeness to her neighbour, having held Lord Cardell's relatives, who had lived at Mulberry Hall previous to this new lord, in the highest regard. Juliet really should learn to guard her tongue, especially where this particular gentleman was concerned. Since they were neighbours, it was in both their interests to reach an amicable acquaintance.

And yet she could not stop her curiosity about him getting the better of her. Despite his self-assurance, she sensed a sadness about him, something frozen and withdrawn, and that he gave of himself sparingly. The only thing she knew about him was that he was a military man. She also knew he had been married and that he had a young daughter. His wife had died early in their marriage apparently. Juliet wondered about her, what she had been like. Did Lord Cardell still mourn her passing, and what kind of a relationship did he have with his daughter, having spent several years in Spain fighting the French with Wellington's army?

She was bemused by him and their meeting and prey to all the emotions churning inside her. She could appreciate his virile good looks, his seductive scamp's eyes and sensual mouth, but that was where it must end, she told herself severely. And yet, despite this, perhaps an apology would be in order on their next meeting. On that thought, she put Lord Cardell from her mind and concentrated on her forthcoming journey to London to confront her brother.

Marcus watched Lady Juliet go, a gleam of interest in his eyes. Aware of his worth and used to being much admired by the female sex, he did not know whether to be amused or insulted by her hostile attitude to him. One thing he did know was that he wanted to get to know her better, and her imperviousness only whetted his appetite. It roused the hunter within him. Having her resist was a novel occurrence for him. He was unable to remember a time when he had turned on his charm and a female had made it so plain that his advances were not desired.

A smile tempted his lips, anticipation stirring inside him. He was going to have to work hard to turn her resentment to desire—and he thought he was going to enjoy the chase immensely. But first he had to journey to West Sussex to see his daughter and to persuade his mother to let him bring her back with him to Mulberry Hall.

It was late when Marcus passed beneath the broken sign of the unwelcoming inn on his way back to London from West Sussex. Going to Cranswick Hall had been a wasted journey. His mother and Adele had left for London a day before he had arrived. They must have passed each other on the road.

The taproom was small and low-ceilinged, and if the hour had not been late, he would have travelled on to look for another. He was met by the nauseating reek of tobacco smoke and alcohol combined with the unappetising odour of cooked food. The tables were occupied by what he would only describe as a drunken rabble. Two soldiers in a similar state, in uniforms of scarlet coats and tight white breeches, clearly having seen much service and which were creased and unwashed, were obviously on their way home from the Peninsular War, their cocked hats and sabres on the bench beside them.

Marcus sat at a table away from them, and a young serving girl came to him. She was small and lacked the lusty sensuality of the other serving girls. He observed that she had caught the eye of one of the soldiers, who reached out to try to touch her as she moved past his table. His advances were unwelcome, and swiftly she darted away. As Marcus ordered food and a room for the night, her pretty young face beneath the starched white cap was scarlet with embarrassment and shame, and her large liquid-brown eyes held the same kind of fear he had seen in those of a frightened young doe facing death.

After he had eaten, he settled into the corner of his seat, slowly savouring his brandy, shutting out the coarse, drunken singing and shouting, and his thoughts turned to Lady Juliet Sinclair. In fact, he had thought of little else since leaving for West Sussex, and how bewitchingly lovely she had looked when he had come upon her in the water meadows.

He sat in deep reflection, sternly attacking his sentimental thoughts until they cowered in meek submission, but they refused to lie down. His attraction to Juliet Sinclair was disquieting—in fact, it was damned annoying. If he wanted an affair or diversion of any kind, he had a string of some of the most beautiful women in London to choose from, so why should he feel this insanely wild attraction to a woman he had met only twice?

Since their parting at the water meadows, he had tried to put her from his mind but failed miserably in his effort. He cursed with silent frustration, seized by a strong desire to call on her and cauterise his need by holding her close and clamping his lips on hers. Instead, he watched the flames in the hearth as they danced against the fireback and forced himself to think of his daughter. Under normal circumstances this was a simple matter, for nothing gave him greater pleasure than being with Adele, but slowly, a face with a pert, dimpled chin, a lovely and expressive mouth with soft, full lips, cheeks as flushed as a peach and thickly fringed amber velvety eyes crept unbidden into his mind—teasing him, tantalising him, laughing, beckoning him.

His attention was again drawn to the young serving girl, who was still trying to avoid the clawing hands of the soldier. Marcus studied him. He had the superior attitude and the trimmings and facings on his uniform of a young officer. His thick pale blond hair fell in a heavy wave over his boyishly handsome face and his eyes were grey with heavy lids, giving him a lazy, insolent look. His fleshy pink lips were parted as he leered and groped at her.

At first Marcus watched with amusement as the young girl eluded his clawing hands, but gradually he became irritated and then angered by the distress the soldier's persistence was causing her. Suddenly, with a shout of triumph, and much to the glee of everyone present, the soldier at last succeeded in pulling the girl onto his knee and thrusting his hand down the front of her low-necked dress. With a wordless cry and unusual strength for one so young, the girl pushed his hands away and scrambled from his knees. Reaching out, she grasped his tankard full of frothing ale and flung it in his face before turning and fleeing from the inn.

Silence fell and all eyes became fixed on the young soldier. His manner changed immediately and his eyes became splintered with ice. It was clear to Marcus that here was a young man who was not used to being rejected or bested by someone he would consider his inferior.

The inn suddenly erupted in a volley of shouts and coarse jokes as the soldier rose, his hair dripping with ale, which he made no attempt to wipe away. His voice, full of a desperate violence, thundered above the din.

'I wager any man here that she's a virgin, and I'll tell you now that I intend to find out.'

A roar of approval went up, and the soldier staggered drunkenly towards the door, dragging one of his legs, which indicated that he had been wounded in the war with France.

Marcus watched and listened, suddenly remembering the fearful look he had seen in the eyes of the serving girl, thinking she could not be more that sixteen years old at the most, and as he was all too aware of the soldier's evil intent, it wasn't long before he followed him outside.

The night was dark and cold when he stepped into the yard but he paid no heed to it. Hearing the strangled cry of the girl pierce the air, it was cut off as if a hand was clapped over her mouth. He turned towards the sound and quickly went across towards the stables, where a light spilled out from the open doorway. The soldier had seized the terrified girl and dragged her inside, where he had brutally flung her on to a pile of straw, crashing on top of her and began tearing at the thin fabric of her dress. Though she screamed and managed to struggle frantically against him as if her very life depended on it, she was no match for the soldier's brute strength, his muscles honed to perfection on the battlefields of Spain. At first her resistance surprised him, but then it excited him and he laughed, a low merciless sound.

'Fight me all you like, my little beauty. I like a girl with spirit.'

The girl's last reserves of strength were almost exhausted when Marcus's tall shadow fell across them from where he stood in the doorway. In surprise the soldier paused for a moment and turned, favouring him with a mocking grin, a glazed expression in his eyes. 'Come to watch the sport, have you? You can have her when I'm done.'

'Enough,' Marcus said with an ominous coolness, noticing the mute appeal in the girl's terrified eyes. Something in his tone made the soldier turn again and look at him.

'Indeed, it is not,' he growled. 'Enough, you say—for what reason? I do not care for anyone to interrupt me in my pleasures. So, whoever you are, be gone. Find your own amusement or wait until I'm done.'

Undeterred, Marcus stepped closer, glowering down at him. 'Then allow me to introduce myself—Marcus Cardell, at your service, and I told you to release the young lady. She has made it quite plain that your over-amorous advances are not welcome.'

Recognising the refined tone and that each word was enunciated slowly and carefully, the soldier staggered to his feet, his clothes dishevelled and his expression deadly. He stood and faced Marcus, several inches taller than himself, who was making a visible effort to control his anger, a faint, scornful smile on his lips that only added to the soldier's rage.

'This is not your affair and I resent your interference.'

'Really?' Marcus mocked. 'But you are bothering the young lady and I am making it my affair.'

'Young lady?' sneered the soldier. 'She is nothing but a common trull.'

There was a faint, animal-like whimper from the straw as the girl, as pale as death and shaking from head to foot, struggled to her feet, modesty causing her to pull her torn skirts together. The soldier turned as if to go back to her.

'Touch her again and I'll break your neck,' drawled Marcus.

The threatening quality in his voice caused the soldier to look at him again, anger blazing from his eyes, and suddenly, unable to restrain himself, he sprang at Marcus with clenched fists. Perhaps, if his brain had not been fogged with drink, he might not have missed his target, but as he raised them to strike, Marcus deftly sidestepped and struck out, hitting the soldier on the side of the face. His eyes rolled in his head and he staggered and fell to the ground, his face bleeding from a cut caused by the blow. All vestige of pride was stripped from the soldier, who was enraged to find himself so humiliated. His body shook with the intensity of his rage, and sheer hatred blazed from his eyes.

'Now get out,' Marcus said, his voice like steel.

The soldier struggled to his feet and in the doorway he turned. 'If ever I have the misfortune to meet you again, I'll make you pay for that. I'll get even— I swear.'

'I doubt our paths will cross again, but perhaps

you'll think twice the next time you are intent on raping anyone.'

Muttering curses beneath his breath, the soldier turned and stumbled out into the night, dragging his injured leg behind him.

Marcus turned and looked at the girl. 'Are you all right?'

She nodded, smiling at him gratefully, too shocked to speak. A woman suddenly appeared by her side.

'Oh, Sal…' and, taking in her torn clothes, she looked at Marcus in alarm. 'Is she all right?'

He nodded. 'I came in time.'

She sighed with relief. 'Thank the Lord. Come on, love. I'll take you home.'

The following morning, Marcus continued his journey to London.

Juliet arrived in St James's Square at the Sinclair residence—for how long it would remain so was a constant worry. Her father's gambling and Richard's affliction to the same, might force them to sell it. The house was of modest proportions but tastefully furnished. It was early afternoon and Richard was nursing a frightful hangover, having spent most of the previous night losing heavily at the tables. He had risen from the bed in which he had fallen into a dissolute, drunken slumber.

On seeing his sister looking unnaturally calm, her

face pale through worry and lack of sleep, his face fell, telling her he wasn't particularly pleased to see her. There was only a slight resemblance between brother and sister. They had the same shade of hair, but there the resemblance ended. Juliet was like a piece of thistledown with a finely structured face, where Richard was six feet and stockily built, with a strong square chin and green eyes.

'Good Lord, Juliet!' he groaned, falling into a chair. 'What are you doing here? And you come alone, without your maid, I see.'

'I had to let her go, Richard,' she said, shocked by her brother's appearance. He looked thoroughly broken, his handsome face creased with deep lines of anxiety, his clothes and hair dishevelled. 'We could no longer afford to pay her—along with some of the other servants. When I discovered you had taken our mother's jewels to pay for your gambling, I had to come. Besides, we are to attend Lord and Lady Wyatt's dinner party tomorrow night—although perhaps with all this going on, you have forgotten about it. Our situation is desperate, you know that. You must stop before it is too late and we have nothing left to sell or gamble but this house and the estate—such as it is.'

'It might be already too late,' he grumbled. 'If things don't improve, then I will have to consult my lawyer.'

Immediately, an icy hand gripped Juliet's heart, and her feeling of dread deepened as she feared the worst.

'We are in a devil of a fix, Juliet.' Richard drew himself up in the chair, staring with a stricken look out of bloodshot eyes at his sister. 'What's to be done? How are we to be saved,' he cried, looking at her as if she knew the answer. 'You really should consider what I suggested. If you were to marry a wealthy man, it may go some way to solving our problems. Our family name still stands for something in the scheme of things. There will be some of the cream of London society there when we attend the Wyatts' dinner party. With any luck, you might attract the attention of an affluent gentleman who is looking for a wife.'

Juliet was aware of a deadening of her senses, and her heart was pounding so hard that she could scarcely breathe. All around them the house was silent. When she looked at her brother, a bitter taste filled her mouth and she wanted to shout hurtful words at him for bringing them to this, this state of ruin and degradation. But when she saw the look on his face, her conscience smote her, and the cruel words died on her lips. What could she say, anyway, that would hurt him? He knew only too well what he had done and it was killing him.

'I have made my feelings plain about that. I refuse to marry a stranger for his money. Besides, your reputation as an inveterate gambler might well deter any prospective bridegroom. There has to be another way.'

'What have I done? That I should have brought us to this.'

The appeal in his voice went straight to Juliet's heart. Without thinking how they could survive, she went to her brother and put her arms around him. Her eyes were soft and tender, and she spoke impulsively, lowering her cheek to his.

'Together we'll think of something. There has to be a way. Something will come up, you'll see.' As she spoke those words that were meant to reassure him, she knew in that moment that there was not even the suspicion of a hope that something would happen to save them.

For the rest of the day, Richard moped about the house in a state of deep depression. She managed to persuade him to put off fetching the deeds to his estate from Surrey and presenting them to his lawyer until a later date, in order to give them more time. She must do all in her power to find a way of keeping the estate and would not recognise defeat. She paced her room, desperately trying to sort out in her mind what she could do. There must be someone who would lend them the money. But then, if some-one did lend them the money, how could they ever hope to repay it?

Chapter Three

The following day Richard's carriage was only one of a glittering array that rattled and streamed through the Portland stone gateway of Wyatt House. How she hated these dinner parties which they were invited to attend while in London. They did so because she knew their mother, who had been a popular socialite in her time, would want them to maintain their place in society. Amid the shouting of coachmen and the jingle of the harness, the carriage came to a halt, waiting for the ones in front to discharge their occupants at the foot of the steps to Wyatt House. Slowly their carriage edged its way along, and Juliet leaned her head against the soft upholstery, thinking with longing of the quiet solitude and leafy green meadows of home.

With Richard by her side, they eventually entered the splendour and opulence of the house, ablaze with lights shining from every window. From somewhere inside, the musicians were already playing, their music filling the rooms, dipping and rising, sweet and sublime, which at any other time she would have found soothing. But not tonight. The strains of the violins matched her nerves, which were as taut as their strings. As she entered the glittering world of fashionable London society, where chandeliers blazed and baskets full of flowers scented the air with a lovely fragrance, she thought, wistfully, how different it would be if Thomas were here to share it with her.

They were greeted by Lady Wyatt, brimming over with her usual exuberance. She was a desirable asset to London's social scene and one of the most popular hostesses at this time—in fact, probably one of the most favoured in London society—giving the most elaborate and brilliant parties, surpassed only by those given by the Prince Regent at Carlton House.

Juliet liked Lord and Lady Wyatt. They had been good friends of her father for many years. Lady Wyatt was a clever, astute woman with an amazing wit. If somewhat domineering and bossy, she was no fool, and her guests could always be assured of some high-level, interesting conversation covering a wide range of topics at her crowded dinner table.

'Why, Juliet,' said Lady Wyatt, taking her gloved hand in her own and squeezing it with affection, while Richard turned away to speak to her husband, 'How lovely you look. I'm so glad you were able to come. Your father would be so proud of you. You do him credit. Now, off you go, my dear, while I talk to your brother. Lydia Davenport was looking for you earlier. She's just dying to tell you about her visit to Brighton. We'll chat later.'

Juliet smiled gratefully, knowing Lady Wyatt was well aware of Richard's overindulgence where both alcohol and gambling were concerned and would be sure to keep a watchful eye on him while he was under her roof. Juliet turned and went in search of Lydia. This was supposed to be an even grander affair than usual, given in honour of the Prince Regent, but Juliet didn't really care. All she was concerned about was getting through it as quickly as possible.

As Juliet made her way down the long gallery, she failed to notice the man standing apart from the rest, leaning casually against an overlarge statue with a calm but bored expression on his darkly handsome face. But then he saw Lady Juliet Sinclair. The glamorous woman who had given him his pedigree was strolling casually through the houseful of wealthy elite. For the first time since arriving in London two days ago, all his senses became alert.

He found himself watching her as she moved with a serene grace along the gallery, her figure swaying slightly as she walked, and he stared, fascinated against his will, remembering the day he had seen her dripping wet in her revealing petticoat when she had emerged from the pond in the water meadows. Forcing his gaze slowly over her figure, coming to rest on the small, high bosom, he could not look away as the most lascivious urges passed through his mind. Good Lord! Had he been *that* long without a woman?

He continued to watch her. With the light from the chandeliers bathing her in a golden glow, she was beautiful in a lavender silk gown, beneath which he could discern all her alluring curves and imagine all the hidden delights of her slender body. The effect was stunning. She aroused envy in almost every woman present and admiration in the eyes of the men, although none could have said whether it was given to the proud beauty of her face, the pale gold hair coiled expertly about her head, or to the exquisite perfection of her body.

Marcus watched her smile and offer words of greeting to people she passed, but her smile was pinned to her face and her actions mechanical—a façade. She appeared remote and detached, totally uninterested in everything that was going on around her, which aroused all his curiosity. Growing tired of watching her, he shoved himself away from the pillar and began his approach.

Juliet was surprised to see Lord Cardell here this evening. The memory of their angry altercation on their previous encounter was still very much on her mind. She stiffened her spine and raised her chin when she saw him heading her way. She looked at him fixedly. Had she wanted to look away, she could not have done so. Never had she seen a figure of such masculine elegance. There was no denying that Marcus Cardell was a gorgeous male with a commanding presence and a potent sexual magnetism that was like a palpable force. She was acutely aware of that force.

Few women would even try to resist a man like this one, she thought, and she was scandalised by the sensations stirring inside her at the mere sight of him. His movements, his habitual air of languid indolence, hung about him like a cloak. He wore no wig, and his own hair was brushed smooth. He looked every inch the well-heeled landowner—and a great deal more dangerous than the average country gentleman. There was something primitive about him, and she felt that his elegant attire and indolence were nothing but a front meant to lull the unwary into believing he was a civilised being while disguising the fact that he was a dangerous savage.

Unlike the other gentleman, who were dressed like peacocks in a multitude of the customary bright colours, the perfect fit of his dark blue coat and the tapering dove grey trousers accentuated the long lines of his body. It was impossible not to respond to this man as his masculine magnetism dominated the scene. A slow half-smile curved his lips and she saw him give a careless shrug and raise his fine, dark eyebrows at some remark. He completely ignored the young women eyeing him with encouraging, flirtatious glances over their fans. Where other women might have succumbed to the irresistible pull to see behind the cool façade and start uncovering the man beneath, Juliet could feel the palpable danger around him. She was a rational person and had the good sense to heed the warning.

Unable to avoid a confrontation, she stood her ground and braced herself as he bowed graciously.

'Lady Juliet! How delightful to see you here tonight. I am surprised.'

Juliet looked at Lord Cardell's shuttered eyes. She could find no trace of gentleness or kindness anywhere in his tough, cynical features. His slashed eyebrows were more accustomed to frowning than smiling, and he had a hard mouth. It was a face that said its owner cared nothing for fools, and in the light blue of his dark lashed eyes, silver flecks stirred dangerously, like small warning lights.

'Lord Cardell! You take me by surprise also. I'm flattered that you remember me,' she said testily.

'You are not an easy person to forget.' He sighed. 'I don't know why you always give me such a hard time when we meet.'

Determined to appear calm and unaffected by their

previous encounter and not indulge in a public display of temper, Juliet forced a smile to her lips. 'I've tried to forget our less than pleasant encounters, Lord Cardell, but it is difficult.'

'Then I can only hope that you will succeed, given time.'

'I will,' she bit back. 'You are acquainted with Lord and Lady Wyatt?'

'They are long-standing friends of the family. Are you enjoying the occasion?'

'My brother and I have only just arrived, but I always enjoy attending Lord and Lady Wyatt's dinner parties. They go to a lot of trouble to satisfy their guests, and the food is always exceptional.'

'No rabbit on the menu?'

'No, I don't expect so…' Her words trailed off when she saw the mischievous twinkle in his eyes and the curve of his lips. She laughed softly. 'I see you are teasing me, Lord Cardell.'

'Do you mind?'

'No, but since our meeting at Mr Ruskin's house and again at the water meadows, I trust you have seen the error of your accusation.'

'I have. I am aware that many a rabbit or a pheasant finds its way into a family pot, but the offence is more serious when deer are killed on a large scale, the ill-gotten gains sold further afield. I now know that Joe Ruskin is not guilty of poaching my game.

My keeper admits he was mistaken, and I have since apologised to Mr Ruskin and his wife for any distress my misjudgement may have caused.'

'I am glad to hear it.'

'This is the first social event I've attended since returning from the Peninsular.'

'You were a soldier I understand, having seen many years of active service in Portugal and Spain.'

'You understand correctly. I've only recently returned.' He looked around at the guests without much enthusiasm. 'I almost didn't come here tonight, but I grew bored watching the world go by in my family's townhouse in Grosvenor Square, so I came to see if the sights were any better here.' He spoke with slow deliberation and the corners of his lips twitched with amusement. His eyes gleamed into hers as he added softly, 'I am happy to report they far exceed my expectations, and I'm glad I came.'

Juliet turned aside, giving him a cool glance askance. 'Have you nothing better to do than ogle the ladies, Lord Cardell?'

'It might look like that, but in truth I was watching just one.'

Juliet ignored the remark, but she could not ignore that seductive lowering of his eyelids or the quickening of her heart. 'The gaming tables will attract a good many gentlemen after we have eaten,' she retorted tightly. 'Why don't you try that?'

'Because I find talking to you more enjoyable than anything else I could come up with. I saw you arrive with your brother. I must renew our acquaintance, not having seen him since we were in our youth. I've heard he is not averse to a game of cards or dice. It's a wonder he hasn't disappeared into the card room before now.'

Juliet stiffened, considering his remark concerning Richard to be in bad taste. 'Lady Wyatt has set rules, Lord Cardell. No gambling until after her guests have eaten.'

'Then, if he has a penchant for the gaming tables, he will probably be the first in the queue.'

Juliet looked to where Richard stood speaking to a close friend of his, James Hockney. They were so heavily engrossed in conversation that they were not aware that she was watching them. Deeply unhappy, she forced a smile to her lips, managing to keep her anxiety hidden. 'Not this evening, Lord Cardell. To-night, he is to refrain from any form of gambling. He has promised to be a passive observer, nothing more.'

'Very wise, Lady Juliet, if I may say so. Do you believe him?'

'He is my brother. He would not lie to me.' Even as she said the words, which she knew to be untrue, she would not give this arrogant lord the satisfaction of saying so, or give him any indication that they were facing financial ruin because of Richard's gambling.

'Then you fool yourself, Lady Juliet. Take my word for it, if he is as keen a player as I have been led to believe, he will weaken eventually.'

'And you would know that, would you?'

'I've met a lot of men like that—reckless young fools—prepared to risk evething over a game of cards or the throw of dice.'

'I am perfectly well aware of that, Lord Cardell,' she responded sharply, 'but that does not mean it applies to Richard.'

'Are you a gambler, Lady Juliet?'

'No, of course not.'

'Pity.'

'Why do you say that?'

'Because I would wager a large sum of money that your brother will find his way to the card tables before the evening is over.'

'Then it's a pity I am not a gambler, Lord Cardell, because you would be out of pocket.'

'Nevertheless, it's a very wise person who knows when to stop.'

Juliet glared at him. 'You really are the most provoking man alive and quite insufferable.'

Instead of being insulted or angered, he looked at her with amusement and shook his head. 'What were you expecting, Lady Juliet? A socially accepted gentleman? A rake or a dandified fop? I am none of these.'

'I have not known you very long, Lord Cardell, but I know exactly what you are. Now if you will excuse me, there is someone I wish to speak to.' Bobbing a stiff curtsy, she turned and walked away, having seen Lydia at the far end of the gallery. For all his devil-may-care attitude and forthright disposition, Lord Cardell was a very intelligent, very perceptive man. Being with him was always stimulating. Her senses seemed to heighten and seemed to be more alive. It was his energy and his vitality, she assured herself. One couldn't help but respond to it.

Lydia smiled broadly on seeing her and hurried towards her. They had become firm friends some years ago when they had both attended Lady Margaret's Academy for Young Ladies here in London. Lydia had been the one good thing about coming up here. She was small with an abundance of glossy auburn hair, which her hairdresser had arranged into fashionable Grecian curls. Lively brown eyes danced in her small elfin face with a smattering of pale gold freckles. She was generous and warm-hearted, and had been a great comfort when Thomas was killed, but she was also vivacious and a terrible flirt, constantly surrounded by a lively circle of friends—especially male friends, whom she not only encouraged but also seemed to thrive on their attention. Juliet was glad of her company tonight and that they were placed together at dinner.

While they were waiting for the first course, Juliet glanced up the table loaded with long-stemmed crystal glasses and gold and silver plates. Richard was seated next to the opulent Lady Melbourne, the two already engaged in lively conversation. Juliet's heart sank despairingly. Her brother's face was already flushed crimson from drinking too much wine. She tore her eyes away from him, praying he wouldn't drink much more, but she knew this was futile. If he didn't gamble, then he would be well and truly drunk when they left. She became desperately anxious for the night to end.

Looking in the opposite direction, she noticed the increasingly popular young poet Lord Byron, his face pale and surrounded by a riot of chestnut curls, his whole attitude tonight being one of disdain. She let her eyes wander to the lady seated beside him, recognising her immediately as being the outrageous Lady Caroline Lamb, whose scandalous behaviour and indiscreet affairs had made her the most notorious, talked-about woman in London, to which she didn't object in the slightest—in fact, she adored being the centre of attention, positively thriving on it.

Sitting right next to Lady Caroline Lamb was Lord Cardell. He was looking directly at her, his eyes unnerving. A crooked smile curved his lips, and Juliet noticed his long and slender hands toying with his napkin on the table. There was no fuss to his dress, and yet there was no denying that he had exquisite style. His presence formed a stark contrast to all the other gentlemen present, who seemed to fade into insignificance beside him. There was an air of complete assurance about him, and he seemed curiously out of place among all this gentility, the overdressed dandies and frills and flounces of Lord and Lady Wyatt's party.

Immediately she dropped her gaze and tried not to look in his direction again, but she was so conscious of him, her nerve endings so raw, her body so primed and aching for something she was too inexperienced to understand, that it was difficult to keep her eyes off him. As each course arrived, she tried to ignore him, uncomfortably conscious of his eyes on her constantly, burning into her flesh.

'That gentleman next to Lady Caroline Lamb looks at you a good deal, Juliet. Are you acquainted with him? He's terribly handsome. If you are, I wouldn't mind if you were to introduce us.'

Juliet shoved the strawberries around on her plate, a faint flush spreading over her cheeks. 'I think you exaggerate, Lydia. It must be you he's looking at.'

Lydia smiled mischievously, her eyes dancing merrily. 'Come on, love. He hasn't taken his eyes off you all night. And you mean to say you don't know who he is? Why, you must be the only person here who doesn't. That's Marcus Cardell, the son of an earl, although as a second son, he's not likely to inherit.' She leaned closer to Juliet, whispering confidentially, 'He was a military man, having distinguished himself in the Peninsular with Wellington's army. Rumour has it that he's now looking for a wife.' Gazing down the table, Lydia shamelessly flashed him a dazzling smile. 'Isn't he wonderfully virile—despite that polite exterior? I wouldn't mind if he chose me, I can tell you.' She sighed dreamily. 'He's as handsome as Narcissus and, I've heard, as rich as King Midas.'

'And we all know what happened to them,' Juliet quipped drily. 'Narcissus was so vain that on gazing into a pool, he fell hopelessly in love with his own reflection and, being unable to endure to possess and yet not possess himself, he plunged a dagger into his heart.'

'Oh dear! And King Midas? What happened to him?'

'After nearly starving to death because everything he touched turned to gold—including his food—and then being given ass's ears, unable to live with the disgrace, he died miserably. No, Lydia. I wouldn't liken Lord Cardell to either of them.'

'Perhaps not, but you can't blame me for wondering what could happen if he were looking at me instead of you. Oh, Juliet, don't you ever dream that one day—'

'No,' Juliet cut in crossly, her expression hard, suspecting that Lydia was about to embark on one of her daydreams about love and romance. 'I don't dream any more, Lydia. I stopped dreaming of romance when Thomas died. He took my heart with him to the grave and there it will remain.'

When she saw Lydia's eyes fill with remorse, she regretted her somewhat harsh and thoughtless words, although Lydia had never shared her own admiration for Thomas. In her opinion, Thomas had been selfish and egotistical, and she had made no secret of the fact. Juliet had never been able to understand why she felt that way about Thomas. She had wondered if Lydia was jealous of her relationship. After all Thomas was one of the most popular, handsome men in town before he had gone to the Peninsular. Being so deeply in love with him herself and not caring much for Lydia's opinion or Richard's, come to think—for had he not voiced his dislike of Thomas on occasion—she had thrust their disparaging comments aside, allowing nothing to cloud her happiness.

Reaching out, Lydia squeezed her hand. 'I'm sorry, Juliet. I didn't mean to hurt you. It was unforgivable of me.'

Juliet sighed and smiled weakly, placing her free hand over Lydia's. 'It's all right, Lydia. It's not your fault that I'm so edgy tonight, but it's not just thinking of Thomas that hurts—it's Richard.' She glanced in his direction just in time to see him pour another glass of wine down his throat.

When the meal was over and some of the guests began to drift towards the rooms where card tables had been set out, and it looked as if Richard—swaying slightly and clutching a glass of liquor—was about to go with them. *Why does he have to drink so much?* she thought angrily. If he has to gamble, then why can't he do it with a clear head? At least then he might stand a better chance of winning some of his money back.

For the next hour, Lydia and other friends and acquaintances claimed Juliet's attention. Having lost sight of Richard, excusing herself, she went in search of him, her instinct taking her in the direction of the card room. Here the noise was curiously muted so as not to distract the players. Small tables for dice, whist, French hazard and other games that took the guests' fancy had been set up. Juliet's eyes scanned the groups of people clustered around the tables, where several games were in progress. The players were obscured from view, but on seeing James Hockney standing in a small group, she moved towards him.

James turned and immediately took her arm and drew her away, but not before she had seen her brother sitting at one of the tables, his body taut and a wild, concentrated gleam in his eyes, which only gamblers had when intent on winning and they could see nothing except the cards in front of them. Shaking off James's arm, Juliet moved towards where Richard was playing.

'Stay back, Juliet,' James said softly. 'Richard won't be pleased to see you in here.'

'I do not care. I am well aware that any self-respecting female with a place in society would be disgraced for all time, but with so much at stake, the ethics of the matter do not concern me. Our situation is desperate—you know that, James. Richard must be made to stop before it is too late and we have nothing left to sell or gamble but the estate, such as it is.'

'I know that, but he is determined. He will not be stopped.'

'Have you tried?'

'Yes, but you know what Richard is like when he has his head set. He will not listen.'

'I will speak to him. He must listen to me,' Juliet said in desperation, making a move towards the table.

'Wait,' James said, putting a restraining hand firmly on her arm. 'Leave him. It may surprise you to know that Richard is winning. He will not thank you for interfering.'

'Winning?' Juliet exclaimed in surprise. 'By how much?'

'Three thousand guineas.'

Juliet gasped, astonishment mingled with relief flooding over her, unable to believe what she was hearing, her mind already racing as she calculated what could be done at Endcliffe House with such an enormous amount of money.

Through a gap in the people crowding round the table, Juliet saw once more her brother's flushed, handsome countenance and his sleek, ash-blond hair falling untidily over his brow. There was a glazed set to his features and a grimness in his eyes. He looked blindly in her direction, his eyes registering surprise and then anger, and his lips curled in disapproval, but he refused to allow himself to become sidetracked from the game in hand by an angry sister who should have known better than to enter the card room. Looking at the table once more, he uttered disappointment when his partner rose, having lost the game and being reluctant to play on.

Juliet was swamped with relief, sure that Richard would finish and come away. But another man came and sat opposite him, putting one of two packs of cards on the table with slender, flexible fingers. She froze on seeing the identity of his partner, for it was none other than Marcus Cardell. She studied him, struck by how different he was to Richard. This man was no fair-haired young man with the face of a choir boy and the manner and air of the privileged. Not one bit. This man with his lean tanned face and a devil-may-care demeanour, wore his impeccably cut clothes with a careless elegance and didn't seem to care a damn.

She felt something inside her plummeting. She couldn't really understand what she was feeling—it seemed to be a terrifying moment of prescience, for she suddenly saw her brother rendered wanting in the presence of Lord Cardell. The man had a way of making everyone he was close to appear somewhat lesser than him even if they were not.

'Why does Richard not stop?' she whispered to James, who was looking on with deep concern. 'No doubt he will blame me if his luck turns.'

'If he loses, it cannot be blamed on you. Not when he is playing Lord Cardell.'

'He's a gambling man?'

'Yes, although he doesn't often come into society, being a military man and only recently back from the Peninsular. He is known for being extremely skilful at cards, and a great number of people have lost whole fortunes to him. His personality is so strong that with a lift of one of his arrogant eyebrows or a flare of a nostril, it is not unknown for his opponent to tremble with fear and drop his cards. He is hard and ruthless and enjoys winning at any form of gambling—and cares little for those who suffer as a consequence.'

'Why is he so unpleasant?'

'It isn't that he's unpleasant. In fact, he can be quite

charming, especially to the ladies, who drool over him, and it's not difficult to see why with his looks.'

Juliet didn't tell James that she was already acquainted with Lord Cardell. Richard, too, having made his acquaintance in the long and distant past, but she was beginning to think that the game of cards Richard was about to play had become something personal for Lord Cardell. That he was about to prove to her that had she taken him up on his wager earlier, she would have lost. Instinct made him look up, as if sensing her gaze. There was a strong, arrogant set to his jaw, and his face was as hard and forbidding as a granite sculpture, his fingers handling the cards with expert ease were long and slender. His eyes locked onto hers, compelling and piercing, and Juliet saw a tightening to his features as his eyes narrowed and swept over her. A confident *I told you so* smile curved his lips before he lowered his eyes to pay attention to the game at hand.

Knowing exactly how the game would end, Juliet was tempted to walk away, but she stood her ground, determined to see it out to the bitter, humiliating end.

They began a game of piquet. It was a game for two people which offered excellent scope for both intelligence and judgement, something Richard would have risen to had his head not been fogged with the fumes of alcohol. Every card he played and lost would have many repercussions. She could feel them now coming at her like ripples when a stone was thrown into a pond. Looking up, he met her eyes, unconcerned by her reaction. Then he looked away, already intent upon the game. She was furious with him. At that moment she was nothing more to him than the cards he played and to be set aside.

Both men became intent on the game, which followed the classic pattern with Richard winning a little, then losing more and more, until he ceased to win anything at all as his partner, who, unlike Richard, was completely unaffected by alcohol, raised the stakes higher and higher. With a mixture of languor and self-assurance, his eyes on the cards did not stir.

For the next half hour, Juliet watched every move of the game with a sinking heart, the tension becoming unbearable as Richard lost more and more of his winnings to Lord Cardell, who presided over the game like a predatory hawk. Her anger was growing by the second, but she tried not to show it. She saw Lord Cardell was experienced, and the more Richard lost, the more Lord Cardell incited him to go on playing, to bid higher and higher. He must have been able to see Richard was drunk and not in possession of his right senses. He would have to be blind not to, but he lounged indifferently across from him, his expression bland as he coolly regarded her brother, whose flushed face and nervousness clearly betrayed his emotions.

When Richard had lost his former winnings, pushing a pile of banknotes into the centre of the table, Lord Cardell raised the stakes yet again by one thousand guineas, and Juliet could not believe it when Richard, in an agitated state, accepted the bet, knowing all he had left to stake were the deeds of Endcliffe House.

No longer able to stand by and watch his friend lose every penny to his name, James stepped forward.

'Don't be a fool, Richard,' he said softly but firmly in his ear. 'You cannot cover the bet if you lose. After losing what you have won tonight, you no longer have one thousand guineas to your name.'

Richard shot him a look which told him not to interfere as he put his signature to a chit and placed it with Lord Cardell's money in the centre of the table. 'I will take the bet and aim to win it back on the next hand.'

Lord Cardell seemed irritated by the interruption, noticing Richard's slight hesitation. 'Do you continue?' he asked curtly.

'I continue,' Richard replied firmly.

Juliet flinched, trying not to look at Lord Cardell's glacial expression, but her anger was also directed at Richard. How could he go on playing when he knew what it would mean if he lost? She continued to watch with the sickening knowledge that because of his reckless stupidity, they were about to lose everything they owned. She turned and left the table just as the last hand was being played, no longer able to watch. No doubt the money Lord Cardell had won was a modest sum to him, whereas to herself and Richard, it was a fortune. Not until the game was over did she turn back to see Lord Cardell rise from the table.

'Thank you. That was an excellent game,' he said as Richard quickly signed the IOU for the money he owed. Richard handed it to him, and Juliet watched Lord Cardell pocket it as her brother slumped in his chair, the knowledge that they would have to face the enormity of his loss quite overwhelming.

Chapter Four

When Richard finally emerged from the card room and came to stand beside her, Juliet caught all of Lord Cardell's attention. He was conversing with Lady Wyatt. Juliet placed a hand gently but firmly on Richard's arm and spoke softly.

'Come, Richard. It's late. I think it's time we left.'

Only then did he become aware of her presence, and he scowled at her, his red eyes full of displeasure and annoyance. 'I can't leave yet,' he said belligerently, slurring his words. 'The hour is not late.'

'Yes, we can—we must, Richard,' Juliet persisted.

'Run along, Juliet. I will not be dictated to by you. I'll leave all in good time.'

Obstinately, Juliet stood her ground, and it was the anger he saw spark in her eyes that prompted Lord Cardell to move towards her, Lady Wyatt following in his wake. The last thing she wanted was a scene.

When Lord Cardell suddenly appeared and introduced himself to Richard as his new neighbour at

Mulberry Hall, Richard looked at him, a trifle non-plussed, unable to understand how a man who could ruin him at cards could then behave as if nothing untoward had occurred. 'Neighbour, you say?'

'I am. We have met—on a couple of occasions when I visited my aunt and uncle at Mulberry Hall many years ago.'

'Ah, yes,' Richard murmured. 'I do recall the occasions. We were visiting with our mother.'

'Lady Juliet and I have already become reacquainted.'

Richard's gaze swung from Lord Cardell to Juliet and back again. 'You are? How?'

'We met before I came to London. I had only recently taken up residence at Mulberry Hall. We encountered each other whilst out riding. Is that not so, Lady Juliet? We shared a somewhat…pleasant few minutes before going our separate ways. I had no idea I had such a charming neighbour.'

His voice was as deep and as smooth as silk, and he exuded a potent masculine allure that was almost impossible to ignore, and, however much Juliet told herself she was immune to it and despite all her efforts, she could not prevent the colour from tinting her cheeks. He must have noticed, for one corner of his mouth lifted in a slight smile, which Juliet found infuriating. How could he behave as though what he had done to Richard was a mere trifle? Had the man no scruples?

'Yes,' Juliet said tightly, inwardly fuming. 'We have met.'

'Humph—oh, I see.' Richard looked accusingly at his sister. 'You never told me.'

'I saw no reason to. The meeting was brief and of no importance.' She turned her attention to Richard. 'I think we should leave now, Richard.'

'Juliet is right, Richard,' Lady Wyatt said. 'The hour is late and our guests will all be leaving shortly.'

'Nonsense. There are a good few hours left yet.'

'I'm afraid not,' she said softly. 'Go home, Richard. Juliet looks quite worn out. Is that not so, Juliet?'

'Yes,' she replied, joining in on the conspiracy. 'I have a headache coming on. Come along, Richard.'

Casting a message with her eyes to one of the footmen when he was close, she asked him to escort Lord Sinclair out to his carriage. Juliet would have liked to follow him as he went down the steps, but the tall figure of Marcus Cardell barred her way. She turned to Lady Wyatt. 'Goodnight, Lady Wyatt, and thank you for a lovely evening.'

'Lovely?' she said not unkindly, reaching out and touching Juliet's arm in an affectionate gesture. 'I think not, Juliet. At least not for you. I know just how painful these parties are for you, having to watch your brother throw more of his money away while all the time your heart is pining to be back in Surrey. And you, Marcus,' she said, turning to Lord Cardell, 'you should have known better than to draw him into a game when he can ill afford it. Lord Sinclair has a hopeless passion for gambling, and if Juliet weren't here to keep an eye on him, then he'd have nothing left.'

Lord Cardell looked at Juliet, his expression suddenly serious, his look questioning. 'It is as bad as that?'

Deflated and unable to deny the truth, she nodded. 'I'm afraid so, Lord Cardell. It is unfortunate, but there it is.'

'But—anyway,' Lady Wyatt said, glancing sharply from one to the other, 'I'm glad you two have met. Might put a sparkle back into her eyes, Marcus, having such a charming neighbour. Juliet has far too many worries for one so young. It's not good for her. By the way,' she said, eyeing him quizzically, seeming reluctant to let either of them go. 'What are you doing here in London? Aren't you supposed to be settling in at Mulberry Hall?'

'I'm here to see Adele—my six-year-old daughter,' he said by way of an explanation to Juliet. 'At present, she is with my mother. I would like to take her back to Mulberry Hall with me when I leave, but my mother obstinately refuses to part with her.'

'I'm sure she will relent. It will be good for the two

of you to be together. Now, all you need is a wife to take care of you both, and if you run true to form, you shouldn't have any difficulty finding one. If my memory serves me correctly, women never used to be a problem. Rumour has it that this is the reason why you are here in London—to look for one.'

'No. That is only one of the reasons.'

Lady Wyatt gave an exaggerated sigh and looked at Juliet. 'If only I were younger, Juliet, and not already married to Henry, but you,' she said, smiling, a mischievous twinkle dancing in her shrewd eyes. 'Now, you would make someone like Marcus an excellent wife.'

'But perhaps Lady Juliet does not wish to marry anyone,' said Lord Cardell, his smile challenging and his light blue eyes darkening to a deeper blue, resting on Juliet's face.

She had listened to the brief interchange between them and was neither shocked nor surprised. She was not at all disconcerted by Lady Wyatt's words, whose laughter made light of them. But Juliet was no fool and knew what lay behind them, that Lady Wyatt thought it high time she stopped thinking of Thomas and what might have been and began looking to the future. Perhaps she was right. Again, she looked directly at Lord Cardell, at the merry gleam dancing in his eyes, one of his winged brows arched as he waited expectantly for her reply. She looked at him with new interest and found herself remembering Lydia's words and her reference to King Midas, and wondered if he really was that rich. She told herself to stop it, not to think like this, but she couldn't help it, and the reply was already on her lips before she realised what she was saying.

'Lord Cardell,' she said coolly, 'I would marry the devil himself if he would settle the debts on Endcliffe House.' She saw the startled look that appeared on his face, quickly followed by a thin smile curving his lips, and she caught a glimpse of very white teeth. 'Now, if you will excuse me, I will bid you goodnight.' And without further ado she turned, following her brother down the steps to the waiting carriage.

'Well now,' said Lady Wyatt, a smile of approval for the way Juliet had responded to their teasing curving her lips. 'There's a challenge if ever there was one. A challenge not to be ignored, I'd say.'

Watching the Sinclair carriage drive away, Marcus nodded thoughtfully. Her reply had been brief but to the point. And it had certainly given him food for thought. It was as if she had thrown down a gauntlet, and he was forced to pick it up.

'You're right, Lady Wyatt,' he replied, having reached the most monumental decision of his life. 'I have no intention of ignoring it.' Come hell or high water, one way or another, he would make Juliet Sinclair his wife.

Lady Wyatt smiled broadly, well satisfied that her words had not fallen on deaf ears. 'No, Marcus. I didn't think you would.'

'How well do you know her?'

'I've known the family for years—her mother since we were children. It was a sad day when she died a couple of years ago, Juliet's father a year later.'

'What's she really like?'

'You've seen her. Surely that should speak for itself.'

'I know, and she's quite a beauty—there's no denying that. But I want to know what she's like beneath that.'

Lady Wyatt smiled slowly. 'This is not just a passing interest?'

'No. She impressed me a great deal and I wish to know more about her.'

'Well, I will tell you all I can and will begin by telling you that she is not like her father—or her brother, for that matter. Her father was a notorious lover of pleasure. He preferred to live in London rather than in Surrey, which he found suffocating. In their time, her father and mother were like a pair of social butterflies, always popular, their presence at any event much sought after. Unlike her father and brother, Juliet deplores London and likes nothing better than to bury herself in the country with her horses, although I believe circumstances have forced them to sell most of them. Most of the young ladies of my acquaintance are sweet-natured, always stitching samplers or dabbling in watercolours or music, a trouble to no one, which cannot be said of Juliet.'

'No? And how is she different?'

'Well, she is quite extraordinary, highly intelligent and enduringly devoted to those she cares about. As a girl, she was defiant of all restrictions and rebellious of all convention. She was complex—untameable, hot-tempered and truculent when she failed to get her own way, and an angel when she did. Her parents despaired of ever making a lady of her, but she has mellowed somewhat since their demise. There was a young man she was to have married—the second son of a baron. They had known each other for years, and devoted to him she was, although I never cared for him myself. Too much of a gad about town for my liking, but she was so deeply in love with him that she was blind to any of his faults and would hear no wrong said about him. He was reported killed at Albuera—which you will know all about, being a military man yourself. It hit her hard at the time, but she's young. She'll get over it.'

So that was it, thought Marcus, understanding at last the reason why Lady Juliet looked so distant, a mournful solemnity in her lovely eyes. She was suffering from a broken heart. But he had no intention of being deterred by this and believed that time would heal her wounds. She had built up a resistance around her inner core, and he had every intention of breaking it down.

'Nevertheless, Lady Wyatt, the man must have been someone quite exceptional to have inspired such love. But what did you mean when you said he was reported missing?'

'His body was never found.'

'So many were killed at Albuera—a bloodbath, it was.'

'We heard. Eyewitnesses have reported seeing him shot down. His father received a letter from his commanding officer, informing him that his son had fallen on the field of battle—seen it himself. Unfortunately, it could not be ascertained whether or not his body had been buried along with many others who had fallen, nor was his name on the list of prisoners.'

'I see,' Marcus said calmly. 'Then there is a possibility that he might not be dead, that he might have been picked up by peasants or the partisans?'

Lady Wyatt nodded. 'There is that possibility, but I doubt it. I believe something would have been heard before now.'

'Then tell me, why does Lady Juliet come to London if she dislikes it so much?'

'Because if she didn't keep an eye on Richard and

his gambling, they'd have nothing left and, if rumour is correct, she has cause to be worried. They're heavily in debt. Since the death of her mother, Juliet has had nothing but heartache, and to add to her worries, she now has poverty staring her in the face. But—if my judgement of her is correct—she will fight tooth and nail to keep Endcliffe House, because if that goes, it will break her heart. No, I feel nothing but admiration for the way she has coped with the arduous task of Richard and his gambling. I am sure she'll come through in the end. She is a very resilient young lady.'

'Yes,' he said, trying to sound casual, but Lady Wyatt could tell that she had caught more than his eye.

'And is it right that you are home to look for a wife?'

'It is one of the reasons. I'm going to have my work cut out getting to know Adele. Lord knows I've missed enough of her young life as it is. My mother's done an excellent job, but it's time she was living with me. A wife would make it a hell of a lot easier, but I have to make sure I marry the right woman.'

Lady Wyatt nodded, understanding. 'If you decided to pursue Juliet, then I approve of your choice. You'll not regret it.'

'Even though it would be like paying court to a powder keg?'

She laughed. 'Even that. She may be nursing the hurt of her betrothed's death, but she's young, she'll get over it, and if I know anything, you're just the man to make her forget. It may cost you a pretty penny though, but I have no doubt you can afford it. Yes, it will be a perfect match, and I guarantee you'll never be bored. Whoever gets Juliet Sinclair will be a lucky man indeed.'

Marcus was conscious of a strange jolt in the region of his heart. Lady Juliet aroused emotions that he had never experienced, not even during his marriage to Elizabeth had he experienced that, which confused him. He was unaware that she and her brother had hit on hard times. Yes, he had known of Richard Sinclair's weakness for gambling, but not to the extent that Lady Wyatt pointed out. Had he known, he would never have drawn him back to the card table when he had been on a winning streak.

On his part, he had wanted to feel nothing but the satisfaction of extracting a measure of revenge because Lady Juliet had been so certain her brother could not be persuaded back to the tables. Marcus had wanted to prove her wrong. It was unsettling knowledge, and there was a faint frown on his forehead as he returned to his home. There was something about Juliet Sinclair that twisted his emotions and made him want to put things right between them.

* * *

Not until they were in the carriage did Juliet or Richard speak, Richard being the first to do so, enraged by his own foolishness.

'I should have taken James's advice and left the table when I was in front.'

'Yes, you should.' Juliet felt the seriousness of the situation had not hit him yet, but when it did, it would be with the force of a hammer blow. 'You promised me you wouldn't gamble tonight, Richard. The whole evening has turned into a disaster. Perhaps if you hadn't drunk so much in the first place, you might have retained a little of what you had won.'

'If Lord Cardell hadn't been there—blast him—I would have won more. Hell and damnation! Just when things were going well for me. It had nothing to do with the drink—it's just that his skill at cards is not to be matched by anyone I know.'

'Then why did you allow yourself to be drawn in by him?'

'Must you always disapprove of everything I do, Juliet?' Richard remarked petulantly.

'Of course I disapprove. I cannot condone your private life or your behaviour. Oh, Richard, how could you?' she accused him bitterly. 'How could you gamble away almost everything we have left?'

'We'll find a way out of it. We always do.'

'How can you say that?' Juliet admonished harshly.

'Don't be stupid. This time we can't. Things are bad, very bad. In fact, they could not be worse. We are in a hole and I cannot see any way out—unless we throw ourselves on Lord Cardell's mercy and persuade him to tear up the IOU. It would bide us a little more time, although it is not enough to save us from ruin in the long run.'

Richard was clearly shocked by her suggestion, which no gentleman would even consider. 'That is quite out of the question, and besides, Lord Cardell would refuse. But if I don't honour the debt, I will be thrown out of my club and spend the rest of my days staring at the walls inside a debtors' prison. I couldn't bear that, Juliet. The shame would be unbearable.'

'Better that than we lose everything. You do realise we will have to sell Endcliffe House, don't you, Richard?' she said despairingly, the mere thought that their home would be gone forever bringing tears to her eyes. 'There is no way we can obtain enough money, and I doubt the bank will grant us a loan.'

As if ashamed of his recklessness and the hurt he had caused Juliet, Richard's expression became contrite. 'Forgive me, Juliet. I do realise that we're in the deuce of a mess. I suppose we could sell this house—although I'd be loathe to do it.'

Juliet looked at him sharply. 'So would I. Mother loved this house. It was where she loved to socialise when she came to town.' She sighed deeply, knowing it might have to be considered if they didn't find a way out of this mess. 'How long before the debt must be paid?'

'A week.'

'As soon as that?' she whispered. 'Then we must work something out.'

As she prepared for bed, she could think of nothing else other than that they might lose everything. She felt weak and defenceless, at the mercy of fate, and then something steely came to the fore. She wasn't going to let it go, not if she could help it. Her mother had told her she was strong, so had her father. Some of that strength came to her aid now. She felt a hard resolve replacing the panic. She wasn't going to let this defeat her.

Two days after Lord and Lady Wyatt's dinner party found Juliet in Mr Marsden's second-hand bookshop in a busy alley just off Paternoster Row. She had come in the hope of obtaining for a few pence a book by William Collins of sentimental lyric poetry, a style that Mr Collins and others had first made fashionable in the middle of the last century. She was also glad of the opportunity to be out in the fresh air, to be alone for a while so that she might think.

She wanted nothing more than to stay at Endcliffe House and never have to leave, but Richard's gambling had made their situation virtually impossible.

He hadn't left the house since Lord and Lady Wyatt's dinner party. Realising the seriousness of their situation had aged him ten years. He looked thoroughly broken, his face creased with lines of anxiety. Not possessing a plethora of relatives they could turn to in order to bail them out, she knew that it would require all their brains and ingenuity if they were to survive.

A bell tinkled pleasantly overhead when she entered Mr Marsden's shop, where the smell of ink, paper and leather-bound books assailing her nostrils was surprisingly pleasant. Like many other establishments, Mr Marsden's shop stocked items other than books, bookselling alone was rarely sufficient to make a prosperous living. The hour was early and apart from two well-dressed matrons who sat gossiping and an elderly gentleman carrying a small parcel of books he had just purchased, the shop was quiet. Juliet loved the bookshop and visited it at every opportunity when she was in town. A table of dusty bargain books invited one to browse. Mr Marsden was unpacking some pamphlets and looked up when she entered, smiling brightly. She told him what she was looking for.

'Let me see, I should have a copy somewhere. You browse, Lady Juliet, while I have a look in the back.'

Happy to wander among the narrow aisles crammed with sagging, dusty shelves of books ranging from classics, educational, drama, romance, prose and many more, she examined books by Fielding and Defoe with avid interest, having read most of them. She picked out *Clarissa*, a book written by Samuel Richardson that was a particular favourite of hers. She had read it several times and agonised over poor Clarissa Harlowe's fate on finding herself in the clutches of her abominable persecutor, Lovelace.

She became lost in the print as she flicked through the well-thumbed pages. She was about to move away from the shelves when a man's heavy tread sounded in the shop, growing closer. He stopped and spoke in a calm, casual voice, unmistakably the voice of a gentleman, a voice she instantly recognised.

'Well, Lady Juliet, here we are again.'

Juliet whirled round at that familiar deep voice and looked into the face of Lord Cardell. For some inexplicable reason, her heart set a wild beat. His face was still, but his eyes were a brilliant, quite dangerous pale blue. He lounged indolently against the bookshelves behind him with the ease of a man discussing nothing more serious than the weather. The remembrance of their previous encounters, all of which had been angry and bitter experiences, touched her deeply. And now he was smiling at her, a friendly quizzical grin.

Taken off guard by his appearance, she started. Ever since their meeting at the dinner party, she had tried not to focus her mind on him, but now that she was facing him once more, her panic increased and she could hardly believe what she had said to him—that she would marry the devil himself if he would settle the debts on Endcliffe House. No doubt Lord Cardell considered her far too outspoken, that what she had said had been foolish in the extreme. She had acted impetuously, rashly and unthinkingly and most importantly without common sense in Lord Cardell's eyes. His name spun through her mind with a combination of anticipation and dread, and now she told herself she would rather do a deal with the devil than her illustrious neighbour.

And yet the feelings she had experienced on the last occasion when they had met took some understanding. She fixed him with a cool, indifferent stare. He was dressed in a tan jacket, buff-coloured breeches and highly polished brown riding boots. The man possessed a commanding presence and was built with all the magnetism and virility of an ancient Greek athlete, with long limbs and powerful shoulders. He seemed to belong to another world, one where the wind and sun had turned his skin the colour of bronze, one that was wild and exciting and far removed from her village in Surrey. Her heart lurched, surprise holding her immobilised for a split second. He seemed to set the whole atmosphere inside Mr Marsden's bookshop vibrating.

'You take me by surprise, Lord Cardell. I did not expect to see you in a bookshop.'

'And why not, pray? I happen to read extensively—when I have the time. I haven't been home very long and there is much to be done at Mulberry Hall. I am on an errand to see an acquaintance of mine and saw you enter the bookshop.'

'And you followed me?'

'Yes. You are recovered from the dinner party, I trust.'

'Recovered? You seem to infer that I was ill. I enjoyed the evening and suffer from no ill effects. Did I look like I was?'

'Not in the slightest. You handled yourself beautifully and with perfect poise.'

'I do my best,' she retorted.

'There's no need to be so defensive. I was merely trying to pay you a compliment. Apparently, I'm out of practice.'

'Apparently you are.'

Idly he inspected the titles on the spines of the books that lined the shelf, selecting one at random. 'Do you mind that I followed you in here?'

'If you had genuinely entered the shop to look at books, then no, but since you admit to following me, then yes, I do mind—although I am sure Mr Marsden who owns the shop will be glad of the custom of such an illustrious gentleman as yourself, Lord Cardell.'

'The informality of my doing so was not meant as an offence, Lady Juliet, and if I offended you when last we met, then I apologise most humbly.'

'You did not offend me, Lord Cardell, although I wish you had not drawn Richard into a game of cards. But worry not. What he owes will be paid before the week is out.'

'That is the procedure, although now I have been made aware of your circumstances, I regret doing so.'

'As much as accusing Joe Ruskin of poaching?' she bit back, unable to stop herself. But she was hurting, and it was a relief to hit out at someone, even though she reproached herself for doing so. Having considered the occurrences on every situation since when they had met, she had to admit Lord Cardell had done no wrong. Of course he had to investigate the poaching situation on his land, and again when he had come upon her swimming in the water meadows and she had accused him of spying on her. He had not been there deliberately to watch her swim. He had come upon her by chance. As for taking four thousand guineas off Richard at the tables, only Richard and his weakness for gambling could be blamed for that.

'I'm sorry,' she conceded. 'I do understand why you acted as you did, and I apologise for accusing you of spying on me at the water meadows. You couldn't have known I would be there. I just wish you had considered the facts before upsetting Mrs Ruskin.'

Watching her closely, Lord Cardell nodded. 'So do I. Where I am concerned, I would like to forget the matter altogether.'

'Yes, I too would like to forget it.'

'And me too I expect.'

'Yes,' she murmured. 'You too.'

He chuckled, unoffended. 'Most of the ladies I meet are more than eager to be amiable to me because of who I am, but you have the unique distinction of being the only woman I have met who is honest enough to tell me to my face that, having met me, she is eager to put me from her mind.'

'Really? And you are not put out?' Juliet asked drily, thinking that what he said must be true, that if he was as wealthy as she had heard he was—and with his kind of looks—he must have women falling at his feet like dominoes in a row, all rendered quite helpless when confronted by his charm and allure.

'Not in the slightest. In fact, I find it a refreshing change. Tell me, are you a frequent visitor to this bookshop?'

'Yes, when I come to town,' she answered, suddenly beginning to feel slightly uneasy. She did not like the way he had followed her inside Mr Marsden's bookshop, nor did she like his easy manner and the steady, unsettling gaze of his penetrating light blue eyes. He was the most lethally attractive man she had ever met, and she would have to take care not to be drawn in by him. Swiftly she raised her defences. 'I do not pretend to be knowledgeable about books, but I do enjoy reading.'

'Has anyone ever told you that you resemble your mother?' he said suddenly, softly, thumbing through the pages of the book.

Juliet stared at him, surprised by his comment. 'You knew my mother?'

'No, not really. I saw her from time to time. I did not often come to Mulberry Hall to see my aunt and uncle—my mother's brother—but there were occasions when your mother came to call on my aunt. As young as I was, I recall she was unforgettable.'

Juliet said nothing to this. The blue-eyed gaze when he turned to look at her was disconcerting, and she was miserably conscious that he had caught her dishevelled from the morning's work of sorting out items of furniture in the attics she and Richard might sell to raise the money to clear his IOU. 'Yes, she was. Tell me, Lord Cardell,' Juliet said, his comment about her mother throwing her for a moment, but not placating her so easily, 'have you caught any more poachers on your estate recently?'

'I've put the matter into the hands of my stewards. They are always vigilant, and there have been no incidents of late. Hopefully, whoever they are, they will have moved on.'

'I sincerely hope so.'

'Has your brother been affected?'

'I… I don't believe so, although it is not unusual for the odd rabbit or pheasant to be taken. It happens.'

'Since the demise of my uncle, there has been no one in the family to oversee the estate for some considerable time. It has been laid wide open to poachers. My uncle might have turned a blind eye to it, being in poor health, but I am no pushover and will not be laughed out of what is rightfully mine.'

'Poachers are usually people who have fallen on hard times and are desperate to feed their families. Does that not concern you?'

'Of course it does, but don't be fooled, Lady Juliet. It does not stop at rabbits or the odd pheasant. When deer go missing, along with sheep and cattle from the home farm, it cannot be ignored. There's a question of money involved.' He placed the book back on the shelf before giving her his full attention once more. 'Since your brother and I are neighbours, let us understand each other,' he said carefully. 'The poaching fraternity—or thieves, as I prefer to call them—is tightly knit, and they keep to their own rules. Certainly they make a living out of what they do—a good living. They are highly organised and they do not stop at the Mulberry Hall estate. Perhaps you should look to your own, Lady Juliet. Your brother's negligence may be seen as an opportunity for the thieves to divest you of some of your own livestock. It is your loss.'

The coldness of his words touched Juliet like ice. With great deliberation she turned away from him, thinking about what he had said. She could not ignore it. The unpleasant thought that there were people out there making a living off their land when they were struggling to keep afloat, she had never considered.

'They—the poachers—they make money out of it?'

'I'm afraid so. They get a good price from butchers in towns farther afield. Your brother should look into it. In this matter, we may be able to help each other. Can you afford to turn a blind eye?'

She shook her head. 'No. You are right, Lord Cardell. Although Endcliffe House needs money so badly that the miserable pounds we might secure is hardly worth thinking about.' She looked down at the book in her hand, tracing the groove of the title with her fingertip. 'Don't you see that once a stage of need is reached, a little money saved here and there does not put a new roof on the house or repair the walls and keep the damp at bay? It would be such a small part of what we need that it wouldn't even begin to patch it up.'

Lord Cardell's eyebrows lifted and his features relaxed. 'Let me see the book that has caught your attention,' he said on a change of subject. He took the volume she was holding. Reading the title on the spine, he raised his eyebrows in surprise. '*Clarissa*! It would not be my choice of good reading, but I can quite see why it appeals to the ladies.'

'No matter your opinion, Lord Cardell, the book has met with considerable success and is a fine work,' Juliet was quick to say in defence of one of her favourites. 'I cannot see why you should pour scorn on it.'

He smiled. 'Clarissa is a nervous young woman of excessive sentiment and sensibility. I confess to having read the book, but she did not endear herself to me in the slightest.'

'And how do you define "sentiment and sensibility," Lord Cardell?'

'As an expression of intense human feelings, of which the heroine in question is in possession to excess. The two words are often confused. *Sentiment* is ruled by the human heart, which is the centre of all emotions, whereas *sensibility* is the key to bodily sensations—touch and such things,' he said softly, his eyes filling with amusement when she flushed and lowered her gaze at his definition and the hidden connotation of the words. He smiled, knowing exactly the effect he was having on her. 'Clearly, you enjoyed the book?'

'Yes,' she replied, wishing she had not asked him to define the two words because she knew she was blushing at the intimacy of his tone. There was altogether something too explicit and intense in his eyes. However, she refused to be deflected. 'So much so that I have read it several times. I confess I was much moved and felt a great deal of sympathy for Clarissa—being pursued and persecuted so cruelly by the abominable Lovelace.'

'Ah, but she did throw herself on his mercy.'

'She accepted Lovelace's offer of help because she was quite desperate to save herself from a dreadful marriage, only to find herself in a worse situation than she was before.'

'And you have an affinity to Clarissa, have you, Lady Juliet?'

Juliet smiled with a faint trace of cynicism. 'Oh, I believe there is a Clarissa in most women, Lord Cardell—just as there is a Lovelace in most men.'

'Perhaps you are right, but we do not all have to resort to kidnapping to engage the affections of the ladies we desire,' he said slowly, meaningfully, in a voice low with seduction that made Juliet think improper things. It was a voice few women would be able to resist, especially not if the man speaking happened to look like Lord Cardell—over six feet tall and built like a Greek god.

She looked at him, suddenly beginning to feel out of her depth, unable to answer his question, and sensing a wave of hot colour burn her cheeks under his close scrutiny. She was relieved when Mr Marsden chose that moment to come shuffling along the aisle towards her.

'I must apologise, Lady Juliet, for taking so long. I thought I had a copy of Mr Collins's poems, but I was mistaken.'

'That's all right, Mr Marsden.' Juliet smiled. 'Thank you for taking the trouble to look.'

When he had moved away, Juliet looked up to see Lord Cardell eyeing her with some amusement and a hint of mockery, his eyelids drooped down over his glorious blue eyes giving him a lazy, sleepy look.

'William Collins! A book of sentimental lyric poetry that was fashionable when first published and much sought after in some circles, I believe.' His smile widened. 'I salute your taste, Lady Juliet—a veritable catalogue of sensation. Perhaps Mr Marsden might order it for you if you are so desirous to obtain it.'

'I'm sure he would. I will give it some thought for another day.' Taking Clarissa out of his hands, she placed it back on the shelf. 'And now, if you will excuse me, Lord Cardell, I must be on my way. I have much to do and little time to do it in.'

Juliet pushed past him and, after bidding Mr Marsden good day, marched out of the shop, relieved that he had not mentioned her parting words at Lord and Lady Wyatt's dinner party, that she would marry the devil if he would settle the debts on Endcliffe House. Having thrown down a challenge, she hoped he had thought no more of it—and yet, did she? She felt a rush of righteous indignation when she recalled how he had drawn Richard into that game of cards and beaten him.

Chapter Five

It was mid-afternoon, St James's Park attracting all manner of people at this time of day. The sun was pleasantly warm, with people strolling along the paths or lounging on the grass in groups, rosy-cheeked children playing all manner of games. Juliet was accompanied by Daphne. Of medium height, dark-haired and with an easy manner and sunny disposition, she was employed at the London residence and had a willingness to turn her hand to any chore. Juliet usually dispensed with a personal maid, but when she was in London, she pressed Daphne into her personal service.

Today they walked side by side, enjoying the day's warmth. Juliet carried a small bag of bread, intending to feed the ducks on the pond. Fallow deer roamed free and were a constant delight to the children, in particular, who loved to feed them. Soldiers, resplendent in their colourful red-and-blue uniforms, paraded at Horse Guards, which was one of the main attractions of the park during the afternoons.

Juliet almost didn't see the group of four people coming towards them—a man and two women and a young girl. Having just replied to something amusing Daphne had said, which had brought a smile to her lips and a sparkle to her eyes, she suddenly noticed their approach, and her smile froze as her gaze became fixed on them.

One of the women, whom she thought to be in her mid-sixties, was quite tall and statuesque, with a regal bearing and strong, handsome features, her gloved hand placed lightly on the gentleman's arm. The other woman, plainly dressed and quite young, Juliet assumed to be the lady's maid. She held the hand of the child, her dark hair arranged in ringlets, which bounced delightfully from beneath her bonnet when she moved her head. But it was the gentleman who caught Juliet's eyes and held them, for it was Lord Cardell.

Both parties stopped, leaving several paces between them. For some inexplicable reason Juliet experienced the depth to which her mind and body were oddly stirred whenever she was in Lord Cardell's presence. His face was still, but his eyes were a brilliant, quite dangerous pale blue. The remembrance of their previous encounters, some volatile and the one at the bookshop not so volatile, touched her deeply.

He wore a plum-coloured cutaway coat and buff knee breeches tucked into highly polished black riding boots, and his neck linen was sparkling white.

'Lady Juliet,' Lord Cardell said, 'I did not expect to find you here.'

'I cannot imagine why not. I enjoy walking and the park is so pleasant.'

'I couldn't agree more,' the older lady said, looking at Juliet. Interest kindled in her eyes. 'Come, Marcus. You must introduce us.'

'Of course. Mother, allow me to present to you Lady Juliet Sinclair of Endcliffe House, a close neighbour of mine. Lady Juliet, my mother the dowager Countess of Cranswick.'

Juliet dipped a curtsy.

'Sinclair?' the Countess said. 'Of course the name is familiar to me. I believe I met your mother on occasion when she visited my sister-in-law at Mulberry Hall. Is that not so?'

'Yes, they were friends as well as neighbours.'

'This is indeed interesting. I learned of your mother's demise some time ago, followed so soon by your father. My condolences, my dear, although it is a little late, I know, but I mean it most sincerely. Are you to return to Surrey?'

'I am staying with my brother at present, but I hope to return to Surrey in the next week or so.' Juliet looked down at the child half hiding behind the other woman's skirts, peering shyly up at Juliet.

'And who is this young lady?' Juliet said, smiling down at her. The little girl's shy awkwardness touched a hidden chord in her, reminding her so much of herself at that age.

'This is my daughter, Adele. She is always shy with strangers,' said Lord Cardell.

Adele took a step towards Juliet a little hesitantly at first, regarding her seriously, and she noticed that she bore a remarkable resemblance to her father, but unlike her father, Adele's eyes, which were wide and as darkly grey as a winter's sea, were from a different strain. There was something rather timid about Adele, dainty and fragile. There was also something cowed about her, contrary to the normal exuberance of children. Juliet prayed silently for acceptance. On impulse she reached out and took her small hand in her own, and bending low, so that her face was on a level with hers, she smiled warmly into her eyes.

'I'm so pleased to meet you, Adele, and what a pretty dress you are wearing. I do hope you're enjoying your walk in the park. There is so much to see, and I always bring Daphne with me for company.'

Adele made no attempt to pull away, and a little smile began to tug at the corners of her mouth. She seemed to be assessing her, and when her eyes ceased to regard Juliet so seriously and her smile gradually broadened, which was a delight to see, it brought a relieved smile to Lord Cardell's features, and he seemed to relax, which told Juliet how apprehensive he was about introducing his daughter to strangers. When Adele's gaze lighted on a small bag in Juliet's hand, Juliet opened it and showed her the contents.

'I've brought some bread to feed the ducks on the pond. Would you like to help me?'

'Oh, yes please,' she said with a bright, eager light shining in her wide eyes, her face taking on a look of enthusiasm, no longer seeing the beautiful lady as a stranger.

Juliet stood up straight and looked at Lord Cardell and his mother. 'Forgive my imposition, but I really have come to feed ducks. Would you permit me to take Adele?'

'Of course,' the Countess said, more than happy to comply. 'I'm sure she would love to. What do you say, Marcus?'

Frowning, Lord Cardell looked down as his daughter.

'Please, Papa,' Adele whispered tentatively. 'Will you let me feed the ducks?'

'Very well,' he conceded, 'it's a wonderful thought.' His eyes lit on a bench close to the pond. 'We'll sit and wait over there.'

Clearly enjoying this exciting moment, holding Juliet's hand, Adele skipped along by her side. Daphne following several paces behind.

* * *

For Marcus, watching his daughter happily throwing bread to the ducks with Lady Juliet, it was a moment of complete enchantment. He began to smile, for their laughter as the ducks noisily competed with each other for their share of the bread was infectious. His face was soft and his eyes were warm. He had a strong sense of responsibility and felt a deep affection for his daughter. It worried him greatly that she was growing up without the influence and love that could only come from a mother.

Equally moved as she watched her granddaughter give way to joyous laughter, his mother said, 'Lady Juliet is a personable young woman, Marcus, pretty too.'

'Yes,' he agreed, watching his daughter as her ringlets bounced against her back and seeing that a rosy glow had sprung to her cheeks as she had skipped alongside Lady Juliet. Skipping! He could not recall seeing her do that. Her bonnet had fallen back off her head and was being held on by the ribbon about her neck. 'She is also the most controversial and unconventional woman I have ever met.'

His mother gave him a quizzical look. 'I see. You must have become well acquainted with her to have formed an opinion.'

'We have met on a few occasions, not all of them amiable.'

'Well, I like her. In fact, I think I recall seeing her at Mulberry Hall when she was quite small, her brother also, although I also seem to recall there was some controversy after one of our visits,' she said, speaking absently. 'Something about Lady Juliet missing for some considerable time…' She shook her head. 'Not that it matters now. It was all so long ago. Clearly, she was found safe and unharmed. Lady Juliet has an easy manner. I like that. Adele seems to be quite taken with her also.'

Marcus glanced at his mother sharply. 'I can see that.' A frown deepened on his brow. 'What are you getting at?'

'You know what I'm getting at, Marcus, so don't pretend you don't. There is nothing that would delight me more than to know you have found someone to marry, a young woman who possesses the requirements of birth and breeding enough to make her worthy of marrying into the Cardell family.'

'I know, Mother, since you never tire of telling me at every opportunity.'

'You are now Lord Cardell, the Earl of Ashleigh, of Mulberry Hall, so you must marry well for duty's sake. I know you would prefer not to remarry at all, but you are not getting any younger, and you must secure an heir for the Mulberry estate and a mother for Adele. My own family is thin on the ground, as well you know, which is why you are in the position you are now. You cannot go on postponing the inevitable any longer. Besides, it's about time you gave me another grandchild. Your brother and his wife had two sons in the first five years of marriage.'

'You seem to forget I've been in the Peninsular for the past eight years fighting Bonaparte, with little time spent at home.'

'Which is why it's important for you to find yourself another wife. I'm no longer a young woman, Marcus, and your brother and his wife have their hands full raising their own children—with another one due shortly. Adele needs guidance and a loving family of her own.'

Marcus didn't argue the matter. He was a widower who had seen little of his family in the past because of his military career. As a young man with a lust for adventure, he'd had little time for marriage and affairs of the heart after Elizabeth's death. Certainly he yielded to the desires of the flesh as much as the next man. Many women had passed through his life. Some had faded from memory and a few he had felt affection for, but he'd never doted on any, not even his wife.

Their marriage had been arranged by their two families. He had been fond of Elizabeth and had grieved when she had died. But it was the army that had been of the utmost importance to him. While the military campaign was ongoing in Spain, he concentrated on developing his mind and spirit for action on the field of battle—until his daughter was born. It changed everything. On inheriting Mulberry Hall, he had resigned his commission.

It was important to him that he got to know his daughter and married again to provide an heir for the Mulberry estate, but he refused to be browbeaten by his mother.

'I am well aware of that, Mother, and I intend to put my mind to it.'

'Well,' she said, a warm gleam in her eye as she looked at her son. 'I do not think you will have far to look.'

Marcus hardly heard his mother's words as he watched Lady Juliet bend down and place her arm protectively about Adele's shoulders, preventing her falling into the water in her excitement, her cheek resting on the child's dark head. Mesmerised by the lovely picture the woman and child created, his expression softened. Looking on, he felt as though he were an intruder, a stranger, and that his daughter belonged to someone else. He was determined to change that. When the last of the bread had been thrown, they slowly made their way back.

He listened intently to Lady Juliet talking to Adele in a way that seemed to come quite naturally to her. Adele looked up at the face of the woman with something akin to adoration, responding to the warmth in her voice. Both the scene and Lady Juliet's words be-witched him and reached out to some unknown part of him that he had not been aware he possessed. It touched and lightened a dark corner for a brief in-stant, and then it was gone. He wondered what it was about her that he found so appealing. She was lovely—beautiful—but there were many kinds of beauty, and the most obvious didn't often appeal to him. There had to be something else, something more than the colour of her eyes, the perfect loveliness of her face and the delectable curvaceousness of her body, though as a red-blooded male he wasn't hypo-critical enough to deny this appeal.

'There,' Lady Juliet said, still hold Adele's hand, 'all the ducks have been well and truly fed. Did you enjoy feeding them, Adele?'

'Oh, yes,' she replied softly, reluctant to let go of her hand. 'Will you come to the park again?'

'While I am in London, I come to the park most days.'

'And can I see you again?' she asked hopefully, 'Can I, Papa?' she asked her father beseechingly.

Marcus smiled down at her. 'Certainly, should we encounter Lady Juliet. Hopefully she will bring more bread for the ducks.'

'I will,' Juliet confirmed. 'It's been lovely meeting you, Adele. You too, Lady Cardell,' she said, bob-bing a small curtsy. 'I won't detain you any longer.'

'It's been a pleasure meeting you, Lady Juliet. Perhaps you will call on us when next we are at Mulberry Hall?'

'Yes, thank you. I would like that.' As Marcus made his way out of the park, he stopped every now and then, his eyes glancing back at the young woman walking in the opposite direction, unaware of the little satisfied smile playing on his mother's lips.

When he had seen her gliding soundlessly over the grass towards him, slender and long-limbed, Marcus had been enchanted by her, his eyes making an instant appraisal. She really was a remarkably beautiful young woman, and it was as if he were seeing it for the first time in his life. Juliet Sinclair was a natural temptress, alluring and lovely. The appeal of this young woman he found hard to explain. His attraction to her was beneath her beauty, it was something else entirely.

As Adele trotted along beside him, it was Lady Juliet he saw dripping wet after her swim in the water meadows. Courageous and lovely, it was Lady Juliet who had faced him squarely at the Wyatts' dinner party, telling him she would marry the devil himself if he would pay the debts on her beloved home. On all their encounters, he'd had no idea she was in such dire straits. She'd been too proud to let him think otherwise, and he admired her for that.

Since returning to England and seriously considering remarrying, when he tried to think of a suitable candidate to be his wife, it was Lady Juliet Sinclair's image that lingered the longest in his thoughts. Yes, she was indeed lovely, but she was much more than that. Highly intelligent, she was proud, wilful and undisciplined. She was also gentle, brave and innocent. She projected a tangible magical aura, and he could almost feel her vibrant inner energy and appetite for life. Her beauty in her home setting had fed his gaze and created a warm hungering ache that would not be easily appeased by anything less than what he desired.

She was different from any other woman he had ever known, but today the smooth skin of her face was marred by mauve shadows circling her eyes, which, he suspected, were the result of worry and sleepless nights. His admiration for her ran deep. As young as she was and dealing with the burden of her ancestral estate while her brother gambled his way through the distinguished halls in London, to keep Endcliffe Hall off the auctioneers block as well as taking care of the servants who remained, she had learned to deal with adversity while holding her head high. He admired her stoicism, her determination to face her trials head on and to deal with them as best she could. Unfortunately, she was running out of options.

But one thing had not changed about her, and at this

he felt a pang of dismay. There was still no warmth in those glorious eyes, which stared out of her pale face with a solemnity that touched him. But instinctively he knew that no matter how sad she was, her sorrow only enhanced her magical power that was capable of enslaving him forever.

When he had been close to her, the faint, heady scent of crushed rose petals had come to him, a scent he would associate with her for evermore. They had looked at each other steadily for a long moment, and Marcus had realised then that if he was to take a wife, then he wanted Lady Juliet Sinclair to be that woman. He wanted her, but more important was the fact that he wanted her to want him, and if he hoped to win her affections, then he was going to have to hold his emotions under restraint, which—not a man known for his patience—would be no simple matter.

As a soldier, he listened to his head and not his heart in all things. Nothing in his life was accidental or unplanned, and everything was carefully thought out. But this was one time when he did not pause to understand the reasons for what he was about to do. He wanted her, and that was reason enough.

Having made a decision to propose marriage to Lady Juliet, Marcus sought Richard Sinclair out in the hallowed rooms of White's, the gentleman's club in St James's. The room was cloaked in the quiet, restrained ambience redolent of the masculine smells of sandalwood, leather and cigars. He scanned the room, his gaze coming to rest on Richard Sinclair. In a sombre mood, he was morosely staring at a goblet of brandy—no doubt nursing his wounds inflicted over his losses at the tables. When Marcus approached, Richard looked up at him, his boyishly handsome face etched with pain.

'May I?' Marcus said, sitting opposite before he could object. Signalling to a servant to bring a decanter of brandy and two snifters, he studied the man opposite.

'If you have come to propose another game of cards Lord Cardell, you can forget it. I'm all cleaned out.'

'Be assured that I did not seek you out for that purpose. I apologise if I have chosen an inopportune time, but what I have to say is of the utmost importance.'

'If you have come to collect on the debt, I still have a couple of days to settle. No matter what your opinion is of me, Cardell, honour my debt to you. Because of my irresponsible behaviour, I have brought shame and dishonour to my family name and ruined whatever chance my sister has of making a decent, respectable marriage in the future. When I have settled my debt to you, with creditors already on my back and the estate mortgaged up to the hilt, I may very well be forced to put it on the market.'

'And you are prepared to do that?' he asked, picking up the decanter and pouring them both a drink.

'Of course. Nothing I can say can excuse my own part in what has happened, and I have reproached myself many times for it. I am to blame and I am deeply ashamed of my past conduct. I have nothing to say in my defence.'

'At least you are man enough to admit that. However, I am here to put to you a proposal—one which, I hope, will benefit us both.'

Lord Sinclair looked at him with the beginning of interest lighting his eyes. 'A proposal?'

Marcus nodded, swirling the brandy around and letting the delicate fumes rise in the air. 'I am well aware of your financial situation. Rents and income from your land are still provided, but it comes in at a trickle and is not sufficient to get you out of the hole you have dug for yourself. I have a bargain to put to you which will wipe out your debt to me and give you some breathing space.'

He had captured all Lord Sinclair's attention. 'I am not a man to turn away a bargain. Let me hear it.'

'It concerns some of the Sinclair land—the water meadows to be precise.'

Lord Sinclair stared at him with astonishment. 'Good Lord. What have the water meadows to do with anything? Although if you intend on making an offer for them, then we could negotiate.'

'That's good to hear. I am interested in coming to an arrangement.'

'You are aware that they are prime pasture?'

'Which is precisely why I have selected that particular stretch of land. Come, Lord Sinclair, think about it. You have just told me that when you have settled your debt to me, with creditors baying at your door and your house mortgaged up to the hilt, you will have no choice but to sell. I am offering you a solution—it is a temporary situation, and it is up to you and your will to stay away from the card tables.'

'You have it all worked out, don't you, Lord Cardell?' Richard said, settling back in his chair.

Marcus nodded. 'They will provide more pasture for livestock on the home farm. According to my steward, the tenant farmers are forever complaining there isn't enough.'

'And what of my own tenant farmers?'

'I'm sure we can come to some arrangement. There's enough pasture to accommodate both.'

'And I pay rent to you—for land that I once owned?'

'Like I said, we'll come to an arrangement satisfactory to both of us.'

Lord Sinclair sat back in his chair, watching as he swirled the amber liquid around the bowl of his glass before looking at Lord Cardell once more. 'An arrangement you say. It seems a queer kind of arrangement to me. It is by no means a fair exchange. I owe you four thousand guineas, Lord Cardell. The water meadows cover fifteen acres. By my reckoning, at roughly fifty pounds an acre, that will leave you out of pocket by something like three thousand guineas. You are either being over generous, or you have something else up your sleeve.'

'I might have. But I ask you to seriously consider the offer.'

'It would seem you leave me with little choice, although how I am going to confront my sister with this, I shudder to think.'

'Come now. You are desperate, are you not, Lord Sinclair? Your present financial situation leaves you with no choice. Settle your debt to me with the land, and you may be able to keep afloat a while longer.'

'You are asking me to sell precious acres, Lord Cardell. It is a difficult decision for me to make.'

'Then let me make it easier for you. Should you agree to my proposal, then I will work with you to help your situation improve. We are neighbours, after all. Your parents were close friends of my uncle and aunt and frequent visitors to Mulberry Hall. That counts as something to me. As you know I have only recently taken up residence at Mulberry Hall following years of military activity in the Peninsular. Managing an estate this size is daunting, but I look forward to the challenge. I also intend to increase my investments in my family's business ventures. I have a flair for business that will guarantee the prosperity for future generations of Cardells. Which brings me to another proposition I would like to put to you.'

'Ah, I thought there might be a catch. Which is?'

'Your sister.'

Lord Sinclair was unable to conceal his shock. 'Juliet?'

Marcus nodded. 'If you will allow me to offer marriage to her, it will benefit us both. I am a widower with a six-year-old daughter. I wish to remarry and settle down.'

'But why Juliet? Forgive me, Lord Cardell—I applaud your taste—but I can't help thinking that if I were to consent to your proposal, it would be like feeding her to the wolves.'

'Do not underestimate your sister. I strongly suspect that she has the courage to pit her will against any man, including me. I choose your sister to be my wife, and in doing so, I confess that I do not make this decision lightly. I know this is sudden, but I have met her on several occasions, and I have discovered she has a temper, is wilful and of an unpredictable disposition, but beneath that, I sense a softer side to her nature.'

'I agree with what you say. She does have a temper and is rebellious, which is our father's fault. He indulged her every whim and allowed her far too much freedom. Mother and I warned him, but he would only laugh and tell us not to worry, that his little Juliet would turn out to be so beautiful that no one would care how stubborn and wilful she was. She will need gentling with a firm hand by the man she marries, should that man be you.'

A smile tempted Marcus's lips. 'It would be a sin to tame such a prize. It is her spirit that I admire most. May God help me if I do anything to change what's inside her.'

'I'm relieved to hear it. She is naive and innocent and refreshingly virtuous—unhampered by caution or wisdom. You ask my permission to marry her, but having just turned twenty-one, she is of an age where she does not need my permission, although I wonder with some trepidation how she will react when she discovers what you intend.' He cast an apologetic glance at him. 'She has no dowry, which is an embarrassment to me.'

'That is immaterial to me. My desire to marry her was not inspired by thoughts of fortune. I am a wealthy man, wealthy enough to keep my wife in the manner to which she is accustomed. She has even met my daughter in the park. They fed the ducks together and Adele has talked of nothing else since.'

'You are aware that she was engaged to be married, that her betrothed was killed at Albuera.'

'I know she was betrothed but not the identity of the man she was to marry. Who was he?'

'Thomas Waring, the son of a baron. Like you, he was a second son who made his career in the army. Did you know him by any chance?'

'I knew of him, but I can't recall meeting him.'

'The family's ancestral home is also in Surrey, just ten miles from my own.'

Marcus nodded. 'There are three sons I believe, somewhat wayward.'

'Thomas was that,' Lord Sinclair said, unable to conceal his dislike of the aforesaid gentleman.

'I sense by your tone that he did not come high in your esteem.'

'No. The truth is that I disliked him intensely. He was never without female distractions. His attitude to love and women had always been easy going, take it or leave it. It was his father who insisted that he marry Juliet. The baron is a fiercely proud man and would not have the ancient line of Warings sullied by having any of his sons marry just any woman. Juliet was the daughter of his good friend—my father. She was the kind of woman he wanted Thomas to marry, to bear his grandchildren, not one of those unsavoury doxies he kept company with in London.'

'He was as bad as that?'

'Absolutely. Thomas took his father's advice and also took advantage of Juliet's naiveté and innocence and courted her, admitting that his father was right. Thomas boasted that she would make a perfect wife, the daughter of an earl. No doubt he thought she would be the perfect wife he could keep tucked away in the country while he continued to enjoy the kind of life he had become accustomed to in London and pursue his military career.'

'Did you not try to dissuade her from marrying him?'

'Yes, constantly. But it was useless. She was hell-bent on marrying him. Her ears were deaf to any criticism.'

'As strong minded as your sister is, I can understand that.'

'Absolutely.' His expression became grave. 'You must want to marry her very much.'

'I do. We have only known each other for a short time, but I have developed a high regard for her. I pray she will accept my proposal.'

'Then, what can I say? I have no objections, but you must realise that in the end, the decision is hers to make. She is not easily persuaded. She has also some idealistic notions concerning marriage, and love plays a prominent part, although the circumstances are such that it will leave her with no choice but to marry you. But what if she doesn't? My debt to you will still remain.'

'I would not like your sister to feel obliged to marry

me simply to get you out of a hole. That is the last thing I want. Are you able to settle the debt?'

Lord Sinclair became silent, thoughtful as he mulled over his options. 'Yes,' he said at length. 'Yes, I can.'

Marcus nodded slowly; his eyes narrowed. 'Forgive me. I thought you were—'

'What? Penniless. Not quite. I still have the house in St James's Square.'

'You would be prepared to sell it?'

'If I have to. I realise it would only be a temporary solution to settling my debts, but it would be a start and give me a little more time to try and get my house in order. Should Juliet turn you down, then that is what I will do. I love my sister dearly, Lord Cardell. I would not like her to think I was forcing her into a marriage that was not agreeable to her.'

'Then the decision is hers. I will not force her into anything, but should I be fortunate and she accepts my proposal, I promise you that I shall woo her like her most ardent suitor and strive to behave impeccably. I have it on good authority that you are seeking to wed yourself, Lord Sinclair, which tells me you are looking to the future.'

'That is correct. There is a lady who is very dear to me, but my financial situation does not extend to marriage at this present time.'

'Your future will not look so bleak should your

sister become my wife. I will do what I can to help you, but you must give me your word that you will keep away from the card tables in future.'

'I know that and I will. I have learned my lesson. Let me assure you that I intend giving the matter of the water meadows serious consideration.'

'I would appreciate that. Now that the most pressing issues have been decided upon, the marriage—should she consent to my proposal—money and business arrangements will be handled by our lawyers.'

Marcus and Richard took their leave of each other, Marcus accepting Richard Sinclair's invitation to dine the following evening to discuss the future with his bride-to-be.

It was early evening when Daphne knocked on Juliet's bedroom door and told her that Lord Cardell had arrived and that he was ensconced in the drawing room with her brother. Having been told by Richard of his meeting with Lord Cardell the previous day at his club and that Lord Cardell had a proposition to make regarding the settling of his IOU, one he hoped Juliet would be in favour of, he had invited him to dine. She told Daphne to inform her brother she would be down shortly. Casting all melancholy thoughts aside, with a firm resolve inside her, she prepared herself to face Marcus Cardell and what he had to offer squarely.

As she went down the stairs, she felt like an actress on the eve of a new performance, all her senses concentrated on making it a success, for on that success, her own and Richard's survival depended. She had to make it the performance of her life, and her instinct told her that if she kept a level head, she could do it. And survival was a question of instinct. *Dear Lord, let it serve me well.*

She entered the drawing room quietly, and although the candles had been lit, the heavy curtains were not yet drawn. Lord Cardell was staring out at the street, his hands joined loosely behind his back. Richard stood by the fireplace raising a glass of brandy to his lips. The soft rustle of her skirts betrayed her presence and Lord Cardell turned sharply. For all the room was quite large and high-ceilinged, his tall broad-shouldered frame appeared to make it smaller. He was as immaculately dressed as he had been at Lord and Lady Wyatt's dinner party with the exception that his long muscular legs were now encased in polished black knee boots. He was standing perfectly still, watching her.

Something in his expression made the breath catch in her throat, and the spell was broken, but the effect of that warmly intimate look in his eyes was vibrantly, alarmingly alive. She did not know this man very well at all, and yet even now he was watching her with a look that was much too personal—and possessive. In the candlelight, his tanned strikingly handsome face had taken on a curiously softer look that she remembered from two days before. But despite this and his polite, correct manner, Juliet sensed something purposeful and intent about him, which troubled her and made her feel uneasy.

'Ah, you're here at last,' Richard said, placing his glass on the mantelpiece.

'I apologise if I've kept you waiting,' she replied, her manner stiff.

'Lord Cardell and I were just reminiscing about the times when he visited his aunt and uncle at Mulberry Hall, Juliet, although Lord Cardell's memory is somewhat vague about the couple of times we were there with Mama.'

Marcus nodded slowly as he tried to recollect. 'My memory is not as vague as I thought, although I confess it is still somewhat hazy,' he said, looking at Juliet. 'I remember a young girl—I assume that was you.'

'Yes, it was. I was four or five, I think.'

'Your sister took an aversion to me when we met recently on my arrival at Mulberry Hall. I cannot for the life of me think why.'

Richard laughed. 'Can you not? Then let me enlighten you. I think it stems back to a game of hide and seek when you shoved her into a cupboard. Unfortunately for her, she couldn't get out. The game ended and you went home. It was hours before we found her. She was terribly upset and never forgot it. She still refuses to sleep in the dark. It was a foul thing to do.'

Marcus looked mortified as the memory of the incident came flooding back. 'Yes, it was, but please believe me when I say it would not have been intentional. I have just a vague memory.' He looked at Juliet. 'Was that you?' She nodded. 'You must have been very scared.'

'Who wouldn't be? Locked in a cupboard for hours in the dark.'

'I didn't lock you in.'

'I discovered that afterwards,' Juliet said quietly. 'The door stuck. You were at Mulberry Hall with your brother and a couple of friends. You hardly noticed me, but I did so want you to involve me in your games.'

Marcus frowned, looking at her hard. 'I do remember now. We were on the point of leaving for London when something went wrong with the coach—a wheel came off or something to that effect—so we decided to have a game of hide and seek while it was being fixed. I remember you looking for somewhere to hide—you were excited and keen not to be found, which was when I shoved you into the cupboard, not realising the door would stick. I can imagine your ordeal, your terror.'

'I couldn't believe you had left me in there. It was very dark, and I couldn't get out no matter how hard I tried. I shouted, but no one came. Everyone was taken up with you leaving. I thought someone would miss me and come looking for me. Even a little time in that place was terrifying. Richard found me three hours later.'

'Good Lord! As long as that? I am so very sorry, Lady Juliet. Little wonder you were hostile towards me when we met. How could you not be afraid to be shut up in that place?'

Richard poured a glass of wine and handed it to Juliet. 'Dinner will be announced shortly. In the meantime, I think we should discuss Lord Cardell's proposition, Juliet. I pray you will be in favour of it.'

'So do I,' she replied, sitting on the sofa and taking a sip of wine before placing it on the small table in front of her. Folding her hands in her lap, she looked from her brother to Lord Cardell expectantly, unable to ignore the look of caution that passed between them and beginning to feel decidedly uneasy all of a sudden. 'Well, which one of you is going to enlighten me?'

Lord Cardell glanced at Richard. 'You haven't told her?'

'Er, no, not yet.'

'Then perhaps you should do so—now.'

Juliet stared at her brother. 'Told me? Told me what? Come, Richard. You know how I hate subterfuge of any kind. If there has been a development, then it concerns me. It's not right to keep it from me.'

Somewhat reluctantly Richard began telling her about Lord Cardell's offer regarding the water meadows, how he was prepared to exchange Richard's IOU for ownership of the fifteen acres.

Juliet listened patiently, hardly able to believe what she was hearing. She stared at him through eyes enormous with disbelief. Suddenly, through the turmoil in her mind, something penetrated, something so awful and humiliating that she fervently hoped neither Richard nor Lord Cardell would confirm it. It was a picture of lush green meadows full of strawberry roan cows munching contentedly on the grass. That Lord Cardell was prepared to buy them in exchange for Richard's IOU was indeed a generous offer, but there was something not quite right about it.

'I see,' she said when Richard fell silent. 'It is indeed generous, but isn't it a bit one sided? The water meadows are worth far less than what you owe Lord Cardell, unless...'

'Unless what?' Lord Cardell said, crossing the room slowly and looking down into her upturned face.

'Unless there is something else, something you haven't told me.'

'Yes, there is,' Richard said, giving her a nervous smile before looking somewhat desperately at Lord Cardell to help him out.

'And?' she asked without taking her eyes from the man looming over her.

'I would be honoured if you would agree to be my wife,' Lord Cardell said softly, watching closely for her reaction.

For a moment Juliet's mind went completely blank. She stared at him in confused, disorientated shock. What colour remained in her face drained away. When the words finally sank in, shock and horror brought her surging to her feet. Her eyes blazing, she glared at him, and when she spoke, her voice shook with the violence of her outrage.

'Of all the conceited, vile, despicable, under-handed... Oh!' she seethed, unable to think of any more expletives to portray her animosity. 'You ask me to be your wife in exchange for—let me see—after the price of the land has been deducted, it will be going on for three thousand pounds.'

'Juliet...' Richard said, clearly cursing perverse fate for making what had already been a difficult situation into one that looked fit to worsen. 'Please listen—'

'Listen? Listen to what?' she flared, glaring at her brother. 'I do not feel particularly complimented by

Lord Cardell's intentions and even less flattered by the manner of his proposal.'

Richard frowned, clearly disappointed by her reaction. 'Do not be too hasty in your rejection of Lord Cardell. This is a great opportunity. What matters is that he wants to make you his wife. He has a large estate, and you would still be close to Endcliffe House. You would find him most generous.'

Juliet glared at her brother in disgust. 'Good heavens, Richard, you make it sound as if I'd been offered a kingdom. I care nothing for his wealth,' she told him, sounding harsher than she had ever sounded when she addressed her brother. But considering the circumstances, it was important that her feelings had to be made plain to Richard so he wouldn't browbeat her into marriage to Lord Cardell. 'I want nothing from him but the settlement of what is owed by you. Next you will be telling me that the matter is already settled.'

'Well, of course I gave him my permission to go ahead and court you.'

'I am of an age where I no longer need permission from you, Richard. But how could you agree for me to marry a man who was almost a stranger to me until not so very long ago without consulting me?' She looked again at Lord Cardell, who had remained infuriatingly calm so far. 'I find the manner in which you have hatched this plot to secure the water meadows and to marry me behind my back, arrogantly expecting me to fall in with your wishes without argument, both insulting and degrading. You must want to marry me very badly if you are willing to *buy* me,' she retorted, her face a stiff mask as she fought the anger and shame churning within her, and the unbelievable hurt that this might be so.

Lord Cardell cocked a handsome brow as his eyes locked on hers with a frowning intensity. 'Well, you certainly know how to turn a man down, Lady Juliet.' He looked at Richard. 'Would you leave us? I would like to speak to your sister alone.'

Richard looked relieved. 'Of course.'

Battered, humiliated and deeply hurt, Juliet watched him leave the room before looking once more at Lord Cardell, feeling the full weight of her misery, her foolishness and for the time she had wasted trying to understand the turbulent, all-consuming emotions this man always managed to arouse in her. At Lord and Lady Wyatt's dinner party and again at the bookshop, she had felt protected and full of a cool self-assurance, but here, in the intimate privacy of the drawing room, where the only sounds to be heard were the clatter of carriage wheels out in the street and the somnolent tick of the clock on the mantelpiece, she was uncomfortably conscious of the overwhelming presence of this man who had come so suddenly into her life at a time when she was lonely and so very vulnerable, when her spirits had sunk to such a low ebb that it would be so easy for her to turn to anyone who offered comfort.

Suddenly Lord Cardell laughed, a soft, velvety sound. 'You're not afraid of being alone with me, are you?' he asked, his eyes and voice challenging.

Juliet looked at him steadily for a long moment, at his darkly handsome face. Fate was moving quicker than she had anticipated. 'No, I'm not afraid of you, Lord Cardell.'

'Thank goodness. I apologise if my proposal has taken you by surprise. I've been too long in the Peninsular, where we do not always stand on ceremony. Perhaps now that we are alone, we can discuss this matter in a civilised manner.'

Juliet's trembling chin raised to a lofty level as she eyed him coolly. 'I do not think much of your methods of procuring a wife. What you did was vile and contemptible. Your deviousness and deceit do you no credit,' she told him bluntly. 'I want nothing from you—absolutely nothing,' she said tonelessly, the repetition with which she issued this statement already beginning to ring a note of insincerity in her mind, the weakening increasing her anger. Her eyes speared him like shards of steel. 'I will not be paid for—certainly not by a man whom I know will demand value for his money. I have my pride, Lord Cardell, and when it comes to the truth of the matter,

I consider myself above the price of fifteen acres of land and three thousand guineas.'

'You are wrong if you think that.'

'Am I?' She raised her brows. 'Richard is to give you his water meadows in part exchange for his debt to you. My own part in this sordid affair is far greater.'

'Believe me when I say that I was not comfortable taking your brother's money. When I proposed a game of cards, I was unaware of his colossal debts. Afterwards, I wanted to make reparation without taking away his dignity.'

'At my expense. Well, it appears you have gotten your wish. I suspected you had your eye on the water meadows when we met that day.'

He nodded. 'Your suspicions were correct. I have gotten my wish, but it is the matter of my proposal of marriage that interests me more.'

The husky sincerity in his deep voice was beginning to make Juliet feel most uncomfortable. The fact that she could even consider entering into a marriage with a man she barely knew was quite outrageous. The fact that she found him far too attractive for her own good roused fresh resentment inside her. She had felt herself being drawn to Marcus Cardell against her will by the compelling magnetism he seemed to radiate, and the memory of his smile and how he had looked at her in the bookshop, how his incredibly light blue eyes had hardly left hers for a moment and the intimacy of his lazy gaze, made her tremble and heat course through her body. She was always stimulated at the way they engaged in a casual repartee she was not accustomed to from her male admirers—not even Thomas, who had been easily bored to converse at length with her on matters that were of interest to her. This had both annoyed and upset her, but she would never have dreamt of saying so.

She reminded herself that Lord Cardell might be the most handsome, exciting man she had ever met—more handsome, even, than Thomas, but then she told herself that he was too conceited, too self-assured by far. He was both these things and more, and she must keep reminding herself of this so that she could keep the fires of resentment alive.

But did she want to? She didn't know that either. The more she delved into the exact nature of her feelings for Marcus Cardell, the more she began to compare him with Thomas and to criticise her former betrothed. Feeling the way she did, it not only seemed silly but wrong and childish to go on resenting Marcus. And why should she? Apart from the poaching incident and the fact that a long time ago he had locked her in a dark cupboard and forgotten about her, he had done nothing to deserve her bitterness and animosity. When the memory of Thomas flashed into her mind and how appalled he would be at a match between herself and the man who was almost a stranger to her, it had a distinctly sobering effect of her but didn't last. Thomas was dead and she must go on, and if marrying someone else who was wealthy would ensure that she could go to bed at night and sleep peacefully without having to worry about money, knowing Endcliffe House and Richard were safe, then she would do it.

He was watching her intently. He smiled, and Juliet was caught up in the powerful charm of his expression. *Dear Lord!* she thought. Her wits must truly have fled if a mere smile from him could bring this spurt of pleasure.

With no small amount of admiration, Marcus watched Juliet struggle to maintain her dignity as she moved away from him, trying hard to hold on to her composure. He should have known that a defiant Juliet Sinclair, with an infuriating stubborn streak and unpredictable disposition, would resent and oppose a proposal of marriage having been made secretly between the prospective suitor and her brother instead of quietly accepting and letting the betrothal run its course until the wedding. Clearly it had been an affront to her pride, and her pride would force her to retaliate by making the whole ordeal as difficult as possible for him.

'Will you at least consider my proposal and what

it would mean for both you and your brother? Can I
not persuade you?'

'I care little for your methods and even less for your
kind of persuasion. You insult me, Lord Cardell—fifteen acres of land and me thrown into the bargain. I
consider myself to be worth more than that. Richard
should have negotiated a better deal.'

Despite her haughty stance, Marcus saw that her
beautiful amber eyes, which were blazing scornfully
at him, were also full of hurt. 'You're right,' he said
gently. 'Anyone knowing you would agree that you
are worth much more.'

'When you told me you were looking for a wife,
I had no idea you would choose me,' she said, looking at him steadily.

'How could you? I didn't even know myself then.
It was too soon.'

'Yes, it was. It was arrogant of you to assume I
would accept a proposal of marriage made in this
manner. I do have a mind of my own.'

His eyes captured hers and held them prisoner. 'I
know. That is one of the things that attracted me to
you in the first place.'

'And I am more than capable of taking care of
myself.'

Marcus moved closer to her. Her wide amber eyes
came to meet the mocking smile in his. 'Were you
able to do that, Juliet Sinclair, you would not be in

the situation you are now,' he pointed out. As clearly as she obviously wanted to throw the statement back in his face, he knew that she could not. Her hauteur faded and was replaced by an expression of pained sadness.

'You think that you know me, Lord Cardell, but you don't. You have much to learn.' Her voice was small and oddly strained. 'I take objection to anyone who believes I can be bought.'

Refusing to believe that all his romantic plans were about to be demolished, Marcus folded his arms across his chest and perched his hip on the arm of the sofa, arching his brows as he looked at her. 'When I decided to ask you to be my wife and approached your brother, I was not buying you, Lady Juliet. If you believe that, then condemn me for it if you must, but I beg you to pardon me afterwards. I was clumsy and in too much of a hurry. I should have approached the subject of marriage between us more cautiously, not rushed in without consulting you first. Clearly my mishandling of the situation has put your back up, and I cannot, in all fairness, say that I blame you for being angry. I confess to being drawn to you on our first encounter. I tried to discount it and put it down to infatuation, but when I met you again in the water meadows and again at Lord and Lady Wyatt's house, I had to finally face the truth—that I wanted you to be my wife.'

'I cannot for the life of me imagine why. You can have no idea of what marriage to me would mean.'

Going to her, he gently placed his hands on her shoulders, his eyes grave but calm. 'Oh, I believe I do,' he said softly, relieved that she did not pull away from him. 'And please believe me when I say that it was not my intention to pry into your circumstances. Apparently, it is no secret that since your father's death, your brother has squandered money in every direction, leaving you hopelessly in debt, and that in order to survive, you will have to sell that which you hold most dear—Endcliffe House. I did not know that at the time when I sat down with your brother to a game of cards.'

She nodded dumbly. 'No, I see that now. There will be no dowry, you do know that?'

'That is immaterial to me,' he said, his gaze lingering on the stubborn set to her jaw. 'I know it is the custom for a bride to bring a dowry to her marriage, but it is something I'm not happy with. As a man, it is my responsibility to provide for you, not the other way round. I mean that Juliet,' he said with cool finality. 'You don't mind me dropping the formalities and calling you by your given name?' She shook her head. 'And you must address me as Marcus.'

'I can see you do mean what you say, Marcus. However, I think you carry the issue of pride too far, but since you feel so deeply about the matter, I will let it rest for now.'

Marcus decided there and then that his bride was going to be a challenge if her defiance was anything to go by. 'It is the woman I marry, not what she might or might not bring to the marriage. I recall you saying that you would marry the devil himself if he would settle the debts on Endcliffe House. Did you mean it?'

'Yes, at the time. I realised afterwards that it was a silly thing to say.'

Looking down into her eyes Marcus searched their depths. 'But you were driven to it, I can see that now. In the eyes of the enemy when I fought in the Peninsular, I was likened to the devil many times, but I hope you never have cause to see me as such. Would you prefer to remain as you are—struggling to pay creditors and eventually losing all you hold dear— or marriage to me? I am offering you a chance to be happy, a future that is secure. I promise you that if you marry me, I will secure your home, since it is so precious to you and if it is to be a condition of your acceptance.' He saw relief flood her eyes and sighed. 'I'm right, aren't I?'

She nodded. 'Yes. Thank you. It means everything to me.'

'Marry me and Endcliffe House will be on your doorstep. I promise I will do all in my power to help your brother get back on his feet and make the End-cliffe estate one to be proud of once more.'

Juliet's eyes widened. There was a softening in their exquisite depths, and he could see some of her belligerence fading.

'You would do that?' she whispered.

'Yes, but your brother must change the way he lives his life. I will neither fund nor advise a gambler.'

'Richard takes after our father, I'm afraid.'

'He was a gambler also?'

'Very much so. Much of what has happened was down to him. His profligacy and lack of judgement had already squandered much of the family fortune before Richard was born. He borrowed money from his friends and was unable to repay it. And so it went on. But Richard has promised me he will change his ways. He understands that and has sworn to me that he will give up gambling. Indeed, there is a lady— the Earl of Bainbridge's daughter, Amelia—they live in Berkshire. Richard is enamoured of her, but her father refuses to consider his suit until he mends his ways, which is another incentive for him not to gam-ble. But why me? Why do you want to marry me?'

'Because I need a wife.'

'But there are thousands of women in London. Why me? With all my debts, I can only be an en-cumbrance to you.'

'Because you are the only one who interests me.

The only one I want—debts and all. I want to make you smile, to laugh, and I want you to savour all I have to offer.'

'I must be frank with you, although I suspect you already know what I am about to tell you. After all, you do seem to know everything else about me,' she said not unkindly. 'But until a short time ago I was betrothed to someone I loved dearly. He—he was killed in Spain, shortly before we were to have been married,' she finished softly.

Marcus nodded, noting how her face changed when she spoke of him, bringing a softness, a mistiness in her wide eyes, and he felt a sudden rush of resentment towards this past love of hers. His face remained impassive when he next spoke. 'Yes, I did know. But time is a great healer, Juliet. You were both very young. You will forget.' Immediately he regretted saying these words, for her eyes were suddenly charged with anger.

'I may not have the benefit of your experience, but I loved him more than life itself, and I know that I shall never forget him.' Her anger melted and she sighed, lowering her eyes. 'I shall probably never love you, Marcus. I shall probably never love any man, so if,' she said, her face pale and tense, 'knowing this, you still want to marry me, and if you will promise to secure the Endcliffe estate, then I accept. However, you must realise that whatever it costs to get the estate back on its feet, it must be considered a loan. Richard, I am sure, will pay it all back, given time—and good harvests and investments.'

Marcus understood what she was saying and was full of admiration for her steadfast loyalty to the man who had brought her to near ruin. But Richard Sinclair was her brother, and whatever he was guilty of, she would cloak his sins and utter no words that would dishonour him in any way. He smiled a strange, crooked smile and placed his fingers gently beneath her chin, tilting her head, forcing her to meet his gaze. 'I am sure he will, Juliet, but believe me when I say that marriage to you will be payment enough. However, there is something I should mention, and do not think too ill of your brother. He told me that should you decide against becoming my wife, he intends on selling this house to cover his debt to me.'

Juliet stared at him aghast. 'He—he said that?'

'Yes. You see, he doesn't want you to feel under any obligation to me. So, Juliet, you do have a choice.'

Shaking her head, she tried to absorb what he had said. 'But—but we have discussed selling the house and Richard decided against it at this time. I—I had no idea he would do this.'

'Despite his weakness for gambling, you are his sister and he loves you enough to not force you into an unwanted marriage. Knowing this, will you still agree to marry me?'

Lowering her head, she turned from him, biting her bottom lip as she considered this new turn of events. Marcus watched her, praying she wouldn't change her mind. At last, she turned and looked at him, her mind made up.

'I am indeed grateful to Richard—that he would do this for me, but no, it makes no difference. Selling this house would be a mere drop in the ocean to what he owes his creditors. I have made my decision. I will marry you, Marcus. Indeed I will be happy to be your wife.' Her lips trembled into a smile. 'We hardly got off to a good start, and I made my resentment towards you quite plain.'

He grinned. 'And the reason for that, your brother has just explained to me. I did not lock you in that cupboard. I thought I was doing you a favour. I merely closed the door so you would not be found, and it stuck.'

'And to make matters worse, you forgot about me and went home without another thought for me.'

'For which you have my most profound apology.'

'When I recovered from the ordeal, my mother told me I would forget it. The memory would fade. It was like a nightmare, but it was not real, though for a long time I dreamt I was still in that cupboard.'

'I regret my thoughtlessness for being to blame

for you having to endure such a terrible experience. You were a quiet, shy child as I recall, a little like Adele is now.'

'I enjoyed meeting her in the park. She is such a charming little girl.'

He nodded, a troubled look entering his eyes. 'She is and I love her dearly. Unfortunately, I have been apart from her too long. My mother has had full charge of her since Elizabeth, my wife, died. It is my intention to make up for the time we have both lost, and to do that I must spend as much time with her as I am able. I am impatient to involve myself fully in the running of the estate, but my mother refuses to let me take Adele to Mulberry Hall until I have found myself a wife.'

'I see. I am beginning to understand your hasty proposal to me,' Juliet said, her tone resentful once more.

'I would have proposed marriage to you regardless of my mother's demands.'

'You would?'

'Yes. You are an original, and I find you considerably more interesting and amusing than any of those simpering young ladies who were present at Lord and Lady Wyatt's dinner party.'

'Is that a compliment?'

He nodded, smiling. 'The first of many. But I have to ask you how you feel about becoming Adele's stepmother. She was quite taken with you when you met in the park, which is unusual for Adele. She has never reached out to anyone the way she did to you that day. Her care is my concern, and it would help me a great deal knowing that the person who will share her upbringing with me is someone I can trust. Of course, a governess will be found for her in due course. Looking after Adele, worrying about her, wearies my mother, and finding the right nursemaids to care for her has often proved a problem in the past. You may find looking after her demanding, and it will require all your patience.'

'What can I say other than I will do my best to take care of her and make her happy? Children have never played a part in my life, but I am sure we will get along just fine.'

'So you will accept my proposal of marriage?'

She nodded, lowering her eyes. 'Yes,' she said softly. 'It would be foolish of me to refuse.'

'I couldn't agree more. Now,' he said, drawing her closer, 'I think a kiss is in order to seal the matter. Do you not agree, Juliet?'

Tilting her head, she looked at him, her eyes wide. 'Yes, I have no objections.'

Something clenched painfully in the region of Marcus's heart as he took her hands and lowered his head to hers, having wanted to kiss her since they had met at the Ruskins' house. His lips captured hers. Her mouth was soft and the texture beyond his imagination. He had wondered what it would be like, suspecting that her lips would be sweet and warm, but he could never have guessed at the powerful desire it would awake within him the moment his mouth touched hers.

She gasped and removed her hands from his, her fingers gripped his shoulders. Her entire body responded to his kiss as instinctively she arched closer. Her mouth clung to his, causing his blood to race in his veins, and warmth flooded through him. Marcus had never felt such explosive desire before, and a warning bell rung in his brain. If he did not bring to a halt this sweet moment of desire, he would be unable to stop, and before he knew it, he would have gone too far. One thing he did know was that she desired him as much as he desired her and that she would not be a reluctant bride. He tore his lips away from hers.

'Dear Lord, Juliet, what are you trying to do to me? That,' he said, his voice low and husky, 'was not what your brother left us alone for.'

Juliet sighed and disentangled herself from his arms. 'No, it wasn't, but at least the matter of our marriage is settled now. Richard will be pleased.'

Her brother took that moment to return to the room.

'Time to eat,' he said, rubbing his hands, looking expectantly from one to the other. 'Please tell me the matter I left you to discuss is now settled and we can move on.'

'Yes, Richard. You will be relieved when I tell you that I have accepted Lord Cardell's proposal of marriage, but you really should have told me that should I have refused, you were prepared to sell this house.'

He grinned sheepishly. 'I wanted you to have the choice, Juliet. It was the least I could do. I am pleased you have agreed to wed, that we will be neighbours as well as brother and sister. Now,' he said, rubbing his hands with glee, for things could not have turned out better, 'let us go in to dinner and we can discuss the details.'

'Of course,' Marcus said quietly, his gaze settling on Juliet's face. 'It is my intention for the wedding to take place as soon as possible.'

Juliet glanced at him. A serious note had entered his voice, and he wasn't smiling any more as his eyes held hers. Startled by his frankness, curiously she felt her nervousness subsiding despite the doubts she felt over becoming his wife. She wasn't at all displeased by his suggestion that they marry as soon as may be. And why should she be? she thought wryly. Wasn't this just what she wanted, an opportunity to hold on to all she held most dear?

Marcus Cardell was conscientious and considerate, a man with a strong responsibility for his estate and his daughter, whom he clearly adored and wanted only the very best. He had proven to be the solution to all her worries, yet it was imperative that she keep all her wits about her. Thoughts of Thomas stirred powerful, painful memories and emotions, especially now when she had decided to relegate him to the past.

When they had become betrothed, she had thought he would come back from Spain and they would be married. She realised now she had been living in a fool's paradise. Nothing had turned out as she had hoped. Now she had to think about making a new home for herself—a stepdaughter and connections and what each partner could bring to a marriage as their relationship developed. She would be mistress of Mulberry Hall. Many women would be thrilled to be in her place. She knew what she had to do. She could not sacrifice her brother because of her own selfish reasons of wanting love as well as marriage. For a moment she felt as if she were suffocating. It was like being back in that cupboard.

Chapter Six

In the dining room, the three of them were seated at the table in the centre of which was a bowl filled with pink roses, each one soft and velvety and perfect, giving off the most gentle, heavenly scent. Marcus was both polite and attentive throughout the meal, keeping the conversation impersonal. The more Juliet relaxed, the more she looked at him, letting her gaze linger.

She was beginning to feel all the power of his gaze when he looked at her, and although she had sworn never to become romantically involved with any man again, she was not immune to Marcus's dazzling good looks and strong personality. But she did wonder if it was his urgent need to find a mother for Adele rather than his desire for a wife which had prompted him to propose marriage to her. But whatever the reason, she was committed to the decision she had made, and for all she held dear, she would abide by that no matter how much heartache it brought her in the future.

After the meal, she walked with him to the door,

where he turned and took her hand. 'Thank you for the meal, Juliet. I want to assure you that Mulberry Hall is a place that will be worthy of you, and you will be able to visit your old home whenever you wish. I don't want to give you any reason to regret marrying me.'

She nodded as she looked at him, feeling strange emotions stirring in her breast. 'I don't think you'll do that. I only hope I don't give you cause for regret. I do promise to make you a good wife and pray that we shall be tolerably happy.' She smiled wryly. 'After all you've done for me and my brother, the last thing I want is to prove a poor investment.'

Marcus looked at her sharply and his eyes suddenly flamed with anger, at which Juliet immediately regretted her thoughtless, impulsive words, and for the first time since she had known him, she felt fear in her heart. He took both her hands in his own hard grip. His eyes were dark and compelling, forcing her to look into them, and his voice was stern when he spoke.

'Tolerably? An investment? I intend for us to be more than tolerably happy, and I never for one moment considered you an investment. I am not given to pretty speeches, Juliet, and unlike your former betrothed whom you professed to love more than life itself, at this point in our relationship, I cannot offer you that, but what I am offering you is a home, wealth and an estate to be proud of.'

'And I am indeed grateful, Marcus,' she said softly, wishing he had not made that reference to Thomas. Wealth and an estate were all very well and meant that she would live in comfort for the rest of her life without having to worry about how to make ends meet, but they were not at the top of her list when it came to marriage. What she wanted was loyalty and respect, to love and to be loved by her husband, and she could only hope and pray that this would come in time.

'You must understand, Juliet, that I asked you to be my wife because it was you I wanted and for no other reason. The fact that your brother was hopelessly in debt was unimportant. You have told me that you will never love me, that your heart went with the soldier to whom you were betrothed to the grave, and I accept that for now, but time heals many wounds, including the invisible ones, and when it does, you will love again. When you become my wife, when you bear my name, which to me is proud and noble, I shall expect some affection from you and respect, but more than anything else, I want you to be happy.' His voice softened when he looked at her sad, downcast face. He placed his fingers gently beneath her chin. 'Look at me, Juliet.'

Slowly she raised her eyes to his, the candlelight

shining into their amber depths. Despite himself, he was touched by the grief he saw there, which brought a bitter taste to his mouth. He sighed deeply, shaking his head slowly, his eyes never leaving hers.

'I am a fool,' he murmured, 'and I have a distinct feeling that I am going to make an even bigger fool of myself where you are concerned, but you cannot live your life searching for something that is gone, that is dead. It is like chasing the wind. You have to let go, Juliet. Do you think you will be punished if, instead, you look for happiness among the living? That you will have to pay penance? For I can tell you that no amount of tears can bring back the dead.'

Juliet stared at him, lulled into a curious sense of well-being by his words as a rush of warmth and gratitude completely pervaded her and her lovely eyes became blurred, shining like stars with her tears. 'I really do not deserve you,' she whispered, 'and I know you are right, only…it's not that easy to let go.'

'Then perhaps this will help,' he murmured, and very slowly he lifted his lean brown hands and placed them on either side of her face. His eyes darkened as he leaned forward, and at his touch Juliet trembled slightly, with nerves or excitement, she didn't know which, but she did not draw away from him as he placed his mouth on her soft, quivering lips, cherishing them with his own slowly and so very tenderly. His gentleness kindled a response and a warm glow spread over her, but also a fear began to possess her, a fear not of him but of herself and the dark, hidden feelings he had aroused.

When he finally drew away, she remained unmoving, as though still suspended in that kiss, her lips moist and slightly parted. She gazed wonderingly into his eyes, and for the first time since she had met him, the grief was gone from hers, which were very bright with unshed tears. 'How do you think your mother will feel about a marriage between us? She might not take too kindly to you marrying your penniless neighbour.'

'My mother will be delighted. She was not only impressed by you when we met in the park but the way you interacted with Adele and she with you. In fact, my daughter has spoken of nothing else since.'

'Really? I look forward to meeting her again and getting to know her. I—I must insist on a modest wedding, Marcus. I don't want any fuss.'

'It suits me perfectly. The sooner we leave London, the better I shall feel.'

'Then what can I say. I hope I shall be worthy of Mulberry Hall, and I promise to do my best to make you a good wife and stepmother to Adele.'

Marcus's lips twisted in a thin smile. 'I am sure you will, but I have to admit that it does nothing for my pride or self-esteem, knowing it's my wealth and not my charming self that you want. However, I do think we both have something to give.'

His face suddenly became a hard, inscrutable mask, and something Juliet could not recognise flickered behind his eyes, and again she sensed in him something purposeful, something vital that made her feel uneasy, and it came to her that Marcus Cardell was not a man to run afoul of. Ignoring this moment of insight and preferring to think instead of the kindness he had shown her and her brother and his obvious sincerity, she fixed him with a steady gaze. Yes, she would marry him. With everything collapsing about her ears, it was the perfect answer to the many problems that beset her.

But how different it had been when she had loved Thomas, with all the passionate intensity of her youth. How she had yearned to marry him, to learn all the overwhelming joys that love had to offer. But this was to be a different kind of marriage—positive and cold. It was to be a union of two people drawn together by circumstances. She wouldn't think about what would come later but would be content for now, knowing the Endcliffe estate and her home was safe.

Marcus's news of his forthcoming marriage to Juliet Sinclair was warmly welcomed by his mother. The fact that Adele liked Lady Juliet and was happy to be in her company was an added bonus and a great relief to her. She had a few qualms about the part Marcus was to play in assisting Lord Sinclair to clear his debts, but she was sure this would be overcome in time should the young man abide by his promise to keep away from the gaming tables.

When Juliet arrived at the house to be presented to her once more, she received her warmly. Attired in a hyacinth blue gown, Juliet stood watching her future mother-in-law, pale with apprehension. Marcus sighed with relief as his mother smiled to put her at her ease, her eyes tender, for she was determined to befriend this lovely young woman who had brought her son once again to the brink of matrimony. Although he wondered how his mother would feel if she knew that beneath Juliet's pleasant exterior, with her soft feminine elegance, there was a will every bit as strong and stubborn as his own.

Juliet entered the Cardell townhouse with trepidation. She was surrounded by wealth: oil paintings of ancestors and country scenes on the walls, carved furniture gleaming with polish, marble underfoot and chandeliers above.

'I am delighted to welcome you into the family, Juliet, and look forward to getting to know you better.'

'Thank you,' Juliet replied a little shyly, seeing she need not have worried about meeting the dowager countess once again, and finding her kindness comforting. She was so gently solicitous that she found herself warming towards her. 'You are very kind.'

'And you are extremely lovely, my dear.' The dowager countess's eyes twinkled. 'Now I begin to understand how impossible it was for Marcus to resist you.'

Juliet flushed, embarrassed by her words, and a frown of disapproval appeared on Marcus's face at his mother's outspokenness, but she laughed lightly, well used to her son's disapproving looks and knowing how to temper them. It was clear to Juliet that she was not in the least sorry that her words might have caused either of them to feel a sense of awkwardness.

'Marcus has made me aware of the circumstances of why you are to marry, of your brother's unfortunate situation and Marcus's willingness to forgo the debt your brother owed him in exchange for some land and to help set him on his feet, Juliet,' she said on a more serious, gentle note, 'which is unfortunate, and I have to say that where marriage is concerned, I cannot countenance such behaviour. I know how forceful Marcus can be, and I do hope he has not made you feel that you are under any obligation to marry him.'

Juliet flushed as she strove to answer the question. 'Why, I—I—no, of course I'm not. He has been most generous.'

'I'm relieved to hear it. Time presses, however, and it is not for me to sit in judgement or to interfere in something which is entirely between your two selves. That is your affair. But I do hope you feel deeply enough about each other to marry in these circumstances.'

Juliet's gaze met Marcus's, but she could read nothing in it. The dowager countess's remark spoken in a quiet, imperious tone would have been enough to daunt even the strongest heart, and Marcus was no exception. Although not the type of man to be easily intimidated by a woman, and had it been said by anyone else, he would have launched a bitter attack. But this was his mother, whom he loved and respected, and he took her gentle reproach lightly, prepared to be tolerant, and Juliet suspected that his mother would not overstep the mark by antagonising her son.

'Is the sermon over, Mother?' Marcus asked tersely.

A smile lit up her face and she laughed easily. 'Absolutely. I promise. It only leaves me to wish you both every happiness. Marcus tells me he is to take you to Mulberry Hall immediately after the wedding, Juliet. Is that not so, Marcus?' she said, looking once more at her son, her seriousness of a moment before having disappeared.

'That is my intention. It is to be a modest affair, but when news of the marriage gets out, it is bound to create a stir. It is my wish to avoid the inevitable curiosity and questions. Besides, I am anxious for

Juliet and Adele to become better acquainted—the sooner the better.'

'I agree. You will like living at Mulberry Hall, Juliet. It's a lovely old house, although as you are already acquainted with the place, you don't need me to sing its praises, but the estate has been in my mother's family for generations. When my brother died without issue and with Marcus's elder brother William already ensconced at Cranswick Hall, and with more titles than is good for any man, it seemed only right that Mulberry Hall should pass to Marcus. Adele is adorable, but unfortunately, I cannot spend as much time with her as I would like to. She is a quiet, shy little girl, but she is young and will soon warm to you. Being many years younger than myself, you might understand her better than I do.'

With a maid in attendance, Adele entered the room quietly. At first, she only had eyes for her adored father, who swept her into his arms and gave her a fierce hug, inhaling the sweet innocence of her before setting her on her feet once more. Marcus's pride as he looked at his daughter could not have been more evident. It was plain for Juliet to see that he loved his daughter and felt a profound need to protect her. Taking Adele's hand, he drew her forward.

'There is someone I want you to meet,' he said gently to the little girl. 'This is Juliet. You remem-

ber meeting her in the park? She is to be my wife—
your stepmother.'

Adele's face broke into a wide smile when she saw
Juliet. Marcus had told her that Adele couldn't remember her own mother and would be unsure what
a stepmother was, but at that moment, when Juliet
smiled and moved towards her, it didn't matter. As
Juliet became reacquainted with Marcus's daughter,
looking beyond her to where his mother sat, watching the proceedings closely, Juliet saw her eyes were
bright with tears—of gratitude or thankfulness that
the child would be well cared for. Juliet thought she
saw a lightening of her spirits, as though a great
weight had been lifted from her shoulders.

Unable to believe their good fortune, throughout
the days leading up to his sister's wedding to Lord
Cardell, Richard walked with a new spring in his
step. His relief in knowing his estate would not have
to be sold after all was enormous, and he lost no time
in making it quite clear to Juliet that he thought she
had done well for herself. Better, he told her, than if
she had married Thomas Waring. His feelings regarding her one-time betrothed had been far from
favourable.

However, she would be devastated if she knew
what Richard had discovered from an acquaintance
he had met at his club, that Thomas had not perished

in Spain after all but was still alive. Apparently, he had been wounded and taken prisoner by the French and rescued by the partisans, where he had lingered in the arms of a dark-haired beauty who had made his time spent in their camp pleasurable—so much so that he had been reluctant to be parted from her.

May God and Juliet forgive him, but he could not tell her, not until after she was safely married to Marcus Cardell. He would pray that Thomas, who, according to his acquaintance, had gone directly to his home, Amberley Park, in Surrey to see his parents, was in no hurry to come to London. But Richard's instinct told him that what he was doing was right. It was far more advantageous to him that Juliet married Marcus Cardell, and she would be far happier with Marcus than she ever would be with Thomas.

If Thomas had been anything like decent, he would not be deceiving her in this way, and besides, he thought as renewed anger possessed him when he remembered how he had not even bothered to write to inform Juliet that he was still alive, it would serve him right when he finally condescended to come to town and found Juliet had married someone else, someone richer even that his own arrogant, conceited self.

The wedding was to take place the following day. Having written to Lydia to inform her of her forthcoming marriage, she arrived to help Juliet prepare for her big day. She swept into the house, her bunches of ringlets bouncing wildly as she moved, her bright eyes shining. Juliet hugged her warmly.

'Thank you for coming, Lydia. I can't tell you how glad I am to see you.'

'And I can't tell you how astounded I was to learn you are to marry the exquisite Lord Cardell. I couldn't believe it,' but then she held Juliet at arm's length. 'It is true, isn't it? You're not jesting?'

Juliet laughed, taking Lydia's hand and leading her into the drawing room. 'Would I jest about so serious a matter?'

'I guess not.' Lydia sighed, a kind of wonder in her eyes as she looked at Juliet, hardly able to believe that what she had told her was true. 'But I recall you saying that after Thomas died in Spain, you'd never marry.'

'I know. I said a lot of things when he was killed, and I meant every word I said—then. But now I have the future to think about. However distasteful the prospect, I thought that if I must marry, if it is not for love, then it must be to someone I could respect. But the most important thing is that he must be rich. Marcus Cardell is all that. Tell me you understand, Lydia.'

'Of course. I can understand that. But to think that

you were on the point of penury and now, well, look at you. Your position is most enviable.'

'Oh, Lydia, no one is more shocked than I am at the speed with which everything has happened.'

'Where is he?'

'Who?'

'Why, the exquisite Marcus Cardell, of course.'

'I don't have the faintest idea. I won't see him again until I arrive at the church. But I am so lucky, Lydia. Just think, I will be living close to Richard and Endcliffe House. I'm going to miss living there, but I know it will be well taken care of with Richard and his future wife—if her father agrees to his suit once he has found his feet. Hopefully my dear brother will become a reformed character and he will have no objections. I have a lot to thank Marcus for. What he has offered me is a lifeline. I have to take it. He's been so kind, so considerate, and I believe he is genuinely fond of me. Why else would he have asked me to marry him?'

'Why else indeed? You know, you've changed, Juliet,' Lydia said on a more serious note.

'Changed? I dare say I have changed a little. You see, I've made up my mind to put the past behind me and look to the future. My marriage will not be clouded with romantic thoughts—at least not for the present. I've been a captive of my emotions once and I vowed never again, and yet,' she said, a soft flush mantling her cheeks when she thought of Marcus and the times when he had kissed her. 'To feel like that—well, I must confess that it was quite wonderful, and I wouldn't mind in the slightest if I could experience it again. But for the present all my aspirations must be realistic. It is important that I marry someone I can trust, someone I can lean on, and if Marcus can do that for me, then I shall try very hard to love him, although I have to admit that marriage to him scares me a bit.'

'You'll soon get used to it.'

'I do realise how lucky I am, but everything has a price, even happiness, and if I have to leave Endcliffe House in order to preserve it, then I am ready to pay that price.'

The day of the wedding dawned sunny and warm. The ceremony was scheduled for midday, and beyond the occasional moment of panic, Juliet felt a strange detachment as Lydia and Daphne fussed with her appearance.

Dressed in a simple gown of champagne-coloured silk gauze and a small flowered headdress, Juliet married Marcus Cardell. Because she had wanted as little fuss as possible, the wedding party was small. The only people present in the church were close family and just a handful of close friends. Richard walked her proudly down the aisle to meet the man who would be her husband. Marcus's brother, William, the Earl of Cranswick, who had come up from West Sussex to see his younger brother married, acted as Marcus's groomsman. His wife, Alice, had not accompanied him since she was close to giving birth to their third child. A serious-minded man, not as tall as Marcus, William had a pleasant disposition. Welcoming her into the family, he had shown her courtesy and friendliness, putting her at her ease at once.

Looking terribly handsome and resplendent in a claret coat and grey trousers, Juliet was aware of nothing but Marcus's close proximity and his firm hands when they'd slipped the gold wedding band gently but firmly on her finger, and for the first time since entering the church she'd met his eyes, darkly serious and intent. She had to quell the ache that rose inside her when she remembered her dreams of how her wedding day would be if Thomas had not disappeared so quickly and tragically from her life.

There was nothing romantic as she had always imagined, nothing but a seal on a promise that must be kept. When Marcus placed his hand over hers, she felt herself possessed. To this man she had committed her life and there would be no going back. But then, becoming aware of his power, his strength, a feeling of wanting to belong to someone, to be cherished almost overwhelmed her. Feeling herself falling under some kind of spell and resentful of it, she was tempted to flee from the church, anything to escape these new, alien feelings Marcus had brought to life inside her.

She knew he was trying to snare her—it was like a clarion warning in her mind—and she knew it would be wise to flee, but she simply couldn't. It was as if her feet were made of clay. Standing there, his hand holding hers, she suddenly realised that she didn't want to run away, that without Marcus, there was an emptiness in her life that she did not want to admit. Her own lack of discipline and restraint frustrated her, but she wasn't entirely certain whether to blame it on him or herself. She liked him to touch her and welcomed his attentions—and the heat and craving he awakened in her.

When the cleric pronounced them man and wife, with the collective eyes of all those present anticipating his next move, Marcus leaned forward to place a light kiss on her lips so as a seal to their union. His mouth was gentle on hers, as befitted the formal occasion in front of witnesses. Their duty done, they departed in the waiting carriage to St James's Square for a private wedding breakfast.

Alone in the carriage with Marcus, Juliet felt as if the whole day had taken on an air of unreality, and she found it almost impossible to believe that the man sitting next to her was now her husband. She had married him but did not know him well. She glanced obliquely at him, telling herself how fortunate she was when she gazed at his clean-cut profile and proud, handsome features. Turning her mind to the physical side of their marriage, of her duty, and all that would come later, she experienced a curious mixture of terror and excitement.

She remembered how, when he had kissed her, he had made her feel suddenly alive, rekindling desires she had suppressed for so long. Desires that she had told herself she would never experience again after Thomas, which proved how little she knew her own body. The memory of those kisses brought colour flooding to her cheeks, and she looked away, but too late, for at that moment Marcus looked at her and laughed softly. Taking her hand in his own, he lightly touched the narrow golden ring on her finger before raising it to his lips.

The simple act of reassurance released her from her anxiety and she began to relax. The cold numbness that had gripped her from the moment she had left for the church began to melt, and the feel of his lips on her fingers sent a strange thrill soaring through her.

'Tell me what you were thinking. What made you look away?'

'Oh, nothing really. I was only thinking how fortunate I am.'

'Are you happy?'

She nodded. 'Yes. Yes, I am.'

'No regrets?'

'No, none that I can think of.'

He contemplated her for a moment, and Juliet was riveted by his gaze. 'Did I tell you that you look exquisite?'

'No, not yet.'

'Then I will tell you now. You are beautiful, Juliet, like some perfect work of art.'

She laughed, a soft flush on her cheeks. 'I'm sure every groom says that to his bride on their wedding day. I am no more beautiful than any other.'

His eyebrows rose. 'I think I should be the judge of that, and perhaps they don't all mean it as sincerely as I. It is no simple passion that torments me, Juliet, but an ever-increasing desire to have you with me every moment.' Drawing her close, his eyes darkened as they fastened on her soft lips, moist and slightly parted, revealing her small white teeth.

His voice was husky when he spoke, which sent a tremor through Juliet. His breath was warm and close to her ear. She could not remain unmoved by the deep, caressing tone that was like a seductive whisper. Looking into his eyes, warm and liquid with desire, she saw what was in them, and she was moved and excited by it. Over the last couple of days, she had thought of him constantly, wondering what it would be like when she was his wife in the true sense, and now that he was close to her, he was more attractive, more desirable than ever, and the urgency to be even closer to him was more vivid than it had ever been. She swallowed, feeling her body grow warm.

'Would you mind if I kissed my wife now that we are alone? For I fear that when we arrive at the house, I shall not have you to myself for—let me see—at least seven or eight hours.'

Juliet's eyes widened in mock amazement and her mouth formed a silent O. 'That long?' and she smiled softly. 'Then in that case, I think you should.'

Sliding his hand around her waist, he pulled her towards him, his eyes dark and full of tenderness. He did not kiss her at once but studied her face, close to his, with a kind of wonder, his eyes gazing intently into hers before settling on her parted lips, which he at last covered with his own, his arm about her waist tightening, drawing her closer, until their bodies were moulded together and Juliet could feel the hardness of his muscular body. Her heart was beating so hard that she was sure he must feel it. His lips, moist and warm, caressed hers, becoming firm and insistent as he felt her respond, kindling a fire inside her with such exquisite slowness, a whole new world exploding inside her. She raised her arms, fastening them around his neck, returning his kiss, her lips soft and clinging, moving upon his in a caress that seemed to last for an eternity.

Marcus's lips left hers, and he buried them in the

soft hollow of her throat. 'I want you, Juliet. You can have no idea how much.' His voice was a soft murmur, a gentle caress, his mouth close to her own once more. He heard the sharp intake of her breath, but she did not pull away from him, and when he lifted his head and looked at her, his eyes burned with naked desire.

Never had Juliet been as aware of another human being as she was of Marcus at that moment. Each of them was aware of a new intensity of feeling between them, a new excitement, both of them victims of the overwhelming forces at work between them. They stared at each other for a second of suspended time, which could as well have been an hour or two, and Juliet had a strange sensation of falling. She saw the deepening light in his eyes and the dark, silken lashes. She saw the defined brows and wanted to touch his face, to know him. She trembled inside, feeling as if she was on the threshold of something unknown, which caused fear to course through her but also something else, a longing so strong that she wanted to pull him towards her, for him to kiss her with all the savage intensity of his desire.

Then slowly, almost haltingly, Marcus lowered his mouth to hers once more in a kiss that warmed her to the centre of her being. Parted lips, tender and insistent, caressed hers, moulding and shaping them to his own while his arms wrapped round her. She had been kissed before by Thomas and then again by Marcus, but never like this. Those kisses had not aroused the passion that the kiss she had just experienced did, a passion so primitive, which swept through her. A passion almost beyond her control, evoking feelings she had never felt before, and this new awareness of her own desire shook her to her very core.

Seeing the hunger in her eyes, Marcus sighed deeply. 'So, I was right.'

'Right?' she whispered. 'What do you mean?'

'That the first time I saw you, to me, a stranger, you seemed to have everything and, I imagined, every young man in London at your feet. But you seemed remote, as if only part of you was alive. There was also a wilfulness about you, a stubborn tenaciousness that told whoever got in your way to have a care. You became an enigma to me, Juliet, and I was determined to get to know you better, convinced that behind that cool façade you presented to me and the world, there beat the heart of a warm and passionate woman. And, it seems, I was right. I hope you will never have cause to regret your marriage to me.'

'How could I? You have given me everything I could possibly want.'

His dark brows knit together as he considered her thoughtfully, a shadow of doubt darkening his eyes. 'Everything?'

Just for a moment her eyes clouded, but quickly

they became clear, as if she had suddenly come to a decision, and then she looked at him directly, a determined tilt to her chin. 'Well, almost everything.' Smiling, she leaned forward and kissed him gently on the lips, just as the carriage came to a halt outside the Sinclair townhouse. 'Companionship, loyalty and love are important in a marriage, Marcus. It's what I want—what I consider important between two people who are to spend the rest of their lives together, and I am certain that will happen between us with time.'

On leaving the church, Marcus had allowed his gaze to linger on Juliet's features, unable to put his feelings into words. His throat constricted at the picture she presented as his bride. He observed how young she looked, how pale and exquisite her face was against the upholstery, making him realise that it would be virtually impossible to keep his hands off her now she was his wife. Pray God, he thought, let me be worthy of her. Before today she had been lovely, but today, as his bride, she was exquisitely perfect.

When he had swept her into his arms in the carriage, he had kissed her slowly, feeling her lips open under his own. In that instant he felt the suppleness of her body, her breasts pressed against him, and when he felt her surrender, a melting sweetness had flowed through his veins. When he finally raised his head, her eyes had lifted to his, and the gentle yielding he saw in their amber depthsd melted his heart. Already he was anticipating the time when all the guests had departed and they would be alone.

On entering the Sinclair house in Henrietta Street, Lydia, who had been following close behind the newlyweds with Richard, hugged Juliet.

'Congratulations, love, and to you too, Lord Cardell. I sincerely hope you will be happy together. 'You made a lovely bride, Juliet.'

'Seconded by me.' Richard pecked his sister's cheek and shook Marcus's hand.

The wedding breakfast was a prolonged and happy affair, the hired butler and extra staff presiding over the proceedings and making sure everyone was taken care of. The food was exquisite, the champagne cold and delicious, the toasts numerous. Juliet chatted and graciously accepted the congratulations given her by the guests and Marcus's brother, all the time aware that the moment when she would be alone with her husband was drawing closer.

Marcus's mother was clearly satisfied and highly delighted that her second son was married again.

'With your brother in charge of the estate, Juliet,' she said when she managed to get the newlyweds alone, 'your dear mother would have been well pleased. I shall look forward to visiting you at Mulberry Hall, but not too frequently. I want you and Marcus to get to know each other and familiarise yourself with the house without me breathing down your neck.'

'You will be welcome always,' Juliet said.

'I know I will, my dear,' the dowager countess said, looking fondly at her new daughter-in-law. 'I hope you will like living at Mulberry Hall. It is natural that you will be filled with trepidation, but you will soon settle down and grow to love the place.'

'I'm sure I shall,' Juliet said, smiling.

Marcus looked at her, his eyes warm and full of affection for his bride. 'And she will love it all the more because I am there,' he teased softly. He arched a brow, amused when Juliet gave him a feigned look of exasperation.

'Why, I see your conceit has not diminished now you are a married man, Marcus,' she chided playfully.

'You're not impressed?'

'Not in the least. You're a complete rogue.'

Marcus gazed at her, his eyes amused. 'I do not deny it. But it cannot bother you too much, otherwise you wouldn't have fallen so readily for my irresistible charm,' he teased, and he smiled, the kind of smile that would melt any woman's heart.

Juliet returned his smile a little shyly. 'I am beginning to see that I was a complete fool to get involved with you. You're quite outrageous.'

'Absolutely,' he grinned.

'He always was,' commented his mother in complete agreement.

As they moved among the guests, Marcus was charming, regaling them with fascinating stories of his time in the Peninsular, taking care not to dwell on battles fought which had taken so many men's lives on both sides. They chatted and laughed until, replete and exhausted, the time came for the guests to depart.

Juliet and Marcus were to spend their wedding night at the Sinclair residence. Tomorrow they would leave London for Mulberry Hall. When the time came for the Countess and Adele to leave for the Cardell residence, Marcus had no intention of going with them, until Adele became tearful on being parted from her beloved father. She implored Marcus not to leave her. Concerned that the day's excitement might have proven too much for her, he gave in to her childish appeal and agreed to accompany her, promising Juliet he would return as soon as she had been put to bed.

Seeing Richard hovering in the doorway, seeming undecided whether he should leave for his club so that the newly-weds could be alone, realising she had hardly exchanged a word with him all day, Juliet went to him.

'The day has gone well, Richard, don't you agree?'

'Absolutely. As you know I intend to make myself scarce so you and Marcus can have the Sinclair house to yourselves. I am to reside with a friend for the time being who has put his house at my disposal.'

'Before you leave, come into the sitting room with me, Richard. It's the first time we've had a chance to be alone together all day.'

Juliet relaxed on the sofa, watching Richard with concern as he sat opposite, sipping a brandy. That he wasn't quite himself was obvious. He fidgeted with his cuffs and crossed and uncrossed his legs, which he always did when nervous. They made small talk for several minutes about the wedding and other unimportant matters, until Juliet could stand it no longer.

'What's wrong, Richard?'

'Wrong?' he asked, somewhat surprised.

'Yes, something's amiss. I can tell.'

He laughed nervously, taking another gulp of his brandy. 'Nonsense. Nothing's wrong,' he replied, trying to sound casual.

Juliet studied his face closely. 'Come, Richard. It's me, remember? I know you too well. I always know when something is not quite right. You cannot deceive me. You've been on edge ever since we left the church. What is it?'

He shrugged. 'Nothing. But if you think I've been on edge, then it's probably just the excitement over the wedding and what your marriage to Marcus means for our future.'

'Are you sure that's it?' asked Juliet, not convinced. 'And that it doesn't concern me?'

'You. Of course not.'

Juliet shook her head and sighed. If there was something wrong and Richard didn't want to tell her, then she couldn't make him. 'Well, if you're sure.'

'Yes, I am sure. Don't trouble your head about me. You have other things to think of now. Your husband, for one. You're so lucky.'

'Yes, you're right. I am lucky, aren't I? And you will be too, when Amelia's father agrees to your suit. My marriage to Marcus will make a difference, I am sure of it. But although you say otherwise, I am still not convinced there isn't something you have to tell me.' Hearing a carriage out in the street come to a halt followed by loud knocking on the door, she sighed. 'Whatever it is will have to wait. I think we have a visitor. More than likely, one of the guests forgot something.'

Getting to her feet, she crossed to the window and drew back the drapes a little, peering out at the gathering dusk, noticing the long shadows cast by the surrounding buildings. She sighed, about to turn away, but her eye was drawn to a large carriage in front of the house. The horses were lathered and the carriage travel-stained, indicating that it had come a long way.

Juliet suddenly turned icy cold when she recognised the familiar coat of arms emblazoned on the door panel. It was the Waring crest.

She stared at it, unable to believe what she saw, but then she told herself that it must be some relation of Thomas's, his father, even, and she reproached herself for not having written to tell him of her marriage. Letting the curtain fall back, she turned and faced the door. A footman stood aside to allow the visitor to enter.

'Lord Thomas Waring, my lady.'

Juliet froze, one hand rising to her throat, the colour draining from her face, her lips, and her eyes fastened on the man who had entered the room sporting a gold-knobbed walking cane. He was quite tall, with a languid, aristocratic grace, his attire elegant. He wore a dark blue coat, and there was white linen spilling from his neck and wrists.

Juliet stared at him, unable to believe her eyes, remembering so vividly the pale blond hair falling in a heavy wave over his forehead and the handsome features, the cynical smile on his lips and hooded lazy grey eyes. She must be dreaming. It could not be true. How could fate play such a cruel trick? Thomas was dead and she was married to someone else.

Chapter Seven

Thomas looked at her and smiled lazily. Juliet felt all the blood drain from her face and with one hand frozen at her throat she watched, feeling an agonising wrench in the region of her heart, as he moved farther into the room. Then she knew her eyes were not deceiving her.

'Thomas,' she breathed, a hazy mist floating before her eyes, darkness threatening to engulf her. 'It—it cannot be you. They told me you were dead.'

He raised his brows in mock surprise. 'Did they really? I assure you, Juliet, that—as you see—I am very much alive.'

It was then that Juliet gave a desperate cry and crumpled to the floor.

Alarmed, Richard hurried to her and fell to his knees beside her, taking her cold hand in his while raising his face to Thomas Waring, utter dislike blazing from his eyes. 'Why did you have to come here? Why couldn't you leave her alone?'

Very slowly Thomas smiled, a thin, cruel smile, his eyes like ice. 'I shouldn't have thought it necessary for me to have to explain my reasons to you, Richard, and, besides, Surrey is a trifle dull just now. Why did you not tell Juliet that I am alive?'

'I didn't want her to know. I hoped and prayed she'd never find out. My God, man! She's better off without you.'

'How could she not find out? This is London, Richard, and gossip spreads like quicksilver. Anyway, shouldn't she be the judge of whether or not she's better off without me? I doubt she would agree with you,' he drawled.

Reassured that Adele was suffering no after effects from the excitement of the wedding, Marcus had returned to the Sinclair townhouse and was going to join Juliet when he heard her strangled cry and halted in shock. Seeing the door to the sitting room open, he hurried inside to find her lying in a crumpled heap on the carpet with Richard by her side. His face clouded with concern.

'Juliet?'

'She's all right,' Richard said quickly. 'She's fainted, that is all.'

Marcus picked her up effortlessly, cradling her in his arms, her head resting against his shoulder. It was only as he straightened up that he became aware of the presence of someone else standing across the room. At first, taken unawares, Marcus was startled by the man's presence, and it was when their eyes met that recognition came to each man simultaneously.

'Permit me to introduce you,' Richard said, his face ashen.

'I think the social distinctions can be ignored, thank you, Richard,' Marcus said tightly. 'We are already acquainted, although his name escapes me.'

'I don't believe we were introduced,' Thomas said, his cold grey eyes narrowed with murderous fury. 'So, it is you. The man I had the misfortune to encounter on my journey back to London.'

'The same, and I observe you have discarded your uniform.'

'Temporarily, I assure you,' he replied, his voice like steel. 'We have an account to settle, you and I. You cannot have forgotten.'

'I have not, and neither have I forgotten the sordidness of the situation in which we met, and I have no doubt you are still the same black-hearted villain who tried to force himself on a defenceless young woman. As I recall, the account was settled. Now, it appears Juliet has received quite a shock. I suggest you leave this house before I do something I would not regret.'

'Wait,' Richard said as he was about to turn away, his face a picture of confusion. 'Marcus, have you no idea who this is?'

'No, nor do I wish to.'

Richard ignored his cutting remark. 'It is Thomas Waring. Thomas, this is Marcus Cardell, Lord Cardell the Earl of Ashleigh. Thomas was betrothed to Juliet before he went to the Peninsular and was reported killed.'

The tension inside the room was ominous, an eerie silence wrapping itself about them.

With anger pouring through his veins like acid, Marcus did not reply at once. He just stared at Thomas Waring, showing neither shock nor surprise, his face a hard, inscrutable mask, the muscles tight. 'Dear God,' he said when he finally did speak, his voice not without contempt. 'How unfortunate for Juliet.'

Still holding Juliet, who was beginning to stir in his arms, he gently laid her on the sofa and stood looking down at her, relieved to see that some of the colour had returned to her face. He was well aware of all the torment, the suffering she would feel when she came to, and it tore at his heart.

The first person Juliet saw when her eyes fluttered open was Marcus, his dark form staring down at her, his eyes full of pain and concern but also something else, which puzzled her—understanding and pity. An anxious Richard stood beside him. Juliet blinked her eyes to clear the mist, wondering what she was doing lying on the sofa, and then she remembered Thomas and that he had come back to her, and her heart leapt and began racing as her eyes moved around the room, searching for him.

Thomas stood, seeming very much at ease at the far side of the room. She stared at him, unable to speak for what seemed to be an eternity, and her eyes shone with the unbelievable comfort of knowing he was alive, and yet why, when he looked the same, did she feel that she was looking into the face of a man she did not know—a stranger?

Seeing her open her eyes, Thomas moved towards her, ignoring Marcus, whose face wore a hard mask of disapproval. With Richard, he stepped back to observe the reunion between his wife and her one-time betrothed.

Aware of and slightly amused by his audience, arrogant in his demeanour, Thomas dropped to one knee beside the sofa and took Juliet's hand in his own. Slowly she reached out with the other and gently touched his cheek with the tips of her fingers to convince herself that it really was him.

'It is you,' she whispered. 'It really is you.'

'Yes. I apologise if my sudden appearance gave you a shock, but I came as soon as I was able.'

'Of course you did,' Richard uttered, unable to conceal his scorn at this barefaced lie. 'But you were reported killed.'

'That I didn't know until later.'

'What happened?' Juliet asked. 'Please, tell me.'

'It was during the battle at Albuera that my horse was shot from under me, and afterwards grapeshot shattered my leg. I was also injured in the chest. I lost consciousness, and I knew nothing else until I came to, only to find myself a prisoner of the French.'

A deathly pallor spread over Juliet's face. So often she had pictured him lying wounded on some battlefield or other, his life's blood ebbing away. She couldn't bear to think of it. 'How did you get back to your regiment? Did you escape?'

'No, it was later, when I began to recover, that I was rescued by the partisans. They came under cover of darkness and freed several prisoners. They returned me to my regiment, but it was only to find that most of it had been wiped out.'

'How dreadful. Are you going back?'

'Yes. I was sent home to recuperate and shall return when the officers who returned with me to England have recruited fresh men.' He smiled down at her. 'Did you miss me, Juliet, as much as I missed you?'

'Yes. Yes of course I did.' Even as she said this, she was vividly aware of Marcus standing behind Thomas as if turned to stone, his hands clenched by his sides, but she did not look at him—she dared not.

Taking her hand, Thomas raised it to his lips and kissed her fingers. 'Would you agree for us to be married before I return to Spain?'

Before she had time to reply, Marcus's voice lashed the air like the crack of a whip. 'That is enough.'

Juliet glanced at him, at his taut face and the thin line of his lips. It was clear he was unable to watch a moment longer this intimate, touching scene and the possessive way Thomas was holding her hand.

'And I would be obliged if you would take your hands off her.'

Thomas turned and stood up straight, fixing him with a cold stare. 'I am baffled as to your presence here, sir. Are you a friend of Richard's? After all, he has a reputation of keeping an odd collection of friends. Juliet and I were betrothed before I left for the Peninsular. We are to be married.'

Marcus stepped forward and he smiled, an absolutely chilling smile, his eyes gleaming with a deadly purpose, his voice cold and lethal. 'I think not. Juliet is no longer free to marry you. She is my wife. We were married today.'

Marcus's words hung like a pall in the air. An unearthly silence fell on the room. The moment was tense. The expression on Thomas's face did not change, but his skin paled and a tiny muscle began to throb at the side of his eye. There was a cold glitter in his eyes when he fixed them on Marcus.

'You lie,' he spat.

'I am not in the habit of lying.'

Thomas spun round on Juliet, who had risen to a

sitting position on the sofa, and his eyes, when they rested on hers, were merciless, his tone cutting. 'Is this true? Is this—this man your husband?' When she hesitated, his voice rang out impatiently. 'Come, Juliet, what have you to say?'

She nodded, gazing up at him, all her wretchedness and pain staring out of tear-filled eyes. 'Yes,' she whispered. 'It is true. But I thought you were dead.'

'Dead or alive, I can see you lost no time in filling my place. How long has it been? Nine or ten months? Were you in such a hurry to be rid of me? The next thing you'll be telling me is how much you love him,' he sneered, 'how you couldn't wait a decent interval of at least a year to marry. For God's sake, spare me that.'

'Thomas, please,' Juliet cried in a terrible anguish, rising to her feet, one hand stretched out to him in her need to make him understand. 'You don't understand—'

Cutting short her protestations, Thomas dashed away her hand. Marcus stepped towards them. The tone of Juliet's one-time betrothed had been deliberately offensive and had provoked his anger further, and he was torn by Juliet's piteous defencelessness.

'Whether he understands or not is of no consequence. The time he has been missing is neither here nor there. You were not married to him, so what does it matter? Juliet is *my* wife.'

Thomas's face was set hard, and a terrible hatred and jealousy directed at this stranger smouldered just beneath the surface to burst like a raging volcano, but an inborn caution seemed to tell him to stay calm, to overcome the overwhelming lust to reach out and tear the man apart with his bare hands. 'Damn you for forcing your attentions on her, knowing she was spoken for.'

'To all intents and purposes, you were dead,' Marcus drawled flatly. 'Or so everyone thought.'

'As you see, I am very much alive.'

'The devil has a way of taking care of his own, and if you intend to remain that way, then I suggest you stay away from me and especially Juliet. So let that be an end to it.'

'An end to it? As far as I am concerned, there will never be an end to it. You have offended my honour. I have a mind to call you out. I want revenge, and I will stop at nothing until I have obtained it.'

Juliet gasped with horror at his words. 'No, Thomas, please, you must not.'

Both men ignored her pleas and their eyes clashed with all the violence born of hatred.

'Honour?' Marcus scorned. 'I dispute that. There isn't an honourable bone in your body, and do not try and fool me. We both know that the revenge you talk of is not, as you would have me believe, for my marrying Juliet. As I remember, you have the disgusting morals of a tomcat, and you make me sorry I didn't kill you when I had the chance. Your sort can only go one way, and I thank God that by marrying Juliet, I have prevented her from being dragged down into the mire.'

Juliet's eyes passed from one to the other in puzzlement as she tried to comprehend what they were talking about. None of it made any sense. That they should feel prejudice towards each other was understandable, but Marcus was talking of another matter which had nothing whatsoever to do with her or their marriage.

'You know each other, don't you?' she asked in shocked disbelief.

'We have met,' Marcus replied. 'But I shall not offend your ears by telling you of the unsavoury circumstances.'

Tell me, Juliet, Thomas had said, *would you have married him if you had known I was alive?*

The echo of his words lingered in the stillness of the room as all eyes became riveted expectantly on her. It was a question she had preferred not to ask herself because she could not endure knowing he might have refused her when he discovered she didn't have penny to her name.

'I—I don't know,' she faltered. 'Please, don't ask me that.'

Slowly and with a deadly purpose, Thomas sauntered to where Richard stood, his limp not quite as pronounced as it had been. Considering the severity of his injured leg, he was lucky in the fact that he had kept his where others had lost theirs. He fixed Richard with a cunning stare, fully aware of what the impact his next words would be.

'Why didn't you tell your sister, Richard? Why didn't you tell Juliet that I was due to come to London? That you spoke with an acquaintance known to both of us, who informed you that my intention was to come to see her just as soon as I had been to Amberley Park to see my parents?'

Juliet's heart suddenly missed a beat and she thought she was going mad. She stared at Richard. 'Tell me it isn't true. Tell me Thomas is lying.'

Richard squared his shoulders, meeting her gaze unflinchingly. 'No. He is telling the truth.'

'So,' breathed Juliet, 'that is what you've been keeping from me. I knew there was something.'

Thomas's lips curled with derision. 'And you are supposed to be her brother, with her best interests at heart.'

Richard looked at him steadily, reading the mockery on his face, but his gaze did not falter. 'You are right. I am her brother,' he said coldly, 'and I have always done what I consider is best for her. That is precisely why I did not tell her. You are a liar and a cheat, Thomas, and many more things besides. I couldn't begin to list them all. You are a man without morals or principles, and you dishonour the very name you bear. You could have written to Juliet, letting her know you were still alive. You had your chances, and then when you returned to London, you could have written or come here, but you chose not to.' His eyes glittered with contempt. 'I don't know who it was that kept you occupied for the time you were a prisoner, but I hope she was worth it.'

Richard heard Juliet gasp and moved towards her. 'God knows, I wanted to tell you, Juliet, but I couldn't. I truly believed—and I still do, I might tell you—that he would have brought you nothing but heartache. For you to marry the likes of him would be like casting pearls before swine.'

'Stop, stop, please stop,' Juliet cried, covering her ears with her hands. 'I cannot bear it. Oh, Thomas, you should have written. You cannot know what it was like for me, the anguish I suffered day after day. I have lain awake night after night, not knowing whether you were alive or dead. Thousands were killed or wounded, yet I heard nothing of you, never a word. All I could do was wonder and pray and—and then your father…he…he wrote and told me you had been killed. I had to come to terms with that. You must understand.'

'You came to terms with it a mite too quickly for my liking, Juliet,' Thomas said with brutal sarcasm.

'However,' and he turned from her sharply, 'I do realise the impropriety of my coming here today. I am well aware that this is your wedding night, and I should hate to rob you of a single minute, so I shall leave you to get on with it.'

'But—but we cannot leave it like this, Thomas,' Juliet cried as he turned and strode towards the door. 'We—we were betrothed. I cannot bear to think I've hurt you. We will meet and talk—not tonight but soon.' She looked imploringly at Marcus, her eyes bright with tears. 'Marcus, please...' But there the words froze on her lips, and she suddenly felt very afraid. His face had paled and his narrowed eyes held a frightening glitter, and she realised that what he felt for Thomas went deeper than anger, deeper even that hatred. It was something she did not recognise and therefore could not understand.

But Marcus had read her mind, and the look he gave her was hard and unyielding, his tone low with contempt. 'No, Juliet. You should know better than to ask that of me. It is inevitable that at some time you will meet socially, but there will be no private meetings between you. He can go and rot in hell for all I care.'

Thomas laughed, a light, brittle sound, but there was no hiding his underlying tension. 'Worry not, Juliet. I will not be far away. You know where I live when I am in town, and should this husband of yours not reach your expectations, then you will know where to find me.' Flinging open the door, he walked out into the hall.

Juliet noticed his limp and was brutally reminded of all he must have suffered in Spain, and her tender heart went out to him. A tearing sob broke from her. He couldn't leave, not now that she had found him again and, gathering up her skirts, she hurried after him, avoiding Marcus's hand when he reached to stop her. 'Thomas, wait. For pity's sake, please wait.'

He stopped and turned, and she came to a halt in front of him, her face awash with tears. 'I'm sorry,' she gulped. 'I know how much I must have hurt you. Please, you must forgive me.'

He looked at her hard for several moments, and his eyes travelled with a lazy insolence over her wedding gown, from the warm glow of the pearls around her slender neck down to her slippered feet before coming to rest on her face. 'Tell me, Juliet, is that the dress you would have worn at our wedding?'

She stared at him in horror. 'Oh, no—no. That would not have been fair.'

'Fair on whom?' he said scathingly. 'Me or the man who is now your husband?' He looked back at Marcus, a cynical curl to his lips. 'As you will know I am a gambling man,' he said slowly, 'and I will lay odds that Juliet will come back to me in the end.'

Marcus's sleek black brows rose mockingly. 'I am

a gambler of some skill myself, and I would not bet on that.'

'Oh, I would. You see, I hold the trump card.'

'And that is?'

'It is me she still loves. Think of that when you lie with her tonight. I shall have her in the end.' With a satisfied smile, he turned and left the house.

Juliet watched him go without a smile or a word of affection or even farewell, and she bowed her head, thinking that he might as well be dead to her. The sound of the closing door and his feet dying away down the steps was like a death knell to her already breaking heart. She stared at the closed door for several moments until, filled with panic that she might never see him again she hurled herself forward. She couldn't let him go, not like this.

'Thomas,' she called, crushed with misery, but suddenly hands caught her, holding her in a firm grip, pulling her back, and she was enraged to find herself helpless.

'Juliet, are you out of your mind? Let him go,' Marcus commanded sharply.

'No,' she cried, whirling round in his arms, a wild expression in her eyes. 'I have to make him understand why I married you. I cannot let him go like this. I might never see him again.'

'And for that I will thank God,' he snapped.

'That's unfair, Marcus,' she said, her voice quivering with anger. 'We were to have been married. Can you blame him for being angry, coming home after what he's been through only to discover that the woman he should have married has married someone else? I don't know what he's done to make you speak of him as you do, but whatever it is, it cannot possibly justify this terrible hatred you feel for him.'

Marcus remained silent, his expression hard, his hands clenched by his sides. 'I met Waring in the most unsavoury situation. I could tell you what took place between us, but I do not want to be the one to shatter your illusions.'

Juliet looked at Marcus, her brother hovering in the doorway to the drawing room, her eyes full of pain and accusation. 'You deceived me, both of you. You should have told me.'

Richard came forward. 'I wanted to—you've no idea how much—but I couldn't. Do you really believe Thomas would have married you, that his father would have allowed him to, when he became aware of our circumstances? He wouldn't. He would have dropped you like a stone.'

Juliet's lips curled scornfully. 'What a low opinion you have of him, Richard. What can he possibly have done to make you hate him so? And yes—yes, I tell you—he would have married me, but you tricked me, both of you, and you had no right. I shall never forgive you for keeping this from me, either of you. I had a right to know so that I could choose for myself.' With a choked sob and a swirl of skirts, she turned sharply and fled up the stairs to seek the sanctuary of her room, but not before Marcus had seen fresh tears shining in her eyes.

Marcus entered Juliet's room. Still attired in her wedding gown, she was standing by the hearth with her back to the door, her body taut, her hands clenched by her sides. She didn't turn as he moved to the centre of the room. Taking a moment to look at her, his throat constricted with pain on seeing her desolation. As she stood there in the flickering golden glow of the fire and candlelight, her hair caressing her shoulders, he thought no one in the whole world was as lovely as she, and he cursed Thomas Waring with every fibre of his being. His very presence had withdrawn her a distance of a thousand miles, and what was in Marcus's heart was like death itself.

Aware of her suffering, rage rose inside him against Waring, and he wondered what manner of man he was that could inspire such a love as hers, but also so much devastating misery. He let his gaze wander around the essentially feminine room he was to have shared for this one night, their wedding night, before they left for Surrey on the morrow but, he thought bitterly, that was unlikely now. He would not make her his wife in the true sense of the word until she had cleansed her heart of Thomas Waring.

Becoming aware of his presence, she turned and looked at him. Her eyes were filled with the pain inflicted on her, her face pale with anger. 'I'm surprised you have come, Marcus. I thought after what has just transpired, you would have left.'

'And why would I do that?' he uttered with a trace of sarcasm, her anger inciting his own. 'Do I have to have a reason for entering my wife's bedroom?'

'Wife?' she scorned, feeding her anger with her words. 'I might not be your wife if you'd been honest with me.'

'Explain what you mean by that?'

'You know perfectly well what I mean. No wonder you were in such haste for the wedding to take place, having me believe it was because you wanted to return to Mulberry Hall when all that time, it was because you knew Thomas was alive and he—'

'Enough,' he snapped harshly. 'Have the grace to hear me out first. Your accusations are unjust. I do not deny that I met him just the once, but I swear to you that I did not know who he was until today, and I will not offend your sensibilities by recounting the sordidness of the situation in which we met.'

'Am I expected to believe this?'

'Believe what you like, but as I told him, I do not lie. What a low creature you must think me, Juliet, but not as low as Thomas Waring. But this I do know. Richard spoke the truth when he said Thomas was a cheat and a liar. The man is utterly corrupt, rotten to the very core, and this worthless libertine is the man you say you love.'

Without taking her eyes from his face, Juliet moved towards him, beside herself with fury. 'How dare you make the one thing I have loved so vile?' she flared. 'I will not listen to your accusations. I do not believe you.'

'Because you don't want to believe me. You cannot get it into your head that your beloved Thomas is anything other than what you know of him, which, it seems, is very little.'

'I knew him well enough to say I would marry him.'

'I doubt that, but just supposing you had married him, do you believe for one minute that he would have loaned Richard the money to save his assets, your home, which you profess is important to you? If you think that, then you are a fool.'

Juliet held her ground while Marcus walked past her to the hearth. Turning, she looked at him. He stood with his back to her, his hands resting on the mantelpiece, his head bowed, his shoulders taut. The cold disdain with which he had uttered the words was like having icy water thrown in her face, and she was suddenly reminded of all he had done for her and was full of contrition. She realised he was just as devastated as she was. He had offered her strength, security and understanding, which she had accepted gladly. She couldn't throw it back at him.

Sighing deeply, some of her anger receded. Nothing could be heard but the rustling of her skirts as she moved towards him. She came to a halt a few feet from him, pausing to gather her wits before she spoke, trying to think where to begin, and because she was so overwhelmed with emotion, she said the first thing that came into her head.

'You're angry, Marcus, and you have every reason to be.' She saw his shoulders stiffen at the sound of her voice, and when he brought himself up straight and turned and looked at her, his expression gave her no reassurance.

'You're right,' he bit out, his mouth set in a bitter line, his black brows drawn in a straight line. 'It would appear that you are already regretting your marriage to *me*.'

Juliet flinched at his enunciation of his last word, which rang with a hollow note. 'But I'm not. Oh, I no longer know what I think. But I am sorry. And perhaps I am a fool. You must think me extremely ungrateful.'

'I did not marry you for your gratitude,' he said coldly. 'That is the last thing I want.'

'Is it true? That you didn't know Thomas was alive?'

'Yes.'

'But Richard knew. He could have told me.'

'Richard loves you, he is your brother, and he would not hurt you intentionally. Because of his past knowledge of your so-called betrothed—which, I might add, seems anything but honourable—he considered that what he was doing was right. He must have gone through hell keeping it from you, but he truly believed he was doing it for your own good.' Smiling crookedly, he moved away from her, paused halfway to the door and turned to look at her again. 'You should thank me, Juliet, for by marrying you, I have saved you from an infinitely worse fate than death. Although I have no doubt you are thinking that you had no need to marry me after all. How could I have been so naive, so stupid? With all my experience and as old as I am, I should have learnt my lesson.'

'Please don't say that, Marcus. You do not understand.'

'What is there to understand? It's simple enough. Before I met you I had only myself and my daughter to take care of. Now, with a wife and a penniless brother-in-law foisted on me, I find I have extra responsibilities I could do without.'

The vicious meaning of his words cut Juliet to the heart. With a surge of genuine anger, her jaw jutted with belligerent indignation, and tension twisted within her as she quickly asserted herself. 'Since you see us as pitiful nuisances—'

'Your words, not mine,' he interrupted harshly.

'Nevertheless,' she seethed, her voice like splintered ice as she took up a stance in front of him, 'that is what you mean, what you were implying. If that is how you see us, then I shall remain in London. You can go to Surrey by yourself.'

'Like hell I will. I will give you a warning, Juliet,' Marcus said in a terrible voice. 'Do not even consider a separation between us. You are my wife, and you will come with me to Surrey when I leave. Is that clear?'

Fury was quick to flare in Juliet's eyes. Moving forwards, she planted her hands on her hips and leaned towards him. 'How dare you, Marcus Cardell! I do not need your permission to do anything, and if I wanted advice, I would not ask you.'

'Then don't. But from now on, you will apply discretion and forethought in your behaviour. I realise how devastated you must feel on finding Waring did not die on the battlefield, and you have my sympathy, but you will never speak with Thomas Waring again. Is that clear?'

Juliet stared at him with hard eyes. 'I shall speak to whomever I choose.' Despite her arrogant words, she felt a spark of fear at the look in her husband's eyes.

'By my faith, Juliet, all I ask is that you do not

speak to him, do not make contact with him.' His soft voice was infinitely more intimidating than a raised one. 'Your loyalty is to me, so let that be an end to the matter. You are my wife, little though I can believe it at this moment. I will have you act your part. You will compose yourself and call upon your dignity. The sooner you accept your position, the better it will be for both of us. You will be accountable to me for your actions. Is that understood?'

Juliet didn't even recoil from his quivering anger. Fury rose up like flames licking inside her, her face as uncompromisingly challenging as his. 'I own no man my superior, least of all you. Ever since I was a child, I have been accountable for my actions to one person or another, being told that women don't have choices, that men make choices for them, but no more. I will not be accountable to you for what I say or do.'

'Yes, you will. Someone should have taught you some sense and tempered that wilful pride of yours years ago,' he said, the anger pouring through his veins making him carelessly cruel. 'Do not defy me, Juliet.'

To her consternation and fury, suddenly Juliet felt close to tears. Rather than let him see her flagging courage and refusing to be humbled, she raised her chin and assumed an expression of remote indifference. 'And if I do?' she ground out in a low voice.

In the face of her defiance, Marcus moved closer and leaned forward until light blue eyes stared into amber from little more than a foot apart. 'You will rue the day. Heed me and heed me well, Juliet. As my wife, you will conduct yourself with proper decorum and never discredit the name you now bear. I am not an unreasonable man, but I can become very unreasonable when I am angry.'

'You are a loathsome, overbearing monster, Marcus Cardell.'

'Yes, I think I have the picture,' he said, stepping away from her.

His eyes narrowed and a murderous glint shone out at her. There was a deep and dreadful silence, a silence so menacing, filled with an unwavering determination of the two to hurt, to destroy one another, that the tension was palpable. 'Do not goad me further, Juliet.'

'But, where are you going?' she asked as he turned away from her.

'I'm leaving. And you needn't worry. I will not be bothering you tonight. I'll spend the night at my home in Mayfair. Tomorrow we'll leave first thing for Surrey. Be ready.'

'What do you mean?' she whispered in bewilderment.

'What I mean,' he said, turning and looking at her once more, his eyes gleaming oddly and one sleek black brow raised, 'is that you can keep your chaste sanctity, my dear. Do you think I would stay with you tonight as, I might remind you, is my right, lie with you, touch you, all the while knowing you were wishing it was your precious Thomas who was beside you?' He looked at her long and cool. 'It is obvious by the way you rush to his defence that you still care for him a great deal, so until the time when it is otherwise, I will bid you goodnight.'

Marcus went out, leaving Juliet staring at the closed door, feeling so utterly bereft, thinking what an awful mess everything was.

A merciful numbness filled her mind as she listened to his footsteps dying away on the landing, and she wanted to go after him, to appeal to his emotions, but she knew that while Thomas was uppermost in her heart, he would remain implacable. He would not yield from his cool verdict and she would continue to sleep alone.

He had been angry and with good reason, and as she stared into the dying embers of the fire, she took stock of all that had happened that day, suddenly so very tired and drained of all emotion. Her feelings towards Thomas were confused and her mind seemed to be going round circles. Why had she been so ready to believe he was dead? Why hadn't she waited before rushing into marriage with someone else? But she told herself, she couldn't have waited if she'd wanted to. Not with Richard's creditors baying at the door.

Her thoughts turned to Marcus. Of her own free will she had married him, nothing could change that and, she thought sadly, it was too late to weep for Thomas and what might have been. She and Marcus were man and wife, and she would honour that, but what her feelings were towards him, she couldn't say, only that they were different from those she felt for Thomas. Marcus had asked her if she believed Thomas would have married her knowing her circumstances, without a dowry and with the added shame of Richard's debts and that they might lose the Endcliffe estate. Would Thomas have secured the estate as Marcus had done? She doubted his father would have agreed to this.

With her heart and mind ravaged by divided loyalty, for her own peace of mind, she had to know so that she could put things right, and to do this she must see Thomas tonight. Marcus intended to leave for Surrey in the morning, so tomorrow would be too late, and if Thomas was to return to the Peninsular, then she might never see him again.

Wishing to avert questions from his mother should he return to his family home in town on his wedding night, Marcus decided against leaving. Occupying another room in the house, lying fully clothed on the bed and hearing the door to the street open and close and a carriage drive off, he went to the window and, looking out, saw the dark silhouette of a carriage disappear. He was filled with a dreadful suspicion that Juliet was inside it.

Cursing softly, he hurried to her room and flung the door wide open. On finding it empty, his eyes darkened until they were almost black, his scorching anger burning a flame in the centre of each one. He knew without doubt that his wife was going to see Thomas Waring. He paused only to enquire of the hired butler the location of the Waring townhouse and to order a horse to be saddled.

Chapter Eight

Juliet was admitted to the Waring house. On being told by the butler that Lord and Lady Waring were not in town, hearing the clink of glass coming from the drawing room, without waiting to be announced, she crossed the hall and pushed open the door and went in. Occupied with pouring himself a drink, Thomas turned. On seeing Juliet, his eyes widened, but then he smiled thinly, a smug, self-satisfied smile, and setting his glass down, he sauntered to where she stood.

He looked untidy without his jacket. His shirt was open at the collar, the fine white linen stained with alcohol. Juliet was disappointed. She had never seen him like this; he had always been so immaculate in the past. It came as some surprise to her to find he had lost some of that magical power to stir the old attraction that had kept her love attached to him for so long. He had also drunk a considerable amount, for his eyes were bloodshot, his aristocratic countenance flushed. She had always been aware of his capacity to absorb large amounts of alcohol, but this was the first time she had seen him lose some of his dignity. When he spoke, his voice was slow and a little thick. He gave her a profoundly mocking bow.

'Why, Juliet, this is a pleasant surprise. I did not expect you quite so soon.'

His lack of elementary politeness irked her somewhat. 'Why were you so sure I would come?'

'Because I knew you would be unable to resist the temptation of seeing me before I left London in the morning. But isn't this a little irregular? I mean, isn't it supposed to be your wedding night? Or is it that your husband doesn't live up to your expectations?'

'Please, Thomas, don't do this. Marcus has no idea that I'm here.'

'Of course he hasn't, otherwise you wouldn't be. But why are you here?'

'You know why.'

'No. Tell me. Is it because now after finding out that I am alive, you are sorry you married Marcus Cardell? Perhaps if I had been dead, it would have saved you the embarrassment of your betrayal, your treachery.'

She gasped, angered by his accusation. 'Treachery? No, never that.'

He moved closer to her, his narrowed eyes fixed on her face. 'I find it hard to believe how easily you forgot me, Juliet.'

'I never forgot you,' she said emphatically. 'You have no idea how I wanted so much for the reports of your death to be untrue. I tried not to believe it, and you can have no idea how I dreamed of your coming home so that we could be married. But...' She sighed, lowering her eyes. 'What's the use in talking now? I am no longer free.'

A cunning glint appeared in Thomas's eyes. 'A sermon doesn't make a marriage. You can be free of him. The wedding can be annulled if you swear it has not been consummated.'

For a moment she dispassionately studied this man she had once sworn to love forever and shook her head slowly. 'No, Thomas. Nothing is the same as when you left. I am not the same, although I am only now becoming aware of it. My marriage cannot be annulled. The vows I made are sacred. I married Marcus of my own free will, and I will not betray him. He is my husband in the sight of man and God.'

At her words, there was a sudden change in Thomas's manner, and his features became taut with a strange glow in the depths of his eyes. Juliet began to feel uneasy. She moved away from him, remembering why she had come, the question she must ask for her own peace of mind.

'There is a reason why I had to see you, something I have to know. Since coming home, what do you know of my circumstances?'

'What do you mean?'

She looked at him directly. 'Would you have married me without a dowry?'

He looked nonplussed. 'Dowry? What has that to do with anything?'

'Before you went to Spain, you were aware of Richard's passion for gambling—be it cards, dice or anything else he could put his money on. Unfortunately, we have creditors demanding money. Indeed, our situation is so bad that there is the possibility that the estate will have to be sold.'

A look of genuine shock and amazement spread over Thomas's face. 'Good Lord! I had no idea. I knew he had debts—what gambler doesn't?—but to be fool enough to lose everything...'

'Yes. Everything. So, Thomas, what I want to know is, would you have still married me penniless and with the shame of what Richard has done? I need to know. Did you love me enough to do that?'

He was taken aback by her question, and for a moment they looked at each other as if both were carved from stone.

'Marriage,' he murmured at last. 'Good Lord, why of—of course I would...' But his voice died away, flat and unconvincing.

Juliet wanted to believe him, but she knew with a sickening sense of reality that he was lying, and the face that looked into hers was not that handsome beloved face it had once been. That was a sweet fantasy, a cherished illusion that had been shattered forever. Thomas did not love her, had never loved her, not in the way she had wanted to be loved. He would have used her to serve his own interests, nothing more. It should hurt, but strangely, it didn't, and if it didn't hurt, then could it be that she didn't love him either?

She smiled bitterly. 'Don't try and fool me any more, Thomas. I can see the truth in your eyes. You wouldn't have married me, even if you had wanted to, and I very much doubt that now. Your father would never have allowed you to marry me anyway.'

He remained silent, looking at her hard, swaying slightly on his feet, the unspoken truth staring from his eyes. She turned from him, eager to leave, to get back home as quickly as possible—back to Marcus. She prayed he would never find out that she had come here tonight. He would never forgive her. Thank goodness he had decided to spend the night elsewhere.

'I don't think there's anything more to be said between us.' She moved to the door, but in an instant, Thomas covered the distance between them, blocking her path, a dangerous, threatening glint in his eyes. She could not repress the icy fear that crept through her. When he spoke, his voice was low and each word he uttered precise, but underlying them,

she could sense the violence that threatened to erupt
at any moment.

'Before you go, Juliet, tell me about Cardell and
how it was that he came to marry you. Did you have
to lie about your circumstances to him?'

'No, I didn't have to. Marcus and I have always
been perfectly honest with each other. He has loaned
Richard enough money to secure the estate.'

For a moment his face did not change its expression, but suddenly, what she had told him caused him
to laugh mirthlessly. 'You mean, he bought you?' he
sneered. 'You sold yourself to the highest bidder?'

'There were no other bidders,' she told him harshly.
'Only Marcus.'

'And he promised to pay all your brother's debts for
your own sweet self,' he scoffed. 'How very touching and how unworthy of you.'

'Unworthy? No, I don't think so. I had no choice.
It is fortunate that his family on his mother's side
owns the Mulberry Hall estate, which adjoins Endcliffe House, so I won't be far away from Richard.'

'Then I wish you a happy life together—while it
lasts. Perhaps I shall visit you there one day.'

'Our life together will be a long and happy one at
Mulberry Hall, and I think you know that you will
not be welcome there.'

'And do you love him?'

'He—he has been very good to me.'

'I asked you if you love him,' he persisted.

'He is a wonderful man.'

'But you don't love him,' he said with an odious smile of triumph, with such finality that she stared at him unbelievingly, noting the immense satisfaction he derived from this knowledge, and she wished with her whole heart that she could have said otherwise, but her feelings for Marcus were still nebulous.

'Move out of my way, Thomas. I wish to leave.'

'Not until I am ready. I am not your husband to order about. You are beautiful in temper. Does your husband tell you that? I've never wanted a woman as much as I want you, Juliet.'

'Why, Thomas? Because you cannot bear the fact that I now belong to someone else? Someone you've clearly had unpleasant dealings with before.'

The meaning of her words and the force with which they were delivered hit home. Thomas's veneer of sham politeness crumbled, and the smile on his face disappeared as he thrust his face close to hers. 'That is true. Cardell and I have a score to settle, and what better way to do that than to take his woman? Why should I let you return to Cardell—the man who has taken the woman I would have married? I will tell you this, Juliet, our last night together will be one to remember. I know you still love me, not Cardell, who you've so foolishly married.'

Juliet paled. Marcus was Thomas's objective, she

knew that now, and he would harm her to get at him. She didn't know fully what warped loathing Thomas harboured against Marcus, but she knew that whatever rebuff Marcus had given him must have festered inside his head and that he was dangerous. He moved closer to her, and she could feel his breath hot on her face. She went numb when she met his gaze. The charismatic façade that had once attracted her was now arrogant, saturnine and cruel, and the cocksure smile had acquired a malevolent twist. She stepped back, her face showing revulsion.

'What you suggest is an adulterous love. The sort I despise.' She smiled scornfully. 'You talk of love, of my love, of not being loyal and accuse me of treachery, but what of your love? Not once in all the time I have known you have you mentioned that.'

'Have I not? Then permit me to show you. I'm going to love you, Juliet. I'm going to make you so happy that you'll never want to leave me to go back to your husband.'

'Never,' she cried angrily. 'I wish to leave now. Let me go.'

'No.'

'Do you intend to hold me here by force?'

'Only if I have to.'

Panic and fear overcame Juliet, and she began to tremble. He noticed and smiled with smug satisfaction.

'Why, you're trembling. Come, Juliet,' he drawled,

his voice thick with passion, 'you think I don't love you, but I do.' He placed his hands heavily on her shoulders, looking deeply into her eyes. At his touch, she struggled to free herself from his grip, but his fingers tightened, refusing to relinquish their hold. 'So,' he hissed, 'you want to fight me? Well, all the better. I like a woman with spirit—one to match my own.'

Juliet was suddenly overcome with fear, but it was a different kind of fear from any she had ever known. Never, in all the time she had known him, had Thomas been anything other than charming, and she had always believed that nothing could touch him, that nothing mattered. But as she faced him, his expression dark and ruthless, she knew that at last something had touched him enough to bring about this ill-mannered, drunken stranger. She was now in no doubt that it was Marcus who had brought about this change and, whatever had passed between them that first time they had met, it must have been something terrible. She knew with a sinking heart that she could have married anyone, and Thomas wouldn't have cared one iota, but because it was Marcus, it was a different matter. Thomas would destroy her if he could to get back at him.

The full consequences of what she had done by coming here swept over her. Thomas saw her fear, but he only laughed, a deep mocking sound that curled his lips, and a look of madness filled and dilated his eyes, which told her that his mere triumph over her, her very resistance, excited him much more than all her passive docility. He wanted her whatever the odds.

A fierce, merciless struggle began between them. Now that she was faced with the terrible prospect of being raped and possibly killed, renewed strength surged through her, and she fought as if her life depended on it, like a wildcat turning on its tormentor. In a blind fury, her nails raked his face, his eyes, anywhere she could see his flesh, feeling an immense, unholy satisfaction when she drew blood. He laughed, a fierce, demonical sound that sent a chill through her.

'That's it. Fight, my beauty,' he hissed, pushing her down onto a sofa. 'Fight all you want. I shall soon have you crying and pleading for mercy. I shall enjoy teaching you to obey me, breaking that stubborn pride of yours.'

Savagely he tore at her clothes. She was finding it harder and harder to defend herself, reality slipping further and further away, and despair overpowered her as she reached the limits of her strength and her struggles became feeble.

And then, abruptly, something happened, and his weight left her. There was a dull thud, and she ceased struggling, trembling in what remained of her clothes. Through a mist, she looked up and discerned a terrifying, faceless figure looming over her. Instinct made her draw her defiled body into a ball, quivering like a terrified child. In the wild tangle of her hair, her eyes, enormous and full of fear, accentuated the transparent whiteness of her face.

She peered up at Marcus, who was in a towering rage, his face contorted out of all recognition as he glared down at her, beside himself with fury. Juliet did not ask herself by what miracle he happened to be there, to save her from what she had been about to suffer at Thomas's hands—it was enough for her than he had come, regardless of the fury and anger he would be sure to vent on her.

Marcus glared down at her dishevelled form bitterly. The spectacle of the vile and contemptible Thomas Waring forcing his attentions on his wife and the pitiful state he had brutally reduced her to made him feel physically sick. In the flickering glow of the candles, she was still lovely, although now tragically so, and he knew the sight of her should sicken him, but it didn't.

'You little fool,' he uttered quietly, his concern for her coming to the fore. 'This was a senseless thing to do. You should not have come here looking for him. Did you think I would not find out? What did you imagine would happen when that animal got his hands on you? You could ask for nothing better—

believe me.' His eyes took in her soft flesh showing through the tattered remnants of her bodice, and quickly he removed his cloak and gently draped it over her.

Straightening up, he looked at Waring, who had gotten up from the floor, where, in his rage, Marcus had thrown him. He stood glowering at Marcus, his fists tightly clenched by his sides, and the scratches of Juliet's fingernails that she had left on his face trickled blood.

'Damn your filthy hide, Waring,' he spat, his voice like a naked blade. 'Can't you get it into your head that Juliet no longer has anything to do with you?'

'Perhaps not, but she did come looking for me, like a bitch in heat.'

Pure madness flamed in Marcus's eyes, and he sprang at his adversary, grasping the front of his shirt and pulling his face close to his own, full of revulsion. 'And you should know all about that, being the dog that you are. Your methods of seduction leave a lot to be desired. I could kill you now, but I will save that pleasure for a later date.'

Waring's lips twisted in an arrogant sneer, his eyes spitting venom as he knocked Marcus's hands away. 'Why, you are jealous—jealous because she preferred my bed to yours. But then, why shouldn't she? And how do you know she hasn't shared it with me before?'

Marcus eyed him with unconcealed scorn. 'Judging by what has occurred here tonight, I doubt very much she would come back a second time.'

'Ah, but you don't know that for certain. How could you? Unless you have pre-empted your wedding vows and taken her yourself.'

For a moment Marcus stared at him in silence, a flicker of doubt entering his eyes as he hoped to God there was no truth in Waring's words. 'What a vicious, callous individual you are, Waring.'

Satisfied that his words had hit home, Thomas smiled smugly. 'I see I have cast the seed of doubt, Cardell. At least I have given you a wedding night to remember. You must have paid quite a price to get her to marry you—debts and all. Perhaps after tonight you'll consider she wasn't worth it.'

Marcus looked at him coldly. 'That doesn't concern you, Waring. You belong to one of England's most noble families, yet you are out of your class. You haven't a noble bone in your body. You are a low, brutal animal not worthy of the blade with which I shall kill you.'

An ugly smile spread across Thomas's features. 'No, it is I who will kill you. I who have been wronged. Had Juliet waited and married me, I would not have had to buy her as you have done.'

Disregarding Waring's insult, Marcus turned back to Juliet, who hadn't moved, and pulling her towards him, wrapped his cloak about her trembling form before again facing Thomas Waring. 'I'm taking my wife home. I would like to say I very much hope our paths do not cross again, but if they should—'

'Oh, they will, Cardell. You can be sure of that. You and I have a score to settle. I demand satisfaction for this night's work.'

Marcus's features tightened. 'You shall have it.'

'It will give me immense pleasure to kill you. I shall not be cheated by you a third time.'

'Don't be too sure. Whatever you might think, having spent several years in the Peninsular myself, I am an expert with both pistol and blade, and I aim to make damned sure you assault no more defenceless women—whether they be high or low born.'

Riding behind the carriage carrying Juliet home, Marcus didn't have the chance to speak to her until they reached the house. They went directly to her room, where Marcus seated himself before the fire. He leaned indolently back in his chair and crossed his long legs at the ankles.

Juliet watched him, waiting for him to speak to her, her very stance defiant, her exquisite features clouded with resentment. She had imagined Marcus would be icy, angry, anything but this cold self-possession. A look had entered his eyes she did not recognise and she felt awkward. She swallowed, shrinking under his scrutiny. Anger had sustained her so far, now fear and something else, something she could not identify, began to nudge. Struggling to steadfastly keep her thoughts on what was happening and aware that in her breast her heart was thumping far too fast for her to claim a mere tolerance of him, surreptitiously she took a step back to minimise contact.

'I imagine you are now ready to explain your behaviour tonight, Juliet.'

The tone of his voice made Juliet's heart contract. No hint of softness showed in the marble severity of his face—no hint of anger, either—which she suspected was stirring just beneath the surface, which was infinitely more disturbing. Anxiety abounded in her heart. After all, what did she know of this husband of hers? She forced herself to remain calm, not to appear ill at ease, not to show the unnerving effect being alone with him was having on her.

'Well?' he demanded impatiently. 'I should like to know precisely what happened between you and Waring before he went off to Spain. As your husband, I have to ask you just how far his attentions have gone. And do not lie to me, Juliet. If there is nothing else, there has to be truth between us from the start.'

Understanding his meaning, Juliet felt the flush start somewhere deep down and rise upwards over her chest and face, and then anger, full-bodied and fortifying, propelled her forward to stand over hm.

'Of all the loathsome, arrogant…' she erupted furiously. 'Despite what happened tonight, which I suspect was brought on by disappointment at my marriage to you, Thomas's behaviour towards me had been impeccable.'

'Thank you for that edifying piece of information,' Marcus remarked coldly. 'And am I to believe that you weren't lovers?'

Juliet was stung by his unjust accusation and the contempt in his voice, and some of her fighting spirit rose to the fore, and her eyes met his, flashing defiance. 'We were never that, but you can believe what you like,' she fumed, stepping back. 'I speak the truth.'

Marcus's face became taut, his eyes boring into hers, plumbing their innermost depths, searching for some sign that would tell him she was lying, but there was none. This woman, his wife, was not only beautiful, she was proud, and her pride would make her oppose him if she thought him unjust. She was also courageous and stubborn, but she was no liar. He believed her, and as he continued to watch her, it was clear to him that after all Waring had meant to her, she was feeling utterly broken by what had happened to her at his hands tonight. She stood in the centre of her room, still clutching his cloak about her like a shield of armour, as if afraid to let it go.

He was suddenly overwhelmed with compassion. He wanted to go to her, to open his arms and gather her to him, to hold her and never let her go, but he couldn't. Not yet. It was hard to swallow what she had done and he could not yet forgive her for going to Thomas Waring. The memory of this night would live with him for a long time, longer than the sight of her bruised and broken body. Her act of betrayal was hard for him to bear.

Getting to his feet, he strode towards the door, and she became alarmed.

'Marcus? You're not leaving?'

He turned and looked at her, his face immobile. 'There is something I have to take care of.'

He watched as his words penetrated Juliet's tortured mind and realisation of where he was going and what he intended dawned on her. Looking sick with horror, distraught, she flung herself across the room. Her eyes were full of desperate pleading. 'No,' she cried. 'I know what you are going to do. Please don't give Thomas the satisfaction of fighting a duel. I beg of you. I have to prevent this happening. It's— it's madness, don't you see?'

'Madness? You should have thought of that before leaving this house to go to him.'

'If I have to, I will get down on my knees to entreat you not to do this.'

A ripple of something stirred in Marcus's breast,

and he marvelled at her courage. She might be stricken and feeling at her lowest ebb on finding that Thomas Waring had not been killed as she had been led to believe, but this wilful young woman had certainly not parted from her temper. Marcus felt a rush of blood through his veins and a hammering in his chest. Like a dangerous illness that desires a desperate remedy, he refused to back down. Before this day was out, he would force her heart to forget Thomas Waring.

'You can't fight a duel,' she persisted. 'One of you will be...'

'What, Juliet? Killed? And which one of us would you prefer to live?'

'Both of you.'

'I intend it will be me.'

'Please, I am begging you, Marcus.' She breathed as if she couldn't inhale enough air. 'How do you expect me to live with you as your wife, to respect you as a wife should, if you take Thomas's life? Don't you understand? Don't—don't make me hate you.'

Marcus looked at the proud beauty and saw the despair that was tearing her apart. When he saw the tears and the fear steal into her luminous eyes, he was beset by a twinge of conscience, which he quickly thrust away. He caught the note of anguish in her voice, which tore at his heart. She was right and he was deeply sorry for the hurt this duel with Waring would cause her, but it was too late to change anything now. It would be a long time, if ever, he thought, feeling a pang of regret, that she would be able to love him as she had loved Thomas Waring, but it would be a long time before he would be able to forget that she had gone to that man on their wedding night. And yet he knew he must if they were to have any sort of life together as man and wife.

'I know you will hate me a good deal more before I am finished, but you appear to forget that it is Waring who has instigated this, not me.'

Lifting his brows, he gazed at her with enigmatic eyes and an impassive expression for several endless, uneasy moments. Her hair lay on her shoulders like a gleaming golden mass. Having thrown off his cape, his gaze dwelt on her torn gown—her beautiful wedding gown. His cool gaze warmed as it rested on her. She was very lovely, this obstinate, spirited young woman he had married. So lovely, in fact, he could almost forgive her for her defence of Thomas Waring.

'Do you know, Juliet, you are one of the very few women who verbally attacks me. The majority of your contemporaries usually find me quite charming. I might even say that some have a great affection for me.'

'Perhaps that is because they have not had the pleasure of being married to you.'

Marcus look at her with disdain. 'The ferocity with which you defend Waring is touching, Juliet.'

'I know how much I must have hurt you, Marcus, but what can I say other than I am sorry. Everything happened so fast. I wasn't thinking. Do not forget that Thomas and I were formally engaged. I foolishly felt that I had to speak to him. We are to leave London tomorrow and he is to return to Spain very soon. I may never see him again.'

'I sincerely hope not.'

'I know you want to settle a score with Thomas, and after seeing the true nature of the man I would have married, I cannot blame you, but do not underestimate him. However confident you might feel about your own prowess, Thomas is a superb marksman and an expert with a sword.'

Marcus looked down at her, a cold glitter in his eyes. 'Don't try and stop me, Juliet. I have to do this. Waring has issued a challenge that cannot be ignored. You are my wife and it is my duty to defend your honour. What you have done, going to another man's house on our wedding night, is beyond the bounds of respectable behaviour.'

He was being uncompromising, he knew, but he was still shaken by what had almost happened to her. Stiffening her spine and with her head held high, as impressive as a tropical storm and a fierce challenging pride on her face, she took a step back imperturbably. She looked as if she were about to do battle, ready to do battle, ready for anything Marcus would aim at her. He impaled her on his gaze, leaving her in no doubt that he intended to seek satisfaction in a duel.

'Promise me you will not kill him. Whatever he has done, he does not deserve that.'

'No? Then perhaps you should have thought of that before you went looking for him.'

'How did you know that I had gone? I—I thought you had left the house.'

'Having no wish to concern my mother, I changed my mind. If she knew there was discord between us already, then she would be reluctant to part with Adele. I cannot risk that. I heard the carriage leave the house. When I found you weren't in your room, I knew you were in that carriage, and where else would you be going if not to Waring? The fact that you have betrayed me, have incurred my displeasure, does not seem to matter,' he said with heavy irony.

'Of course it does, and you have every right to be angry, but I did love him once—only I realise now that I did not know him, what he was capable of. I—I was so afraid.'

'Of course you were, when you discovered to what depraved depths he would sink to get his own way. If anything has been achieved by tonight's events, it is that all romantic thoughts of that man will at last be banished from your mind.'

'Yes, you are right. I had no idea he would behave as he did. It was as if some kind of monster had been unleashed.'

'And yet you want him to live.'

'Yes, of course I do,' she said, her eyes blazing with anger. 'Even though I pity him, if the events of this night have taught me anything, it is that his soul is a cold quagmire of cruelty, deceit, selfishness and wickedness. I loathe him, and to think I would have married him.'

'I am sure his feelings for you have not changed, but your circumstances have. You are my wife in name, and soon to be my wife in fact, should you need reminding of the vows you spoke earlier today. Juliet, that man has abused you and damn near destroyed you. Don't ask me to ignore what he did tonight. I would rather hang.'

'And hang you shall if you kill him.'

He looked down at her, feeling her hand clinging to his arm with all her strength. Unsmiling, he looked at her seriously for a moment, one eyebrow lifted almost imperceptibly. 'The minute he walked through the door, he addled your wits. If you had known he was still alive, would you have married me? Tell me, Juliet. I have a right to know.'

'I cannot answer that. The truth is I don't know,' she replied miserably. 'Truly.'

'Now that you have seen him again and know what he is capable of, do you still have feelings for him?' he went on remorselessly.

'I told you. I hate him for what he has done this night. Whatever feelings I had left for him, he killed tonight. He is a brute, and I would like to see him punished for what he has done, but I beg you not to fight a duel. I no longer love him, but I cannot be the one to bring about his death. All this has come about because of my foolishness, and I have no wish to have the death of either of you to be the result of me making the wrong decision. If you kill him, I shall blame myself as surely as if I had pulled the trigger or wielded the sword. I shall have killed him, and I cannot live with that. The guilt would be too heavy for me to bear. Please,' she whispered softly, 'if you kill him, his death will stand between us forever.'

The anguish and pain on her pale face had their effect, touching some hidden chord deep inside him. Marcus didn't know how to react to this display of grief, but he had to acknowledge the sense of her words, fully aware that he had allowed his hurt masculine pride and anger to cloud his judgement.

'Has it not crossed your mind what will happen if you do kill Thomas, that despite being who you are, you will be arrested? I cannot bear to think of the punishment that will be meted out to you. It is too horrendous to imagine.'

He considered her intently and nodded slowly. 'Yes, I have thought about it. But put it another way, Juliet. What if Waring proves to be stronger than me? Has it not occurred to you for one moment that *I* might not return? Have you thought what will happen if he kills me?'

At his words, she stared at him, mortified. 'I have indeed thought of this, but believing you are stronger and more proficient than Thomas, I have tried not to dwell on it. Tonight my feelings have undergone a considerable change so that I no longer know what to think. But, dear God, not that. After all that has happened, after all I have lost, I could not bear that—to lose you. It would break my heart.'

Deeply touched by her words, Marcus's heart swelled with thankfulness that she should feel this way. 'Very well, Juliet. Should I gain the upper hand, I promise you that I shall not kill him. Merely teach him a lesson he will not forget. But he should not go unpunished, leaving him free to assault other innocent women. He is to return to Spain in the near future. Perhaps army discipline will knock some of the wickedness out of him.'

On that note Marcus turned on his heel. At the door he hesitated and looked back at her. 'Goodnight, Juliet. I trust tomorrow we can put this behind us.

* * *

Juliet stood and looked at the closed door through which her husband had disappeared, his face set in such lines of implacability that it left her feeling thoroughly chastened, stupid, and what little fight she had left within her drained away. Her behaviour had caused a hidden force to erupt inside him, and she was seeing a side of him she hadn't known existed. Could that cold, angry stranger be her husband? The man she had married, who had promised her and Richard so much for the future?

Crushed by the full weight of responsibility for her stupidity, her gullibility that had wreaked such havoc, she sank onto a chair. The hideous events of the night had unleashed in Marcus all the fury of his passionate nature. Within the past twenty-four hours, her life had been torn asunder, and she prayed fervently that Marcus would return to her unharmed, for she had come to depend on him like the very air she breathed and whose quiet strength she valued a great deal.

Feeling bruised and defiled and weighted down with terrible misery and despair, the thought that she had to go on living beyond this night was inconceivable. Covering her face with her trembling hands, she wept, silently praying for his safe return.

Chapter Nine

Marcus's anger died the moment he entered his room. Throwing his jacket on the bed and moving to the fireplace, he rested his arms on the mantelpiece, his mind going over the night's events as he stared down into the flames. He could not find words to describe his defiant young wife. He was enraged by her attitude, yet at the same time, he could not help but admire her courage. She had spirit, too much damned spirit, he thought. He didn't know another woman who would stand up to his wrath as she did. She had stood up to him from their first encounter, and then angered him by taking it upon herself to visit Waring at his home.

Juliet wasn't a woman he could wrap around his finger and charm with an irresistible smile. With her back straight, head held high, her hair caressing her spine and her eyes flashing a desperate amber, she had faced up to him. He was intrigued by her eyes, for they would glow with fervour, and at other times they were quiet, looking inward and sad, and it mattered to him. He thought about everything she had said, how vehemently she had expressed her feelings. For a long time he stood there, knowing he must try and make amends for all the wrongs he had caused her, before her hurt really did harden into hatred.

Perhaps his anger had made him hasty. If he was honest with himself, then he had to admit that he didn't want to kill Waring. He was a villain and he despised him, and it was right that he should be punished for what he had done, but he did not deserve to die for it. The last thing he wanted was his death on his conscience. He would prefer to put the whole ugly episode behind him.

But that was before one of the servants brought him a note that had just been delivered to the house. It was from Thomas Waring, and the short missive told him that he would meet him at dawn in Hyde Park, where they would settle their differences with swords. Marcus uttered a sigh of resignation. So, he had no choice. He would have to fight. If he did not meet him, he would be branded a coward, and that was unthinkable.

It was just before daybreak that he went to rouse Walter, his valet of many years, urging him to get dressed quickly and meet him in the hall. After briefly informing Walter what was required of him, they did a short detour to collect his sword from his home before riding in the direction of Hyde Park. Initially he had considered asking William to be his second, but finding the mere thought of explaining to his brother the sordidness that had brought about the duel and not wishing to cause his mother undue concern should she get wind of it, he had decided against it.

The world as the two men rode through the park in a thick blanket of grey cloud was cold, everything about them dormant, gripped by a beautiful desolation. A slight breeze snaked its pathway round the trees, pointing their leaf-covered branches up to the sky.

Grim-faced they rode hard, the only sound being the heavy breathing of their horses and the rhythmic pounding of their hoofs. As they approached the desired spot where the duel was to take place, it was oddly silent and deserted, the park hereabouts deeply wooded. They entered a circular glade, slowing their pace. They scanned the dark shadows not only for Thomas Waring and his second but also for others, for the constables, for if the law had got wind that a duel was to be fought, then it would spell disaster for them all.

Waring and his second were already there. Accompanied by a physician he had had to pay well for his services, they rode out of the dark shadows as they entered the glade. Quickly they all dismounted, Marcus divesting himself of his cloak and handing it to Walter, eyed Waring carefully as he moved closer. In the cold light of dawn, there was no trace of the drunken creature of last night, when the fumes of alcohol had clouded his mind. Now he met Marcus's gaze coldly.

'I trust you slept well,' he said with sarcasm, 'and that you said farewell to your bride, for I doubt you shall see her again on this day or any other.'

'No, I did not, for I do not expect to die.'

Waring smiled almost pleasantly. 'Then you were too confident, for I promise you, you will not live to see another dawn.'

'We shall see,' Marcus said, taking off his jacket and throwing it on the ground.

The two men faced each other in shirts of fine lawn, and Marcus read clearly the evil intent to kill in Waring's eyes. Both men loosed their swords, freeing the naked blades from their sheaths.

Waring saluted his opponent with a sardonic smile. *'En garde.'*

They circled each other warily before their blades engaged, ferociously slicing the air. The swords clashed, and at first, neither bore the initiative, but they fought with all the violence born of hatred. Both men were evenly matched, although Marcus was the taller and appeared the most powerful of the two with his strong, muscular frame, but Waring possessed a lithe agility and fought with all the skill of an experienced duellist.

It was only after Waring stumbled slightly on stepping back, his weakened leg letting him down, that Marcus seized his chance and immediately took the initiative, lunging, pressing home his attack. Enraged at finding himself at a disadvantage, Waring fought like a man possessed, and their blades clashed faster and faster. A fierce, determined light shone in Marcus's eyes, but not a muscle in his face moved as his sword flashed, the clash of steel on steel rending the air. With everything to lose, Waring began to fight dementedly, but however hard he tried to attack, he could not penetrate that unwavering guard and was constantly driven back as Marcus proved the stronger, his blade fiercely hissing through the air.

Pure cold fury filled Waring's eyes at being held constantly at bay, and in desperation, he began lunging wildly, carelessly, while Marcus retained his calm. And at last pressed home his advantage, sliding the point of his sword through the soft flesh of Waring's right shoulder.

Waring's eyes opened wide in absolute surprise, his sword slipping from his hand, bright red blood staining the white purity of his shirt as he stumbled and fell, crumpling onto the ground. Marcus stepped back and stared down at him.

Waring cursed softly and attempted to get up but, his chest heaving, the effort proved too much and, smiling bitterly, he looked up at Marcus. 'Well, what are you waiting for? Aren't you going to finish me?'

'I shall not kill you, but only because before I came here, Juliet begged me not to. It is she you have to thank for your life, though God knows why after what she suffered at your hands. But be under no illusion, because it would give me immense pleasure to finish you for good.'

'Then do so,' hissed Waring, 'because I swear that while ever there is breath in my body, I shall hunt you down. I shall be avenged. I swear it! You shall regret not killing me. This I promise you.'

Marcus's eyes were like cold pieces of flint as they met his adversary's. 'I doubt that. When we parted on our first encounter, I was aware of your insane hatred, but I did not know what such bitter resentment might lead you to do until I met you again last night. And now this. If I ever catch you on my property or in close proximity to my wife again, I will arrange your judgement day to come sooner than you expect.'

'You…threaten me?' Waring's tone was mockingly incredulous. 'Don't be too sure about that, Cardell. It's your life and all you hold dear hanging in the balance, not mine.'

'I am stating what our future relationship will be,' Marcus said coldly. 'We have fought a duel. I won.

You had your chance to get rid of me and failed. You are a sad excuse for a man, Waring. I pity you.'

Thwarted of triumph, Waring's fury burst. 'Pity? You pity me? His face darkened with rage as he watched his adversary begin to move away.

'That is what I said.' Marcus stepped back. 'Come, Walter, our business here is done. Waring is not dead and it was a fair fight. Whatever he threatens, I doubt he will bother us again.'

And without paying further attention to the recumbent figure with the doctor ministering to his wound, he turned and strode away, firmly believing as he did so that he would never set eyes on Thomas Waring again.

Back at the house Marcus found Juliet in the drawing room pacing up and down as she waited anxiously for him to return. When he entered the room, he paused for a moment and looked at her, so still that she might have been carved out of stone. Her face was white, one hand at her throat as she waited, taut with suspense.

'Marcus,' she uttered softly. 'Thank God you are safe, that you have returned to me unscathed, haven't you?' Hope that this was so was mirrored in her eyes, plain for him to see.

'I am unharmed.'

'I was—I was so worried. I could not have borne

it if... You are telling me the truth, Marcus? Thomas did not hurt you?'

'Cease your worrying, Juliet. I come back to you in one piece.'

She swallowed hard. 'And Thomas? Is he—is he dead?'

Marcus saw that she trembled slightly with fear at what he might tell her, and the intonation of his voice when he spoke was cold and distant as he replied, 'You will be relieved to know that I spared him. When I left him, I regret to tell you he was very much alive.'

At the relief that flooded her eyes, his face hardened and he was conscious of a sudden surge of anger.

'Thank you. Was—was he badly wounded?' she whispered, her voice dying away into the silence of the room.

Marcus looked at her incredulously. 'You astound me, Juliet. Does it matter to you so much? Is it possible that after all the harm he has done, you can still feel compassion for Waring?'

'It is natural for me to feel concern.' She looked down at her hands despairingly. 'How can I make you understand the torment I have been through since you left? How can I make you believe that I never want to see Thomas again—ever? But that neither do I want him to die at the hands of my husband. And how can I make you believe that after much soul-searching, I realise that if one man had to forfeit his life during the course of the duel, then I would rather it have been Thomas?' She stared up at him, and as she met his gaze miserably, she said, 'This has been the most terrible night of my life. I shall never forget it as long as I live.'

'Then you must forget it. For your sake as well as for mine,' he said. 'And I will tell you this, Juliet. I never want to hear the name of Thomas Waring mentioned again. Do you understand? You are my wife now and I expect you to behave as such. I will fight no more duels on your behalf. I have Adele to consider. She has already lost her mother. I cannot risk leaving her an orphan.' He turned from her. 'And now perhaps you would be good enough to be ready to leave for Surrey as soon as possible. I have to go and collect Adele. William is to leave for Sussex with my mother, to welcome a new addition to the Cardell family, I expect. With such a long journey ahead of him, my brother will not thank me if I am late.'

'Yes—yes, of course. I have instructed Daphne to begin packing my things.'

Following him out of the room, with her head held high, she proceeded up the stairs. Marcus watched her, aware of the wretchedness she must be feeling and detesting himself for venting his anger on her, knowing that the manner in which he had spoken to her was unforgivable. On reaching his house, he strode quickly into the dining room cursing angrily and, taking a decanter, poured a generous helping of brandy into a glass, but not even when he drank deeply, feeling the fiery liquid course through his veins, did it lessen his self-loathing.

Juliet was glad to be leaving London for Mulberry Hall. Daphne had completed the packing and, to Juliet's delight and relief, had agreed to go with her to the country to act as her maid.

When Juliet considered what her life would be like from now on, she felt that it would be like spinning about in some great vortex without the stable influence of Endcliffe House, on which she had always depended and from which she had been wrenched, and she was totally unprepared for the scale of misery that engulfed her.

Adele, who was supposed to be travelling in the coach behind with her nursemaid, Daphne and Marcus's valet, became fractious and tearful to find she was to be separated from her adored father.

'Adele can surely travel with us,' Juliet suggested, hoping Marcus would agree, because Adele's presence in the coach would go some way to alleviating the tension that existed between them.

Adele immediately caught on to the suggestion, and her little face became alight with hope. 'Please, Papa, let me go with you.'

Marcus looked down with concern at his daughter and his expression softened. 'If she's going to be difficult, then I suppose she must.'

Juliet was pleasantly surprised when he reached down and lifted Adele into the carriage.

The little girl was clearly delighted to be travelling with her father and her new stepmother. A happy smile stretched her pink lips as she nestled as close to Marcus as was possible, which made him smile.

He cocked a dark brow at Juliet as she settled herself opposite, waiting for the nursemaid to join them. 'How I wish I could pacify all the women in my life as easily as I can my daughter.'

Juliet responded with a wry smile. 'Perhaps if you didn't go around with such a stern expression on your face all the time, you wouldn't find it such a problem,' she dared to say, amused when she turned her head away and heard him chuckle softly.

It was late afternoon, and the clouds were gilded with sunshine when the carriage passed through a huge stone gateway with the heraldic bearings of Marcus's mother's family. They travelled slowly up a hill, the drive lined with giant beech trees, offering a cool, gentle shade. Adele had drifted off to sleep before halfway through the journey and was cradled close to her nurse. Before they topped the rise, Marcus ordered the driver to stop the carriage. He climbed down, holding his hand out to Juliet.

'Come, I'll show you Mulberry Hall.'

'But I've seen it many times, visiting it when I was a girl, if you recall, and on the occasions when I ride out.'

'I know that, but I want to show it to you myself.'

Holding her hand, he led her to the top of the rise. Touched that Marcus wanted her to see it with him, without realising she was doing so, Juliet held her breath when she gazed in wonder at what she always thought must be a dream. The gentle sweep of the valley unfolding before her eyes, the acres of fields and woods stretching almost as far as the eye could see and the pastures full of cattle never failed to move her. Seeing it with Marcus filled her with enchantment. This was her husband's domain, and when her eyes rested on the house, the stones of which it was built glowing rose-pink in the late-afternoon sun, her heart swelled. The house rose stately and supreme in timeless splendour, like a jewel beneath the dark shade of tall oaks and elms, surpassing the quiet beauty of her own Endcliffe House.

Watching her reaction, Marcus smiled slowly. 'It's beautiful, is it not, Juliet?' he said with pride.

'Yes,' she breathed, 'it is quite splendid.'

'I think this is the best spot to see the house. It never changes,' he murmured. 'It smiles, it beckons, it invites and welcomes. I have loved it since I was a child. There is nowhere quite like it.'

'Has it always been in your mother's family?'

'Yes. It was my great-grandfather who gained favour from Queen Anne and acquired the earldom, then built the house. It was only after many trials and adversities that he at last achieved success and created a rich estate—the one you now see. One to be handed down with pride to his descendants. Sadly, over the years, the family were not blessed with male heirs, hence my own ascendance to the title and estate.'

'But your brother William? Should it not have passed to him?'

'William has titles and properties enough on the Cardell side. Knowing this, my grandfather bequeathed Mulberry Hall and the title to me on his demise.' Marcus looked down at her. 'It will be handed down to our children. All this is yours now, and I want you to feel for it as I do. I want you to be happy here, and not miss Endcliffe House too much.'

She smiled up at him. 'I don't think that will be too difficult.' At that moment she had no doubt that Mulberry Hall was part of her destiny, that she belonged here, that she could be happy here. She told herself that these thoughts were fanciful, but she truly believed it was possible. 'Endcliffe House was my home for too long for me not to miss it, but Mulberry Hall is my home now. I'm sure I shall be very happy here.

Indeed, who would not be? It is a beautiful house. How did the house get its name?'

'My great-grandfather was something of a botanist. He cultivated the mulberry trees for their berries. The leaves can also be fed to livestock. The trees grow to quite a height, so they need pruning. '

'Are the berries not excellent food for silkworms in the silk trade?'

'I believe the leaves of the white mulberry are. The Romans first brought the trees to Britain. The leaves are said to have medicinal purposes, but they became most prized for their succulent berries.'

'Have any of the trees survived that your ancestor planted?'

'Several, I believe, though they are somewhat gnarled now, but they still bear fruit.'

'Then I shall look forward to seeing them—and tasting the berries.'

'I sent word on ahead, so we are expected. I am sure you will be familiar with some members of staff since they are from the locality. Having run Endcliffe House since your mother's demise, you will be no stranger to what is expected of you, but don't worry. You'll soon get used to it. The housekeeper, Mrs Cherry, who has been at Mulberry Hall for some years now, will familiarise you with everything. I mean to entertain quite often—local dignitaries and such like. But you can rest assured that I have no plans to entertain anyone for the present, and nothing too strenuous will be required of you.'

'I have no worries about that. It will be no different to running Endcliffe House, but on a larger scale.'

'Come,' Marcus said, turning and slowly escorting her back to the carriage. 'Let us be on our way to the house.'

The two coaches pulled up in front of the house. What seemed like a dozen servants suddenly appeared and began unloading the baggage while the occupants entered the house. The large hall was surprisingly cool, with doors leading off to other rooms, all tastefully furnished.

Juliet hadn't visited Mulberry Hall since she was a child, but it was much as she remembered. As soon as she entered the house, she was greeted with unaffected warmth. The magnificence and antiquity with which she was surrounded overwhelmed her. She had the strange feeling of passing into another world and that life would never be the same again. She could feel the past closing in on her, wrapping itself around her, but it was in no way threatening or unpleasant; in fact, it was quite the opposite, for it gave her a warm, welcoming glow deep inside. It was a house where courtesy and mutual affection ruled in perfect harmony. As she absorbed the atmosphere of the great house, it seemed alive but dormant, quietly waiting for the return of a family to fill its rooms with the voices and laughter of children, to make it a home again.

The staff had gathered to welcome them home. Some of them who came from the surrounding area Juliet already knew. Adele was whisked off to the nursery, and Mrs Cherry, who had been housekeeper since before Juliet was born and remembered her mother, escorted her up the long flight of stairs, pointing out the merits of her new home. The long gallery, crossing the width of the house, was of tremendous proportions. Its floor was of polished oak and its walls supported a huge vaulted ceiling of decorative plaster. Set in rows along the walls and giving the visitor the impression that they had stepped into the presence of gathered nobility were paintings of Marcus's ancestors on his mother's side—men and women who had coloured the exclusive world of Mulberry Hall for generations, all housed in elaborately gilded frames. Her bedchamber, which was one of gracious elegance, sumptuous in both design and colour, was decorated in delicate shades of green and ivory.

'I can't tell you how happy I am to have you here, Lady Juliet,' Mrs Cherry said warmly. 'Your dear mother would be happy for you.'

'Yes,' Juliet replied softly, 'yes, she would. She always loved visiting this house.'

'You have brought your own maid along with you I see.'

'Yes, Daphne. She has been employed at the house in London and is a highly competent and capable young woman. Having spent all her life in town, I was so pleased when she agreed to come with me to Mulberry Hall.'

'I'm sure she will soon settle down. I hope the room is to your liking. Facing south, it gets plenty of sun, and it overlooks the deer park and the lake.'

'Yes, I like it very well, Mrs Cherry. It's perfect.'

The heavy brocade curtains moved gently with the soft, refreshing breeze blowing in through the open windows. There was a door connecting Marcus's room to hers, through which he could come to her any time. It was only then that Juliet, staring at the large bed, felt a sudden dart of panic when she thought of the nights Marcus would share it with her.

Mrs Cherry departed when Daphne came in, unable to suppress a gasp of delight at the extravagance of her new surroundings. She flitted about the room, inspecting the dressing room leading off from the main bedchamber and delighting at the wardrobe space where Juliet's beautiful gowns would be hung.

Impatient for her mistress's trunks to be brought up so she could unpack them, Daphne made herself scarce when Marcus entered.

'I see the bed has given you pause for thought, Juliet. Does it displease you knowing we will occupy it together?'

She spun round, startled by the sound of his voice. 'No—no, of course not,' she stammered. 'Only, I—I thought—'

'Thought what?' he said brusquely. 'That because of the unpleasantness that followed our wedding I didn't wish to share a bed with my wife? Well, whatever thoughts might have passed through that pretty head of yours, I can tell you now that I find the possibility quite appealing. Although it seems that I will have to wait, for I will not make love to my wife, or any other woman, come to that, while her heart lies elsewhere.' He threw her a mocking smile. 'Rather like having three in a bed, don't you think?'

He moved to the window and stood looking out. Juliet stared at his stony profile, his jaw set firm. With a sudden surge of longing to go to him and run her hands over the broad set of his shoulders welling up inside her, she didn't move. His relaxed, easy manner when they had stood together to look at the house had gone. She swallowed hard, sensing the tension inside him. She thought back to all that had happened since their wedding, which now felt as if it had happened in some other lifetime. But one thing was clear to her: they couldn't go on like this. They would have to talk, to bring down this invisible wall he had erected between them. She had sensed a softening in him when they had stopped to look at the house, but the reticence was back.

She moved towards him. 'Please, Marcus,' she said softly. 'We have to talk. We can't go on like this.'

'No, you're right, we can't.'

Juliet watched as he lifted one hand and massaged the taut muscles in his neck, his expression becoming darker and more ominous as his mind went over what had occurred. He was deeply troubled, Juliet could see that, and naturally so, with everything that had transpired. Weren't things difficult enough between them without the added pressure of Thomas standing between them? In a desperate attempt to make things right, Juliet moved closer to his side.

'I'm sorry about all this, Marcus. Believe me, if I could change things, I would.'

He turned his head and looked down at her, barely concealed doubt cloaking his eyes. 'Would you, Juliet? Would you really?'

'Yes, of course I would. There was a time, not so long ago, when I could never have imagined being close to any other man but Thomas. But times and emotions change, and they have changed me. When will you realise that I no longer love him?'

'Then tell me,' he said, his voice low and controlled, 'why did you go to him last night? I have to know, Juliet.'

He had told her he never wanted to hear Thomas's

name mentioned again, and since leaving London neither of them had, but she knew the man remained uppermost in Marcus's mind.

'I have already told you why. Do we have to go over it all again?'

'Tell me again.'

'I went to him,' she said quietly, 'because I had to know if he would have married me when he became aware of my circumstances. I had to know—it was important to me—before I went away, for my own peace of mind.'

Marcus turned sharply and looked at her, and she cringed inwardly at his cold expression. 'And would he?'

She shook her head. 'No.'

'Then it was fortunate for you, after all, that I came along when I did, wasn't it?'

'That isn't fair,' she gasped, stung by his words. 'You knew my situation when you asked me to marry you. I made no secret of what my feelings were for Thomas.'

'Of course,' he said, his lips twisting with sarcasm. 'You must forgive me for forgetting. But do you expect me to believe that you went to him on our wedding night for no other reason than to talk to him?'

'Yes, I do,' she said, moving closer to him. 'As far as I am concerned, Thomas is dead, and if we are to find any happiness in our marriage, then he must be dead for you too. Nothing can change what has happened, so we must learn to put it behind us. I no longer love him—I realised that before I went to his home to see him—and in fact, I don't know if I ever did. This I have told you, so why can't that stubborn pride of yours let you accept it?' She sighed deeply, her anger of a moment before leaving her.

Aware of his indecision and that he continued to doubt her words, she moved closer to him. 'Please listen to me,' she pleaded fervently, gripping his arm. 'I find it hard to see myself as I used to be—living my life believing Thomas would be a part of it forever. That was another lifetime. Then I was somebody else. I want to discover a different life—with you and Adele here at Mulberry Hall. I cannot conceive of anything different.'

'I am touched by what you say, Juliet, and more than anything, I want to believe you. In the beginning, I did wonder how you could ever respect me as a wife should—a man who had virtually bought your affections, and yet when you spoke your vows, I hoped you had truly put Thomas Waring behind you.'

'I fully intend to do that,' she murmured, placing her hand timidly on his arm. Summoning up all her courage, she gazed beseechingly into his eyes. 'Have you made up your mind to hate me all your life? How much longer will you continue to spurn me? Can you not find it in your heart to forgive me? None of this has been easy for me either.'

Marcus tried hard to shove her away with hands that secretly asked nothing more than to hold on to her. She had taken the first step toward a reconciliation, and she expected him to take the next, which, after all that had transpired within the past two days, he found difficult. Despite having told him otherwise, he suspected that deep down, Juliet still harboured tender thoughts for Waring, and he could not bear the thought of making love to her while she was thinking of someone else.

He looked into the imploring softness of her eyes, so bewitchingly beautiful, and he was moved in spite of himself, wanting nothing more at that moment than to atone for his sharp words and win her forgiveness. With some concern he noted the dark smudges beneath her eyes.

This is not good, he thought, despairing. *We can't go on behaving like enemies.*

She looked so piteous, so defenceless, and she spoke so passionately that the hard gleam went from his eyes and there was a softer tone to his voice when he spoke.

Taking her hand from his arm, he tenderly drew her close. 'I don't hate you, Juliet—don't ever think that. No man in his right mind would spurn you intentionally. You are far too lovely for that. I know that none of this is easy for you, that it is far easier for me than you.' He smiled slowly. 'I've been a selfish brute, haven't I? You deserved better after what you've been through.'

Juliet smiled with relief at the tenderness filling his eyes, and she trembled with a quiet joy. 'Then we are friends again?'

'More than that, I hope. But how does it feel to know you have the power to make me suffer, to make my life hell? You have bewitched me, Juliet. No other woman has done that.'

'I—I'm sorry, Marcus.'

'What for?'

'My stupidity. Did I hurt you very much?'

'More than you will ever know, but you are right. We will put all that has happened behind us. We must not allow it to poison our happiness, and besides, the days ahead—of settling in to living at Mulberry Hall and building on your relationship with Adele, will be difficult enough for you without that. Having made a hasty marriage, I regret there was no time for courtship, but it is not the first time that virtual strangers have found themselves married to each other.'

'Not entirely strangers. We had met before.'

'You were a child, Juliet. A long time has passed since then, and I have been away fighting a war. While all this is strange and unfamiliar at this time,

we have our whole lives to learn to know each other.'
Gazing down into the magnificent amber depths of
her eyes, he raised her hand to his lips, feeling desire surge through him, and he was impatient for the
night to come when he could make her his wife in
flesh as well as in name. But however soft and inviting the large bed looked, now was not the time.
'Much as I would like to remain with you at present,
I have matters to attend to and you must settle in,'
he said huskily.

Disappointment clouded her eyes. 'Yes, of course.'

'Later, we will spend time together. I promise,'
he said, bending his head and brushing her soft lips
with his own. 'Wild horses won't be able to keep me
from you tonight.' He looked down at her, a wicked
light dancing in his eyes. 'No objections, Juliet. It has
been delayed, I know, but we will count this as our
wedding night, and you are my adorable bride. I do
not intend to waste one minute of it.'

'I do not object,' she murmured.

'That's what I wanted to hear. I will leave you to
wash and change and I'll see you at dinner.'

Before joining Marcus in the dining room, Juliet
went to check on Adele. After being confined to the
coach for the journey to Mulberry Hall, the child
was clearly thrilled to have been let loose at last and
to explore her new domain. She had set about drag-

ging toys out of boxes and cupboards and enthused excitedly over a particularly fine rocking horse. She insisted on showing Juliet her new playthings and in particular the books with stories of children's exploits, of fairies and elves and princes rescuing beautiful princesses, making Juliet promise to read them to her in the coming days. Leaving the nursemaid to settle her down for the night, Juliet went down to the dining room, where Marcus, washed and changed and looking terribly handsome in grey trousers and a dark blue jacket, which was stretched smoothly over his broad shoulders, was already partaking of a pre-dinner glass of wine.

'To us,' Marcus said as he handed her a glass of red wine.

'To us,' she murmured, raising her glass and gently tapping his before taking a sip of wine, 'and to a new beginning.'

There was a pause as their eyes held for a moment, the peace between them unspoken but there all the same. It had been a while coming, and they both felt it deeply. She felt herself tremble with wonder, and the relief at being here with him surged through her entire body. But it was more than that. With Thomas receding into the past, Marcus had released what had been lost inside her, had set free her ability to feel the emotions that swelled her heart—her ability to love.

She was ready to relinquish her guard, like a snake shedding its skin.

'What do you think of Mulberry Hall? Although having grown up in the grandeur of Endcliffe House and surrounded by the trappings of the nobility, perhaps it does not impress you as much as it would some.'

Juliet's eyes were alight with interest as she gazed at the pictures and furniture that harmonised perfectly. Turning to look at her husband, she realised he was awaiting her reaction. There was an expectant hope in his handsome face, and she could not deny him.

'On the contrary. I am impressed. It is very fine indeed,' she murmured, taking a seat by the hearth, 'and just as I remember. Few brides are presented with so much. Usually, it is the groom who receives what his wife brings to him as a dowry, which I have failed to provide.'

'I told you. None of that matters. You will find that I am a generous man in that regard.'

'What was she like, Marcus—your first wife, Elizabeth? I imagine she didn't enter into marriage as impoverished as I.'

'No. She came from an impressive, wealthy family. Our families were friends of long standing. It had been in the cards for some time that we would marry.

Elizabeth was young—no more than eighteen—simple and good and pretty.'

'Biddable?'

'Yes, she was.'

'Unlike me.'

Marcus grinned, capturing her gaze. 'Exactly. Never were two people less alike.'

'I see. And did you love her very much?'

Marcus looked at the glass of wine in his hand and swirled the liquid round in the glass, seeming to think how best to answer her question. 'I don't think love entered into it. We liked and respected each other—there was affection—indeed we were the best of friends, but love? Elizabeth wanted nothing more than to be my wife. For the short time we were together, she was content. She died giving birth to Adele.'

There was a husky rasp to his voice, an edge of sadness. 'I'm sorry,' Juliet said quietly.

'There's no need for you to be. It happened. I did love her in a way, but I wasn't in love with her. It was a long time ago. She is but a memory to me now.'

'Kept alive by Adele.'

He nodded. 'I can't tell you how important it is to me to be here, to take care of her. I returned home for a brief period when she was born, but the war in the Peninsular got in the way, and I was duty-bound to return. Now that I am home and she is with me, I will be able to devote more time to her.'

Their conversation was curtailed when a footman came to tell them dinner was ready to be served.

Chapter Ten

Attired in just her nightdress Juliet moved aimlessly to the open window, nervous but impatient for Marcus to come to her. As she looked into the distance, in the darkness she could imagine Endcliffe House. Part of her wanted to be back there but, she thought wistfully, if she were back there, then Marcus wouldn't be with her, and suddenly all those girlish dreams of Thomas and the bulwark of her security—Endcliffe House—began to slip into the past and didn't seem to matter now.

Suddenly, without her noticing, Marcus had become a very important part of her life. He had stood by her, offering her his name, risking his money and his reputation. No man would have done all these things for a woman he did not care about, and she knew she would rather be here with him than without him at Endcliffe House. But what did she feel for him? Did she love him? This she did not know. After Thomas, she would never trust her judgement again, but when she thought of him, of his darkly handsome face and flashing smile, her body trembled with an unaccustomed desire to have him hold her. To feel his strong arms about her and to rest her head on his broad chest—to have him love her. She was more than ready to become his wife in every sense of the word.

Her vigil was rewarded when she heard footsteps on the other side of the door that connected their rooms. With feverish anticipation she turned. Her heart began to beat quickly and her mouth became dry, the palms of her hands clammy, and then suddenly he was there, standing in the open doorway. His flame-coloured robe was partly open at the front to reveal the strong muscles of his chest, with its crisp matting of hair just visible. Broad-shouldered and with his dark hair curling about his face, his jaw lean and firm, with his wicked eyes and lazy smile, he would have made the most handsome pirate, she thought.

They stared at each other, the air crackling with unexpressed emotion. Marcus's awesome presence seemed to fill the room. She could sense his eyes on her, sense his penetrating gaze stripping her body bare. She watched him close the door and move closer with the same rapt attention a rabbit gives a stalking fox, feeling his presence with every fibre of her being. A growing warmth suffused her, and she was achingly aware of her own newly formed desires.

He cocked a handsome brow as he gave her a lengthy inspection. Her nightdress clung to her slender form and the pins had been removed from her hair, allowing the thick tresses free to tumble about her shoulders. 'I see you are expecting me,' he murmured, raising his hand and tracing her bare arm with his finger.

'Yes. I—I expected you sooner.'

'I apologise if I have kept you waiting, Juliet, but I want you to be sure you are ready to become my wife in more than name. After your ordeal at Waring's hands, I would like to make sure I will be welcome in your bed.'

She laughed lightly, touched that he would still be concerned how Thomas's assault may have affected her. 'Worry not, Marcus. What happened has not scarred me in any way. I know you would never harm me physically. I have no fear of what you will do to me. Indeed,' she said, flushing slightly as she anticipated the night to come with a tremor of excitement, 'it is quite the opposite. In fact, I am as impatient as you are to begin our lives together—already I am anticipating exploring the sensual side to our marriage.'

'Then I shall do my best not to disappoint you. Be assured, I shall be a proficient and considerate teacher.'

'Did you say goodnight to Adele?'

'I went to the nursery only to find she was asleep. She is quite exhausted, poor lamb.'

'I—I looked in on her earlier,' Juliet said haltingly, trying to subdue her nervousness. 'She is thrilled with her new toys, in particular the rocking horse.'

'I had it brought here from Cranswick,' he said, his fingers moving upwards to caress her shoulder. 'I intend buying her a pony of her own when she is settled. She loves horses.'

'She will like that,' she said, her heart pounding with a deafening beat as he bent his head and placed his lips where his fingers had gone before. She was tense and still as she allowed him to continue his caress. Closing her eyes, she tilted her head back, feeling delicious sensations stirring inside her. 'Marcus, please,' she gasped. 'Should we not wait—and—'

'Juliet,' he murmured, 'stop talking.' Looking into her eyes, he caressed her fingers with his mouth. He could feel her melting, feel it in the way her fingers trembled.

'But we—'

He stopped her sentence with his thumb gently pressed against her lips. 'Shh.'

The tone of his voice was so soft and inviting that for one mad moment, Juliet almost surrendered herself there and then. She felt herself tremble with the need that he always invoked in her when he was close.

Taking her shoulders, he drew her lithe form towards him, capturing her in a gentle embrace, his eyes feasting on the delicate creaminess of her face and her shining hair spilling down over her shoulders. The sweet fragrance of her body drifted through his senses, and the throbbing hunger to possess her began anew.

'You must learn to relax, Juliet,' he whispered, his mouth against hers. 'The attraction between us has been denied for too long. It is my hope that come daylight, we will have reached an understanding.'

'But there is nothing to understand.'

'There is, my love,' he said, his voice a ragged whisper as he slid his tongue across her lips. 'Let me show you.'

His voice had deepened. His strength and the heat of him were palpable. When he lowered his head, she lost sight of his eyes and fixed her own on his lips. They brushed hers, gently testing their resilience, teasing, savouring, then, with the confidence that there would be a welcome, he covered her lips assuredly. That kiss almost sent her to her knees. Sensations she had never imagined overwhelmed her. The feel of him, the smell of him sank into her flesh, into the bones of her. In response, she slid her hands up his chest to his shoulders.

The kiss ended and he drew back slightly, sliding his hands down her bare arms.

Taking her hand, he drew her towards the bed, seizing her lips once more, drawing her senses again into the heated depths of a kiss, devouring her sweetness, languidly coaxing and parting, his tongue probing and plundering the honeyed cavern, as if he had an eternity to explore and savour.

The sweet urgency of it made Juliet lose touch with reality. It filled her soul. The embers that had glowed and heated her rebellion in the early days of their relationship now burned with passion, her protestations having become raw hunger. It was a kiss so exquisite that whatever doubts had plagued her over the days before becoming his wife died as she became imprisoned in a haze of dangerous, terrifying sensuality over which she had no control.

His hand deftly slipped the narrow straps of her nightdress off her shoulders, revealing the cleft between the round fullness of her breasts. Her cheeks flushed scarlet at his boldness. Raising his head, he laughed softly. There was still so much of the girl in her at war with the assertive young woman, and Marcus had the knack of bringing it quickly to the surface. It was clear to Juliet that in this particular arena, he had absolute control.

Bending his head to pay homage to the soft flesh glowing like creamy pearls in the soft light, he placed his lips in the hollow of her throat where a pulse throbbed. The contact was a shock to Juliet, a delicious one. Heat blossomed and spread. But the heat building inside Marcus, fed and steadily stoked, was escalating into urgency. As he awoke from their kiss, his long fingers divested her of what remained of her nightdress. Her glorious body was a lustrous shade of pale gold in the wavering blur of the flickering candles. Juliet's throat dried. Marcus's gaze focused upon her figure and the ardour in his dark gaze was like a flame to her senses. She was unable to free her rational mind from the overwhelming tide of desire that claimed her, fuelled by a whirlpool of emotions she didn't recognise, much less understand.

'When you've finished ogling me, Marcus, kindly remember you're supposed to be a gentleman and take off your clothes too, unless you intend to make love to me with them on.'

Marcus continued to drink his fill, noting her shallow breathing, sensing anticipation rising like scent around them. Chest tight, eager to seize, to devour, to slake the lust that drove him, every nerve Marcus possessed stilled as slowly his gaze traced up the curves of her long legs, the gentle swell of her thighs, over her taut stomach and minuscule waist to her breasts, full and tipped with rosy peaks. Proceeding to remove his robe, he struggled impatiently with the restricting belt.

Surrendering to the call of her blood, impatient to resume contact between them, with nimble fingers Juliet undid the knot herself. She felt a tremor of alarm and embarrassed admiration pass through her as his body was exposed to her. He had the form of a tall, lithe athlete. His shoulders and thighs were firmly muscled, his belly flat and taut. He was splendid, magnificent, and as she stared at him, her heart gave a tremendous leap, unable to believe how handsome he was. He laughed when she flushed and averted her maidenly eyes away from his manhood, and his teeth gleamed white from between his parted lips as he threw back the bedcovers, and then they were together once more, locked in each other's arms. Never had Juliet been as aware of another human being as she was of Marcus at that moment. Each of them was aware of a new intensity of feeling between them, a new excitement.

'You are an inviting, haunting temptress,' Marcus murmured against her lips. 'And you are about to experience a night of passion and sensual delights such as you cannot have imagined.'

Juliet saw the deepening light in Marcus's eyes. She saw the defined brows and wanted to touch his face, to know him. Then slowly, almost haltingly, he captured her mouth once more in a kiss that warmed her to the core of her being. Parted lips, tender and insistent, caressed hers, moulding and shaping them to his own while his hand touched her bare skin, which felt like liquid satin, his lips following where fingers had gone before, wandering at will over the contours of her.

Juliet was on fire. With a low moan, she stretched alongside him and the hard pressure of his loins. So lost was she in the desire he was skilfully building in her that when his hand travelled along more intimate ground, her thighs loosened of their own accord and quivered beneath his questing hands. She almost drowned as wave after wave of pleasure washed over her.

Hesitantly she half opened her eyes and met her husband's intense gaze, hearing the drumming of her heart until her ears were full of the sound. Faintness drifted on the edge of her vision. She wanted him. She ached for him. And she clutched at him with the awkward desperation of inexperience. Anticipating the pain she would feel in the next moment, she stiffened her body, her arms going round him.

Sensing her apprehension, he gentled the moment of entry. The pain was mild, and when it had subsided, in its place was a hungering, throbbing ache. He filled her fully, touching all of her. It was incredible, something new that burst inside her, and as she slowly began to move as he moved and arched to meet him to the full, she was so carried along on a rapturous glow of passion by the driving force of his powerful strokes deep within her that she was almost delirious. When the explosion came, it broke in a wave of ecstasy and she felt her body soar.

When the weight of his strong body lifted off her, sated and happy, Juliet looked up at him, fighting her way back from oblivion. She sighed and closed her eyes. Marcus lowered his head and ran his tongue provocatively over her lower lip.

'Are you happy, my love?'

'Mm,' she breathed without opening her eyes.

'What are you thinking?' he asked with a tender smile, stroking her satiny skin.

On a sigh, like a kitten she nestled close beneath the sensual onslaught of his caressing hand and mouth. 'My thoughts are most unladylike, I'm afraid. I will not offend your ear by airing them.'

Opening her eyes, she saw the gleam of an ugly silver scar on his shoulder. She touched it with her finger, tracing its smooth line. Lifting her head, she looked at him, imagining the pain he must have felt on being wounded.

'How the war in the Peninsular has hurt you,' she whispered.

'Nay, Juliet. The scar is one of several. I like to think I gave the Frenchies as much as I received on the battlefield. I'm relieved you are not repulsed by it.'

As if to heal his scar, she kissed it before wrapping her arms around him. 'Is every night to be like this one?'

'It is my hope.'

'Then I shall be well satisfied.'

'You speak as if this one is already over and done with, sweetheart. If that is what you think, then you are mistaken,' he said and, as if to prove it, he took her lips in a devouring kiss, renewed desire already pouring through him as he proceeded to kiss and caress her into mindless insensibility.

Later, as Juliet slept, the silky mass of her hair draped about her, his mind still reeling when he thought of the flagrant sensuality of the creature lying next to him, Marcus lay on his side, resting on his elbow, the fingers of his free hand gently brushing strands of hair from her face. His eyes were drawn compulsively to her, and he looked at her with part reverence, part awe, unable to believe this woman, his wife, had succeeded in sending him to unparalleled heights of satisfaction and desire. A deep contentment engulfed him as he gloried in the sweet, wild essence of her.

Conscious of the languor that weighted his limbs, of the satiation that was bone deep, he realised that this state had been reached not by mere self-gratification, but by a deep contentment more profound than at any other time in his life. Juliet had succeeded in tapping the source of his well-being where every other woman he had known had failed.

He was engulfed in a swirling mass of emotions, emotions that were new to him, emotions he could not recognise and could not put a name to. His every instinct reacted to the fact that he had this woman in thrall, that he'd finally breached the walls and captured the elusive creature at its core. He had always known that when he finally made love to her, they would be a combustible combination, but what he had just experienced had been the most splendidly erotic sexual encounter of his life.

In the light of a single candle and the sanctuary of their bed, he had gloried in her beauty—her tiny waist and rounded hips and full breasts. He had lingered over his wife of two days as he had begun to seal their vows securely in a physical knot of passion, determined that he would make her body sing with rapture before he was done. But it had been no easy matter ignoring the urgent heat and throbbing in his loins, and as gentle fingers had shyly explored his naked body, slowly gathering courage, they had ignited too many fires for his rapidly splintering restraint.

When he had entered that most intimate part of her, she had gasped at his invasion, and with the blood pouring through his veins like molten lava, he had gloried in the joy of the woman in his arms, feeling her yield to his caress.

* * *

Juliet sensed the presence of a warm, naked masculine form pressed against her as she floated in a comforting grey mist, drifting in and out of sleep. Lying soft and acquiescent beside him, she could smell his skin, his hair, and he was drawing her to him like a magnet.

'Good morning,' Marcus murmured. 'I trust you slept well.'

Opening her sleepy eyes, she gazed up at him. His tousled hair was dark against the snowy whiteness of the pillows, and sleep had softened the rugged contours of his handsome face. She thought of the times that he had made love to her throughout the night. The first time he had loved her with wild abandon, but thereafter he had exercised more control, lingering over her, holding himself back while he guided her to peak after peak of quivering ecstasy, caressing and kissing her with the skill and expertise of a virtuoso playing a violin.

With these memories occupying her mind, she felt her lips, swollen from his kisses, part in a smile. 'I seem to recall you gave me little time for such luxury,' she answered, her voice low, throaty and warm. 'How long have you been lying there watching me?'

His smouldering gaze passed over her naked shoulders, lingering on the twin peaks straining beneath the sheet. 'Long enough to come to the conclusion that you are too much temptation for a man not long away from the battlefield and starved of a woman's company. In fact, my love, if you were not already married, after our night making passionate love, I would have to marry you,' he teased, kissing the tip of her nose.

'Then it's a good thing I'm a married woman,' she purred, trailing her finger slightly across his chest, 'although I shudder to think what my husband will have to say about it. Why, he might even insist on divorcing me.'

'You may strive at times to drive him to it, being the stubborn and temperamental female that you are, but I can promise you that he will never divorce you,' Marcus stated. His voice still held a hint of teasing, but his eyes were dark and deadly serious.

'What time is it?' she asked, stretching like a sated cat, her gaze going towards the window. Seeing the brightness of the sun penetrating a crack in the drawn curtains, she sat up. 'Heavens, it's daylight. I'm ravenous and ready for my breakfast.'

Laughing softly, Marcus swung his legs over the side of the bed. 'Then I will leave you to your ablutions and see you at breakfast shortly.'

Left alone, Juliet felt as if she were a different person from the day before. Marcus had awoken feelings inside her that she had not known existed. She was no longer a naive innocent but a woman, with a woman's wants and needs that could match those of any other, and she knew that only one man could fill those needs.

What she had felt for Thomas had not been like this. That had been warm and gentle and pure, whereas what she felt for Marcus she couldn't begin to analyse or understand. It was dark and mysterious and all-consuming, a highly volatile combination of terror, danger and excitement, and the force of it terrified her.

Last night he had come to her room to seduce her, to make her want him, and he had succeeded. Her face exploded in a blaze of scarlet when she thought of how she had lain with him and kissed him, had let him fondle her in the most intimate places, exploring her body with the sureness of an experienced and knowledgeable lover, and she felt the pleasurably wanton feelings tearing through her again at the memory.

The smell of his elusive scent still lingered, and she could still taste his kisses and remember how urgent and hungry his mouth had been on hers. Not even in her wildest dreams had she imagined that a man could make her body come to life like that, and she doubted that anyone else ever would but Marcus. It was instinct with him and, being a demanding male, with a dominating sensuality, it was the most natural thing in the world for him to make love.

She gazed at herself in the dressing table mirror, seeing her lips slightly swollen from Marcus's kisses, and her skin seemed to glow from his touch. At the transformation, a sense of triumph swept through her, for the face reflected in the mirror was the face of a woman, all trace of innocence having disappeared, and when Daphne tapped on her door and entered, smiling broadly, one look at Juliet's face, and she too noticed the transformation and welcomed it. Never had her maid seen her look so radiant, so happy.

Later, when Juliet was dressed, she went down to join Marcus in the breakfast room. She entered in a state of spiralling apprehension at the thought of seeing him again. In the cold light of day, how would they react to one another after the intimacies they had shared in her bed, and how could she appear calm and matter-of-fact when she could remember every intimate detail of what she had done with him? She found him already seated at the table. On seeing her, he rose.

'Ah, here you are, Juliet. I waited for you.'

'There was no need.'

'Yes, there was.'

Juliet found it difficult to hide her treacherous heart's reaction to the deep timbre of his voice. Why, she wondered desperately, did she feel different from the way she had felt yesterday? Why could she still feel his hands on her bare flesh and his kisses on her lips? Slowly, she walked toward him, trying to still the trembling in her legs. He seemed extraordinarily tall and broad-shouldered to her this morning, his face more striking and handsome than ever.

As he stood looking down at her, there was a small quirk of a smile on his lips, and though his gaze travelled leisurely from the top of her bright head, lingering meaningfully on her soft mouth, it lacked the roguish gleam that often brought a flush to her cheeks. She felt heat in her face, felt it spread at that naked, desirous look. It was a look that spoke of invitation and need.

'I was thinking of you. How lovely you look this morning. I was half afraid you were not real but a ghost of the night.'

Juliet laughed. 'I assure you I am flesh and blood.'

He nodded and smiled knowingly. 'So you are. Come and sit down,' he said, pulling out a chair. 'Cook has prepared a breakfast fit for a king, so I hope you will do it justice.'

Which she did. As she began to eat her eggs and delectable little mushrooms done in butter, she was amazed by how hungry she was. They made small talk until Juliet laid her napkin down after finishing her last piece of toast and slowly drank her coffee.

'I have certain important matters to take care of today, Juliet. It will be a good opportunity for you to familiarise yourself with the house and servants. It's a skeleton staff at present, but we can employ more when you have taken stock of things.'

'I will. I plan to speak to Mrs Cherry and ask her advice on staffing matters. I would also like to spend some time with Adele. I thought we would go for a walk.'

'She will like that. I expect she is eager to explore the house. When I was in Spain, I would think of Mulberry Hall, remembering how much I loved the house when I was a boy. I want Adele to feel that way about it.'

'The war must seem very far away now.'

'It is. I spent a long time there.'

'What was it like?' she asked, taking a sip of her coffee as she tried to envisage him as a soldier, thinking how handsome he would look in uniform.

'Hot for the most part, dusty, although the winters, especially in the mountains, could be freezing. Food was frequently in short supply because resources failed to get through.'

'Did you see much fighting?'

'A great deal, as a matter of fact.'

'And did you suffer any injuries?'

'Several, minor ones. I was lucky.'

He hesitated. Thinking of the scar she had seen on his shoulder, Juliet was strangely sensitive to his thoughts and understood. 'You don't have to talk about it, Marcus. I have spoken to several soldiers who have returned from the Peninsular, so I do have a picture in my mind of what it was like.'

'Unless you were there, at Albuera or Badajoz, you can never know, and it's as well that you don't. Thank God we've almost seen the last of it. But there were times when I saw the real Spain, and at times like those, when the sun set over the brooding mountains and crimson lit the sky, like it does now, in a way that belongs to the radiance of late summer, we saw the beauty of the country and it felt good to be alive.'

As one day passed into the next and the wonderful shades of autumn began to colour the trees, Marcus was kept extremely busy with estate affairs and Juliet saw little of him during the daylight hours. He would ride off in the early morning with his steward or someone else, and she would often not see him again until late afternoon. On occasion he would ride over to Endcliffe House to see how Richard was managing his affairs, giving advice where necessary and reporting back to Juliet that he was working hard to put things right.

Juliet made a point of getting to know the servants and familiarising herself with the house, which was run efficiently by Mrs Cherry. She also spent a great deal of her time with Adele, realising that she had a talent for entertaining the child that surprised her. In spite of her lack of experience with children, she had no trouble winning her trust and arousing her eager curiosity for most things. Adele loved to draw and paint and play simple games. But her greatest love was to be outdoors. They would walk together in the grounds of the house and often go beyond to the surrounding deer park and sit by the lake and feed the ducks that clamoured for the bread they brought.

But there were times when Adele could be difficult. Often, she would be quiet for long periods and unable to concentrate for any length of time on any one thing. She was quite wilful, and there were tears if she could not get her own way. But on the whole, she brought much pleasure to Juliet.

It was Marcus who, knowing of her love of reading, proudly gave Juliet her first glimpse of the library. It was vast, a treasure trove of books, of precious tomes of history, religion and theology, the gems of poetry and fiction. It was as she perused these books that Marcus placed a small package in her hands. She looked at him in puzzlement.

'Is this a gift for me?' she asked.

'It is indeed. One more book to be added to the poetry collection, one I know you will like.'

She unwrapped it carefully, expectantly, gasping when it was revealed to be the book of sentimental lyric poetry by William Collins. She stared at it with delight.

'Oh, Marcus, how did you know?' and then she recalled the day they had met in Mr Marsden's bookshop, when she had gone there in the hope of purchasing this very book. She looked up at him, seeing in his eyes the pleasure it gave him to present her with this gift. 'You remembered.'

'I did. I managed to find it in another bookshop in London. I hope it will give you many hours of pleasurable reading.'

'It will. And thank you, Marcus. I will treasure it always—more so because you gave it to me.'

'I know you will, and who knows,' he murmured with a roguish quirk to his lips. 'What you read on the pages of Mr Collins's book of poetry just might spill over into our bedroom.'

Juliet laughed at his teasing audacity. 'Are you telling me that I need educating in the arts of making love, my lord?'

He smiled an amiable smile and lightly touched her cheek with his finger. 'You've learned a great deal. I am proud of you, my love. On the whole, you've been a marvellously satisfying student.'

'Are you saying that I have still more to learn?' she asked, her eyes sparkling with humour, thinking how wonderfully attractive he looked, his hair still a bit damp from his bath and smelling of pine-scented shaving lotion. He really was the most appealing man she had ever met.

'There are more delightful things you have to know, and between Mr Collins and myself, I am certain we can improve matters.'

'Thank you, Marcus. Every girl likes to be called inadequate.'

'You are never that,' he said, laughing quietly. 'And I guarantee you will not find your lessons too difficult a task.'

'I sincerely hope not, otherwise I shall be too exhausted to do my daily chores.'

'Then you shall have the day off.'

Tossing her head, Juliet laughed and walked toward the door.

'Where are you going?'

'To the garden to read Mr Collins's poems. His words happen to be more subtle than yours.'

'Ah, but not nearly as interesting,' he said, following in her wake.

'You, my lord,' she said, turning and poking him in the ribs with her fingertip, 'are outrageous.'

'Utterly,' he agreed, taking her arm and escorting her into the garden, where they would sit and together read Mr Collins's delightful and informative poems.

They had not been at Mulberry Hall a week when the invitations to visit neighbours began to arrive. And so began the endless round of social events as Juliet was swept along as if on a tidal wave. She never failed to look stunning, and Marcus proudly escorted her to all the events. They were the much sought after attraction at any event they attended and were received warmly. Never had Juliet believed she could be so happy.

The lives of the people in local society in which they mixed were varied and full. Most of them managed their estates, visited their neighbours, hunted, danced and gambled, making frequent visits to the city, and many of these privileged landowners also engaged in politics, dominating society and local government, the titled gentlemen taking their seat in the House of Lords. New to the area and committed to the management of his estate with the help of his stewards, at this present time, Marcus was not as deeply committed to British politics as some of his neighbours. This would come later.

Feeling restless and longing to stretch her legs and maybe ride out on one of Marcus's fine mounts, she entered the dim interior of the stables, the smell of hay, horses, manure and leather strong, though not unpleasant. Juliet observed several people at work. Her gaze became focused on a man forking straw out of one of the stalls. Her eyes opened wide. Tall and thin, the man was in his late thirties. He also had a wooden leg upon which he seemed to manage very well. She hurried towards him.

'Joe? Joe Ruskin—I am glad to see you have found work.'

Joe stopped what he was doing and looked at her, a wide smile breaking on his face. 'Lady Juliet! I can't tell you what a relief it was when Lord Cardell came to see me and set me on. It upset me, it did, when I was accused of poaching, but that was a mistake and His Lordship was quick to show how sorry he was to have believed the rumour and told me that I had you to thank for making him find out the truth of the matter.'

'I only did what I thought was right, Joe. I knew you were innocent.'

'Aye, I was, though it caused Rose a lot of grief at the time.'

'I know. And you are happy working here?'

'More than that. I love working with horses. That's what I was doing out in the Peninsular—taking care of the horses—until I lost my leg when I got too close to the battlefield. I thought I would never work again and shuddered to think what would become of Rose and the bairns. But Lord Cardell told me that since he was to expand his stable, there was always a need for an extra pair of hands.'

'I'm so happy to see you settled, Joe. You…are aware that Lord Cardell is my husband now? We were married in London.'

'I do know that and wish you both every happiness. It's good to know you won't be leaving the area.'

'Yes, that is one of the advantages.'

Having heard the voice of his wife, the man in the next stall jerked erect. 'Only one?' his voice rang out. 'I shall be interested to learn the rest.'

As Juliet turned her head, their eyes met instantly, and so abrupt was Marcus's appearance that Juliet started. Then she laughed. 'Marcus! I might have known you would be lurking somewhere. I've just been having a word with Mr Ruskin. I was surprised to find him working here. You should have told me.'

'It slipped my mind. Joe is a welcome addition to the stables—knows all there is to know about horses apparently, having looked after them for the army in Spain. Is that not so, Joe?'

'It is. Thank you, sir,' Joe replied. 'I was just telling Her Ladyship.'

Looking from one to the other, Juliet knew that because Marcus had given him this chance, Joe would be his servant forever. Grateful to Marcus for doing this for Joe, she regretted all the bitter words she had accused him of on their first encounter.

Walking into the stable-yard with Marcus, she said, 'Thank you for finding work for Joe. I am grateful to you for giving him a place, although now that Richard is home, and when things begin to improve at End-cliffe House, I am sure we could have found work for him.' Juliet looked at Marcus and smiled, meeting his gaze directly. 'You do realise that by treating Joe with courtesy, you have engendered his respect, and you can be assured of his lifelong devotion.'

'Which is what I strive to do with my wife,' Marcus remarked on a teasing note.

Juliet ignored his remark and averted her gaze. 'I came to see if I could find a suitable horse to ride. It's such a lovely day.'

'You should have said at breakfast. I will ride with you.'

'I know how busy you are, Marcus. Are you sure you can spare the time?'

'For my wife, anything.'

Chapter Eleven

Later that same day, after enjoying a vigorous ride with Marcus, with it being so lovely, she suggested taking a walk to the lake with Adele. Marcus was in favour of spending time with his two favourite ladies, even going so far as to suggest taking a hamper of food along with them and making an afternoon of it.

Adele gazed at the hamper her father was carrying with excitement. 'What's in that basket?' she asked. 'Is it a present for me?'

'Well, kind of,' Juliet replied. 'It's full of lovely food Cook has packed for us.'

Adele looked nonplussed. 'Why? Is it for the ducks?'

Juliet laughed, taking hold of her hand. 'Only a little bread is for the ducks. The hamper is filled with all sorts of nice things for us to eat. It's such a lovely day that your father and I thought we would eat it by the lake.'

'Do you mean we are going to eat outside?'

'Exactly,' Marcus said. 'It's a splendid idea, don't you agree, Adele?'

'Ooh, yes,' she replied happily, letting go of Juliet's hand as she skipped on ahead.

All the lazy heat of late summer was in the air as they walked around the lake, which was fed by fast flowing streams at one end, swelling its banks before cascading over a weir at the other, where it fell into a turbulent deep dark pool. It was a dangerous place to be and was to be avoided by the unwary. Finding the perfect spot, discarding her bonnet to reveal the glorious, luxuriant hair upswept in glossy curls that almost took Marcus's breath away, unaware of the effect she had created with such a simple act, Juliet spread a large blanket on the ground. Adele helped her take the food out of the hamper and place it on a separate cloth, thinking it great fun.

'This is what I do when I give a tea party for my dolls,' she told them, happily kneeling on the edge of the cloth and helping herself to a sandwich.

As they talked and ate, Juliet was vaguely aware of Marcus's appreciative gaze on her animated face as she handed Adele a cup of lemonade. When the child had eaten and drunk her fill, she picked up some bread and ran off to feed the ducks on the edge of the lake.

'You have a way with Adele,' Marcus said. 'It's good to see her so happy.'

'She's an easy child to get along with.' Sitting beside him and tucking her feet beneath her, she looked at him. 'During the short time I have spent at Mulberry Hall, I have gained a deeper understanding of why you married me—your generosity towards Richard, how you are helping him regain his standing in the community. My attitude toward you has become more sympathetic and my thoughts more favourable. Of course you were furious when Thomas turned up on the day of our wedding, and in your place, I would have felt the same. But there are times when I really don't understand you. In the short time I have known you, you have gone from being an irritable neighbour to a considerate husband.'

His eyes slid over her face, trapping her in their burning gaze. 'Which is what I will always be, but I could never be indifferent to you. One must either love you to distraction or want to strangle you.'

'And what would you like to do to me, Marcus? Tell me.'

He grinned. 'I haven't made up my mind yet.'

'Then kindly let me know when you have.' Drawing up her knees and wrapping her arms around them, she watched Adele trying to make friends with a moorhen which skittered among the tall rushes skirting the lake. The day was perfect. They talked of ordinary and extraordinary things, about his childhood and his close relationship with his family and in particular his brother, of how his father had been killed in a riding accident during a hunt, and as he talked, his voice seemed to ring inside her head. When he fell silent, content to sit and watch his daughter, Juliet was miles away, thinking of nothing other than this incredible moment. Nothing could match this quiet joy she felt.

'This is such a wonderful place,' she murmured at length. 'Here by the lake and surrounded by wooded hills, one feels quite small and vulnerable—rather humble, in fact.'

Marcus's expression gentled, and a glint of amusement came into his eyes as he slanted her a wicked look. 'You couldn't be humble, my love, if you tried. You're unpredictable and quite outrageous, and you never cease to amaze me.'

She looked at him and laughed. 'And isn't that how you want your wife to be? Predictability can be so dull—much more exciting for her to have many interesting and diverting contradictions to her character.'

'Not so many that she would take some keeping up with.'

'Then, what is your idea of an ideal wife? A woman who should lose her individuality completely and live only for her husband? To always be at his beck and call and spend her days carrying out her part of the marriage contract?'

Marcus stretched out on his back and closed his

eyes, and the mobile line of his mouth quirked in a half-smile. 'Carry on, my love. It gets better all the time. I'm certainly in favour of a married woman knowing her duty is to take care of her husband, to cook his meals and to clean the house. And do not forget that the husband always likes his wife to be gentle and sympathetic to himself, to place him on a pedestal and be humorous, witty and cheerful at all times.'

Juliet was momentarily dumbstruck by his speech, then she burst out laughing at his teasing. 'While he doesn't always concern himself very particularly about the means to make and keep her so. And what are your opinions concerning an intelligent wife? Would that be acceptable to you, or would you be afraid that if she were too intelligent, she would be capable of perceiving the mind of her husband—should he be of lesser intelligence than herself, of course.'

Marcus opened his eyes and grinned up at her. 'Which he never is,' he uttered conceitedly, closing his eyes once more.

'Is that right?' she retorted with mock indignation. 'If women were more forthright and didn't appear to be dim-witted half the time, convincing their menfolk that they are smarter and wiser than we are, their egos would be well and truly shattered.'

'Then if that should prove to be the case, men would use their brute strength to gain supremacy over them in the time-honoured way.' A seductive languor appeared in his eyes when he opened them and looked at his wife, and it made her heart turn over. 'A man may treat his wife in any way he sees fit—within reason, of course.'

'But of course,' she scoffed, almost choking on the laughter that was bubbling up inside her. 'Like a possession, you mean!'

Marcus smiled, closing his eyes and nodded smugly. 'I could not put it better myself. However, I'd consider it necessary that my wife should be intelligent if she is to conduct my concerns through life, but not too intelligent, just enough to appreciate my own intellectual mind.'

'But you would allow her to have some freedom of her own?'

'The truth of it is that I would not have to permit my wife to do anything. In law you are my wife, so whatever is yours is mine also. I can, if I choose, treat you harshly and without consideration, and confine you to the kitchen and the bedroom.'

Unable to contain her mirth any longer, Juliet laughed out loud at the sheer arrogance of her husband, relieved since now that she had come to know him, she understood he was teasing her and enjoying every minute of it. 'You would not. You wouldn't dare. I would kill you first.'

Marcus linked his hands behind his head, staring

up at the blue sky dotted with white clouds. 'You have a beautiful laugh, Juliet. You should laugh more often.'

Wriggling herself into a more comfortable position, Juliet looked down at him. 'You're only saying that to change the subject. Please don't tell me you meant all that rubbish about wives being completely subservient to their husbands?'

Marcus half raised his eyelids and looked into her eyes, shining softly so close above him. 'I was just making a point—and a valid one at that. Many a husband would not allow you so free a rein as you have, my sweet.'

Juliet sighed, stretching out beside him and rolling onto her stomach. Cupping her chin in her hands, she feigned despondency. 'I am beginning to think I would be better off if I were a widow.' That said, she very quickly changed her mind as she let her gaze travel down the long, superbly fit and muscled body stretched out beside her.

'It's a good thing we have servants since I could not do all the things you would expect of me. You would be sadly disappointed. I've had no practice in the ways of a wife. I can't cook—at least I don't think I can since I have never tried—although I do know quite a lot about keeping house. I do have other interests and accomplishments, but I don't think they would be of much use to you.'

'Worry not, my love. I expect my wife to be happy with what I can give her. I would promise her that she will always have clothes to wear and food to eat and a roof over her head that does not leak, and if she loves me, she will accept that.'

Juliet's brow puckered in a thoughtful frown and she turned her face away. 'Love? In truth, Marcus, I don't know what I feel. What I do know is that ever since you came into my life, I have been so confused, with my emotions all over the place. I—I have also come to have a strong attraction to you, which you already know.'

Reaching out, Marcus gently cupped her cheek to turn her face towards him. 'And I have an extremely strong and passionate desire for you, Juliet, and if we were alone, I would show you.'

She met his gaze steadily, strangely disappointed that he couldn't think of a stronger emotion to describe what was between them other than desire. 'Desire, as wonderful as it is, is not enough to base a marriage on, Marcus. It is only a temporary emotion, and I have no wish to become trapped in a loveless marriage.'

'It won't be, that I promise you. Do not forget that it was a mutual decision for us to take our marriage vows, Juliet. Honour and duty must run side by side with our emotions.'

In his expression Juliet saw a resolute determination that he would have his way. It was an expression she was coming to know quite well. 'I will not be your duty, Marcus. I want more from you than that.'

Adele chose that moment to come for more bread to feed the ducks.

'Here you are, Adele.' Juliet handed her more bread. 'They must be very hungry today—or just greedy.'

'No,' Adele replied. 'They really are very hungry,' she said over her shoulder as she went off to give the ducks more bread. Juliet began packing things away in the hamper when she suddenly found her wrist taken and looked up.

'That was not the most romantic thing I have ever said, Juliet. If I have hurt you by discussing our marriage in such a blunt fashion, then I apologise. Our marriage was not an ideal affair. I wish it could have been different.'

'So do I.'

'If you want the truth, I will tell you that in my eyes, you are as alluring and desirable as any woman I have ever known. I want you, and I shall go on wanting you. You are beautiful and vibrant, and you were made for love. On the nights when you lie in my arms, I find something that binds me to another human being more assuredly than anything else in my life. There is a sense of rightness to it, as if that is where you are meant to be. You have become a passion to me, and I cannot bear the thought of losing you. If I could, I would lay the whole world at your feet, and I have never been so serious in my whole life.'

Perhaps it was the way his head was slightly tilted to one side, perhaps it was a trick of the light, perhaps it was the yearning softness of his voice, but whatever the reason, Juliet had the impression that his face had changed. His features were relaxed, making him look younger, less hard and cynical. She had a momentary glimpse of the young man he must have been before he had gone to Spain.

'I don't want the world, Marcus. I will be satisfied for a very small and humble part of it, if it is somewhere we can call home.'

They sat for a moment in silence, each with their own thoughts. Juliet looked towards the lake where Adele was still feeding the ducks, feeling that nothing existed but the feelings of her body as she lusted for her husband with increasing desire. She was happy to be with him, satisfied that the unfortunate events that had clouded their wedding had been resolved between them. She could think of nothing but that glorious fact. The more they were together, they discovered things about each other that were entirely new. They both had such strong views on everything, and arguments flared easily, but they both agreed that a placid partnership would not have suited them, and they soon realised that it made the making up all the more passionate and exciting.

Juliet turned back to him, seeing how the sun caught his head in a halo of light. She gazed at his face and caught her breath at something she saw there. No man had ever looked at her quite like that before. She cursed herself for being unable to free herself from the sensual trap he had set for her.

She was falling in love with him. She knew she was.

It was an idyllic time for them, a time when they were suspended in some kind of dream, reluctant to let the outside world into their lives. But it was inevitable that it would intrude sometime, which it did when Richard took time off from his many duties and came to call. Juliet was amazed by the change in him and by the way he had taken over the running of things on the estate, without any mention of returning to his pleasurable pursuits in London.

His life had been taken over by work as he set about finding ways to increase the income of the estate, contracting better rents, which had been set some years back, without being excessive, and renting out more grazing land to the neighbouring farms to allow them to increase their herds and flocks. However, until things were seen to improve, economy had to remain a rule.

'I'm surprised I haven't seen anything of you since you came home, Richard,' Juliet said when he entered the drawing room with Marcus.

'There is much to be done on the estate, Juliet—as you well know—if I am to bring it back to what it once was. Your husband has been doing much to help me in that, for which I thank you, Marcus. I came to tell you that I'm off to Berkshire for a few days. Amelia's father, the Earl of Bainbridge, has invited me.'

Juliet gasped with delight. 'This is happy news indeed, Richard. Is he to consider your suit at last?'

Richard flushed slightly and smiled, looking a little bashful. 'It would appear so. If all goes well, then Amelia and I will be married at her home in Berkshire, possibly in the spring of next year. I do hope you will both be able to attend.'

'We shall be delighted. I doubt you will be able to keep your sister away,' Marcus said, pouring them both a glass of brandy. 'Do you not miss the London social scene?'

'Not really. Now that there is a chance that Amelia and I can be married, I am quite content to be at Endcliffe. I have not been drawn into a game of cards since I left town. You were my last opponent, and after that unfortunate experience, I have no desire for another.'

'I am overjoyed to hear that,' Juliet said, looking fondly at her brother.

Marcus sat down and crossed one leg over the other as he studied Richard. 'I'm glad you have seen the error of your ways, Richard, and decided to settle down to a more sedate and sensible lifestyle, which means less for Juliet to worry about. No doubt the delightful Amelia has had much to do with that.'

'She most certainly has,' Richard answered with a beaming smile, having observed that marriage to Juliet had certainly made his brother-in-law less formidable and more approachable. 'I have just seen Adele setting out on a walk with her nursemaid. She seems to be a happy little soul.'

Juliet laughed. 'And so she is. She's adorable. I think they are to walk to the lake to feed the ducks. It's Adele's favourite pastime, I'm afraid.'

'She really is quite delightful, but then, any child who is fortunate enough to have you for their stepmother would be.'

Marcus's face became set in serious lines. 'My sentiments entirely—in fact, Adele has begun addressing her as Mama, is that not so, Juliet?'

'Yes, she has. I am quite touched by it, but we have become close.'

'Your sister is a truly remarkable woman, Richard. She has become very dear to me. That game of cards, which was so disastrous for yourself, turned out to be a blessing in disguise for me—my salvation, you might say. Out of your misfortune came the luckiest moment of my life,' Marcus said quietly, his expression grave, intending to leave Richard in no doubt as to the strong bond of love that had grown between Marcus and his sister.

Juliet was always impatient for the days to end and the nights when Marcus would come to her room and take her in his arms. When at last a blissful aura broke over them, spent and exhausted, slowly they would drift back to earth, drained and incapable of any movement other than to hold each other close. Juliet sighed, the physicality of their lovemaking, her vulnerability and her implicit surrender sweeping over her as her hand caressed Marcus's chest.

They would make love until towards dawn, when at last they would fall into a short, blissful sleep, but before Juliet closed her eyes, curled within her husband's warm embrace. She knew with a feverish joy, as sure as night followed day, that she loved him. She accepted the truth with every fibre of her being. He was part of her, branded on her very soul, and she would never be free again. With this glorious revelation, everything she had found so difficult to understand suddenly seemed so simple. She wished to stay by his side for always.

Marcus was with his steward inspecting some land that was to be cleared of scrub to make room for more crops to be planted. The day had begun sunny and warm, but clouds were gathering overhead threatening a storm. At a loose end and deciding to take a walk in the grounds with Adele before the storm broke, Juliet summoned one of the maids to fetch Adele from the nursery. She was surprised when the child's nursemaid in a state of agitation came to inform her that Miss Adele was nowhere to be found.

Juliet stared at her in disbelief. 'But she cannot have disappeared. She might be hiding. Where have you searched?'

'Everywhere, but she seems to have disappeared into thin air,' the maid cried.

'When did you last see her?'

'Just after breakfast. She didn't eat much, said she wasn't hungry. I left the room for just a moment and when I returned, she wasn't there, and her breakfast plates were empty, so I assumed she might have eaten it after all and gone to see her father or you.'

'Lord Cardell is not here and I have not seen her. I'll summon the servants to mount a search,' Juliet said, not unduly alarmed, for Adele couldn't have wandered very far.

A search was mounted but without success. Going to the upper story herself, where some of the servants had their rooms, her eyes lighted on the large cupboard, a cupboard that was all too familiar to her. Immediately her mind went back to her own ordeal inside it when she was no more than Adele's age. She approached it with some trepidation, memories of that awful time flooding back. Gingerly she pulled the door open with effort. It was still stiff and would be impossible for a small child to open. With some trepidation she peered inside. Thankfully it was empty, but she decided there and then to have the cupboard removed from the house.

Going back down to the hall and being told that there was no sign of Adele, she became seriously worried. Outside she scanned the gardens and beyond, looking towards the lake. Thinking of what the nursemaid had said, that Adele had not eaten her breakfast and on returning to the nursery had found that both the breakfast and Adele had disappeared, she reached the conclusion that it was possible that Adele just might have taken what remained of her breakfast to feed the ducks. She felt sick at the thought of the child going all that way alone.

Juliet turned to find Joe Ruskin coming up behind her.

'Have you found her, Lady Juliet?'

'No, but I have a feeling she will be heading for the lake. I need to find her as soon as possible.'

'Storm's coming,' Joe said as lightning cracked and thunder rumbled in the distance. 'It'll be with us soon.'

Ominous grey clouds loomed overhead, and the

wind was rising, buffeting the trees. Scanning the parkland and looking towards the lake, she was certain she saw the flash of something in the distance. Two figures, one tall, the other a child. The tall one looked like a man walking with a limp, and she saw that he was leading a child by the hand, heading in the direction of the calm, still water of the lake that was slate grey beneath the leaden sky. When the figures disappeared into a wooded area, at first, she thought her mind was playing strange tricks, but then she saw them emerge from the trees and stop beside the lake.

She stared in disbelief, sure they were about to step into the water, which was shallow there, until she saw them climb into a small rowboat that was one of three kept tethered to a small landing stage. The lake was teaming with pike, trout and carp, and the boats were frequently used by the gamekeepers to provide fish for the house.

'Goodness! I can see her, and she's with a person who is known to me. Thomas!' she gasped, her stomach twisting as she realised who it was that had Adele. 'I must go after them. Get help, Joe. Send them to the lake and tell them to hurry.'

Without stopping to think, Juliet began to run, her cloak dropping from her shoulders onto the ground. She ran as if her very life depended on it, taking air into her lungs, breathing in and out, putting one leg in front of the other. She was oblivious to the rain as it began to fall. The clothes she wore were not thick enough to shelter her from her nightmares of her wedding night and Thomas's vicious assault on her person, which rose to the surface of her mind to taunt her as she hurried onward, running harder, faster. Almost spent on reaching the edge of the lake, wiping the rain from her eyes, Juliet stared ahead, sucking great gulping breaths into her lungs. Suddenly there came another flash of lightning that pierced the sky, followed immediately by a deafening rumble that seemed to shake the very foundations of the trees. The storm had come.

Teeth gritted, bodily exhausted, she looked across the water at the boat. Thomas was manning the oars and Adele sat across from him, the waves tossing the little wooden boat from side to side. The child sat very still in her now sodden clothes, a frightened look on her young face as she clutched a small package to her chest, no doubt bread meant for the ducks. They were crossing the lake to the other side, where a variety of waterbirds collected.

Hearing the loud noise of the water as it cascaded over the weir at the far end of the lake into a deep whirling pool, Juliet was profoundly concerned for Adele's safety. There was a strong current in the middle of the lake that drew the unwary towards the weir. Looking to the other side of the lake where the road led away from Mulberry Hall was a carriage. It was stationary, and the awful thought of what Thomas intended—not only to abduct Adele but to secrete her away somewhere in retaliation for the humiliation he had suffered at Marcus's hands—was too much to bear.

'Thomas!' she called, waving her arms. She called out again, and Thomas turned his head and looked at her, making Juliet's blood run cold when she beheld the expression on his face. His eyes were as dark as the leaden water of the lake, his look one of madness, as if he had completely lost all reason.

With no other thought than to reach Adele before the boat was taken over the weir, she stepped into the water. If that were to happen, then Adele would surely drown, she thought suddenly, horror striking at her very soul. She must get help from somewhere. But how could she? There was no time. The house was too far away. By the time Joe had summoned help, it would be too late.

Without thought for her own mortal danger she stepped farther into the water and began wading out into the lake, shuddering when the cold water invaded her shoes. Her feet stirred up the muddy silt on the bottom, which clouded the water about her. With her eyes fixed on the boat, she shouted for Thomas to come back, but he carried on rowing, paying no heed to her entreaties.

Despite being hampered by her heavy skirts, reaching deeper water, she began to swim for all she was worth.

When Marcus returned to the house, he was aware of a strange quietness all around him. With a feeling of alarm, seeing an anxious-looking Mrs Cherry appear from the domestic quarters, he strode towards her.

'What is it? Has something happened?' he demanded.

Relief that he had come flooded Mrs Cherry's eyes. 'Thank goodness you're back, Lord Cardell. I'm afraid there is. Miss Adele has gone missing. The house has been searched, but there's no sign of her anywhere.'

All Marcus's senses became alert. 'Where is my wife?'

'She went to look outside in case she had wandered from the house.'

'What else has been done to find her?'

'Everyone is looking for her—inside and outside— even the stables have been searched. Lady Cardell was quite beside herself when she couldn't be found, and now she too appears to have disappeared. With rain threatening, she was wearing her cloak, but it was found on the drive and no sign of her.'

'I see. I'll see what's being done.' He left the house

and looked around, taking stock of the indoor and outdoor servants searching the grounds. He looked at them hard, as if willing them to tell him what had happened, but he wasn't seeing anything. Something black and formless and terrifying in its secrecy had come alive inside him, almost stopping his breath and wrapping itself around his pounding heart. Joe Ruskin approached him as the first heavy drops of rain began to spear down on them.

'Have you seen my wife?'

'She's heading in the direction of the lake, said she'd seen a man leading a child in that direction. Told me to fetch help.'

Marcus stared at him. 'A man—with a child?'

'Yes, sir.'

'And what did this man look like? Have you a description.'

'No, sir, other than he looked like a gentleman and he had a limp.'

'A limp?' Marcus could think of only one man he knew with a limp, and that did not bear thinking about just then. 'And was nothing done to apprehend them?'

'Some of the grooms and lads from the stables have gone after them.'

'How long ago?'

'About ten minutes, sir.'

Marcus turned and began striding away, his eyes

springing fiercely to life and his uncompromising jaw set as hard as granite as he looked in the direction of the lake, the rain slanting down as another flash of lightning forked across the sky in the distance followed by a hollow roll of thunder. A man with a limp? Thomas Waring was the only man he could think of, and remembering his parting words after that ill-fated duel they had fought, Marcus had no doubt that he was the man who had taken his daughter.

Richard, who had just arrived, was ashen-faced and came to stand beside him. 'I've just heard Juliet has gone missing?'

Marcus nodded, his face grim. 'And Adele. I have every reason to believe she has been abducted.'

'But I cannot think of any reason why anyone would want to abduct a child?'

'Can you not? There is one person who springs to mind, Richard. One person who wants to avenge me for marrying Juliet, along with an incident before that. He is desperate and demented enough to go to any lengths to exact his revenge.'

Richard blanched, swallowing hard, knowing after one devastating, heart-stopping moment who he was referring to. 'You think it is Thomas, don't you?'

'Yes. I know it.'

'Thomas may be a libertine and accused of many things, but I cannot believe he would resort to this.

What is the object of doing such a thing as to seize a child?'

'The man is so demented and determined on revenge that I doubt he knows it himself. You are aware of his dissolute reputation, Richard. Why, you were against him marrying Juliet because of it, so to show any kind of loyalty now is misplaced. He threatened revenge. He is devious enough to resort to anything. Now come. We must hurry.'

'Where to?'

'The lake.'

'Good Lord! Little wonder you are worried. But he wouldn't stoop to—'

'To what, Richard? Murder?'

'He wouldn't.'

Marcus looked at him and their eyes locked in fervent prayer to God that he was right. Waring's threats had become reality. It would appear that Adele must have wandered off and Juliet had gone after her.

'I'll head for the lake. Some of the grooms have already set off. Get more men together and come after me.'

Knowing without a doubt that his beloved daughter was in the hands of Thomas Waring, he became like a man in the grip of a nightmare, cursing himself for having shrugged off Waring's threat. Marcus knew what the man was capable of, but he would never have thought he would stoop to anything as base as abducting a child. The thought of his daughter and Juliet, bewildered and terrified in the hands of a man who would go to any lengths to enact his revenge on Marcus for marrying Juliet, caused a violent rage to fill his being, which increased with each passing moment as ran swiftly to the lake, reaching it in just a few minutes.

Seeing the boat with his daughter and Thomas Waring heading for the weir, and his wife struggling to stay afloat, he flung off his jacket as he ran and pulled off his boots before entering the water. With powerful strokes, he began to swim out to Juliet across the lake, desperate to get to her, while he could see the boat with his daughter and Waring was being carried swiftly towards the weir. He could also see that men were already in situ at the head of the weir, ready to snatch Adele before the boat went over.

Chapter Twelve

Juliet did not see Marcus emerge from the trees, nor did she see the people running towards the lake from the house, or hear one of them calling her name in frantic desperation. Death stared her in the face as she went under the water, her legs, as they thrashed about, becoming entangled and held fast by long trailing weeds, resembling the long strands of her hair that had become unpinned. It was like a nightmare from which there was no awakening, and because of the water, she could not cry out.

She managed to surface briefly and gasp for air, at the same time seeing the boat being carried in the fast-flowing water towards the weir. Gradually she became unaware of the intensity of the cold seeping into her, of the numbness taking over her entire body. The last thing she saw before she closed her eyes was Adele's white face as she clung to the side of the boat, which was beginning to spin around with the force of the water close to the weir. Like a captive bird, she was visibly trembling, her eyes wide. But there was nothing Juliet could do. There was water in her mouth, her eyes, her ears, the force of it pulling at her, taking her farther and farther down to the murky depths of the lake.

It would be so easy to give way to weightlessness, so easy to surrender, to give herself up to the darkness waiting to claim her completely. A pleasant stupor stole over her and time lost all meaning, but from somewhere in the centre of her mind, the instinct for self-preservation made her fight the darkness in one last scramble for life. She flailed her arms, struggled to the surface and gulped for air as her head surfaced again, before darkness claimed her one more time.

Just when she thought all was lost, when she thought all the breath had been driven from her and her lungs would burst, she was sure she heard someone calling her name from up above, commanding her to live, and she felt herself being grasped and pulled upwards, strong arms encircling her waist. Again, her head appeared above the water, and this time someone was holding her, making it impossible for her to sink back into the slimy dark abyss of the lake.

Briefly her eyes flickered open and her heart soared when they became focused on Marcus's familiar beloved features. She was in no condition to ask what miracle had brought him to her when she needed help most, to snatch her from the very jaws of death. It was enough for her that he had come.

Barely conscious, she heard more voices as a boat was brought alongside and more arms reached out and pulled her up out of the water. Only when she felt the hard boards of the boat beneath her back did she realise she was safe. She felt her lips move, but no sound came for she was trembling too much. Hearing a buzz of voices coming from somewhere, her eyes flickered open for a brief moment, her vision obscured by mist, but she saw a blurred outline of someone bending over her. The excruciating terror of her ordeal had seeped into the deepest places of her mind and she was too weak, still too terrified to do anything other than shake, and giving a long shuddering sigh, she surrendered to the mist swirling all about her.

Marcus knelt beside his wife, cradling her head in his arms, unwinding her long sleek hair which had become tangled about her body. Her eyes were closed and circled with purple shadows, emphasised by the deathly pallor of her face. He called for someone to find something warm to wrap her in, and a blanket was quickly produced, which he wrapped around her, wiping her wet hair from her face before gripping her shoulders.

'Juliet, open your eyes. Please. I implore you.' He

shook her in an attempt to get her to look at him, the hideous fear which had gripped him when he thought he might lose her beginning to recede when he saw she was breathing. 'Juliet, look at me. For God's sake, open your eyes and let me see you are all right.' He watched as she gradually came out of the darkness that had engulfed her and opened her eyes. 'Thank God,' he said, feeling that nothing could be compared to the joy he felt. His voice and the expression on his face gave evidence to the relief he felt at that moment, but he cringed when he saw they were wild with terror. Death may have receded, but fear would take longer.

Feeling a surge of deep compassion, he drew her into his arms, holding her tight in an effort to convey to her some of his warmth. His love. In her fear and desperate need for comfort, he felt her press against him.

'Be still, my love, be still,' he murmured, gently placing his lips on her brow, speaking the words naturally, for never would he know such anguish, such agonising pain, as he had felt when, on being told both his daughter and his wife were missing, his instinct as well as the last sightings of them had drawn him to the lake.

When he had seen Juliet swimming in the dark water struggling in pursuit of the boat, all the demons in hell had broken loose inside his head. If he didn't reach her in time, she would be lost to him forever. He had seen half a dozen of his outdoor workers congregated on the head of the weir to apprehend the boat before it could be swept over the edge, where it would be in danger of tossing its passengers into the swirling, frothing whirlpool below.

'I will take care of you. Don't be afraid. Come, calm yourself. You're all right now. You're safe. It's all over.'

'Adele…' she croaked, the wildness back in her eyes as she remembered why she had been in the water.

'Adele is unharmed and quite safe,' he informed her, having seen his daughter plucked from the boat before it went over the edge of the weir, its other occupant not so lucky. Men were trying to retrieve Waring from the churning waters. 'We'll get you to the house. There you will be tended to. Do you understand what I am saying?'

Juliet managed to nod her head, the mist receding from her eyes, making Marcus's face clear to her. She saw his clothes were wet, his shirt clinging to his skin and his black hair glistening with droplets of water. Her eyes left his and became fixed on the glassy, rippling water of the lake, so calm now the storm had passed, giving no evidence of the tragedy which had taken place within its depths just a short while before. When the boat reached the shore, she was lifted out. Marcus carried her to the waiting carriage which had been sent from the house, as effortlessly as if she weighed nothing at all. On the journey back to the house, she clung to him, shaking uncontrollably, trying to speak, but her words were disconnected.

As Marcus carried her up to her room, where he was met by an anxious Daphne and an anxious Mrs Cherry following in her wake, her terror and trembling began to lessen as she became comforted by his warmth, by his strength, which stole over her, giving her security.

When he turned to leave her and knowing where he was heading, she sat up in alarm. 'You will be careful, Marcus,' she begged as he shrugged himself into his jacket over his wet clothes. 'I couldn't bear it if anything should happen to you.'

'I will,' he said hoarsely. 'Waring planned his strike with evil cunning. After what he has done this day, he has much to answer for. I do not intend to let him escape.'

With Juliet safe, Marcus went in search of his daughter and the perpetrator of this vicious deed. He left the house as Adele was being lifted out of the carriage swaddled in a warm blanket and being carried by one of the grooms. Overwhelmed with relief,

Marcus hugged and kissed her, trying not to imagine how he would have felt had she suffered the same fate as Waring. Having come to no harm except a soaking, her little face was smiling now, for the whole thing had turned into one big adventure she couldn't wait to tell her stepmother and her nurse about.

On reaching the weir, where the water tumbled over to the roiling depths below, he stood and watched the men at the water's edge trying to haul in the capsized boat that was bobbing about like a cork. One of his grooms turned when he saw the master.

'What's happening?' Marcus asked, having to raise his voice in order to be heard above the noise of the tumbling water.

'No sign of the man in the boat. It's thought he might be underneath, but until we can secure it, we can't be sure.'

'Has he surfaced at all?'

'Not that we know of. You can see for yourself how strong the current is. It will have dragged him under.'

Marcus stood and watched helplessly as his men worked frantically to overturn the boat. Eventually they succeeded and with poles with hooks attached, Thomas Waring was dragged from the water. He was laid on his back, his eyes wide open and staring, water trickling from his mouth. Marcus did not have to place his head on his chest and listen for a heartbeat that did not exist to know that Waring was dead.

* * *

Relief was clearly felt in the household when Juliet and Adele returned, mercifully virtually unharmed. On hearing of the events leading up to Adele's abduction, that she was taking her breakfast to the ducks on the lake when a gentleman had approached her and offered to assist her, after scolding her severely for going off and causing so much concern, making her promise that she would never wander off again without an adult, Marcus hugged his beloved daughter.

After removing her clothes and placing her in a hot mustard bath, her nursemaid put her to bed, where she was cosseted and pampered and fed by everyone, which pleased her enormously. Fortunately, she suffered no after-effects from the ordeal, not even a chill after getting a soaking from the rain and the spume of water overlapping the boat, but the story of all that had happened to her would be an adventure she would never tire of telling.

The day of Adele's abduction was like a grotesque nightmare to Juliet. It was as though all the energy she had concentrated on getting Adele out of Thomas's evil clutches had drained out of her, and her spirits sank to such a low ebb that for a while, as Daphne and Mrs Cherry fussed around her, she almost ceased to function.

When she heard the news of Thomas's death from

Daphne, who had been told of it from one of the searchers, who called at the house with the news, she was overcome with shock. When Marcus returned, he came straight to her. The house was quiet now, everyone having settled down to their work after the worry and excitement of the day's events.

As she came towards him, her hands outstretched, rage rose inside Marcus when he saw how deeply her ordeal at Waring's hands had affected her. Her eyes were enormous in her pale face, the dark circles of pain and worry making them look even larger. He opened his arms and she walked into them like a child seeking succour, but before she laid her head against his chest, he saw her chin tremble and tears she could no longer hold back brimming in her eyes and spilling over.

'Oh, Marcus, thank goodness you came in time.' She wept, over and over again, with her face against his chest, letting the violence of all the raw emotions that would not come before now flow uncontrollably out of her. He held her for a long time, rocking her and kissing her hair, murmuring sweet, gentle words of comfort while she sobbed, quietly and wretchedly, waiting patiently until she had mastered her tears, aching with a love for her that was like a deep, physical pain.

He cradled her in his arms, holding her close while

she poured out all her anguish and misery. Everything that had happened to her that day came out in a torrent of words, and he listened, knowing that it was good for her to talk like this, that it would help cleanse her of the evil Waring had perpetrated against her and Marcus and Adele. That it would help with the healing process later.

When she became still and quiet in his arms, feeling an unbelievable comfort of knowing he was holding her, that she was safe, she sighed, wiping her tears with her hands.

'My poor darling,' Marcus murmured, his lips against her hair. 'What has he done to you?'

'Nothing that won't heal,' she whispered bravely. 'I thank God that Adele is safe, that she is all right. According to Mrs Cherry, she has survived it well—better that I have myself, it would seem,' she said, smiling up at him through her damp lashes.

'Thank God.'

'I have been told that Thomas has drowned. Where is he? Where has he been taken?'

'He is here. Richard is taking care of everything. The carriage driver who brought him here is waiting. He is to write a letter to notify his father of what has occurred and have his body taken to Amberley Park.'

Juliet leaned back in Marcus's arms and looked up at him, her eyes luminous with tears. 'Thomas tried to destroy me, Marcus, to destroy us both—using your daughter to do it. If he had succeeded in getting to the other side of the lake, then I am certain he would have taken her away somewhere, and we would never have found her...'

Marcus's arms tightened around her. 'If he had succeeded in his vile plan, I would have found him, and he would not have escaped with his life,' he said hoarsely, his voice shaking with angry emotions. Taking her hand, he led her to the window seat, where they sat close together. He placed his arm around her, reluctant to let her go ever again. 'How are you feeling now?'

'Overwhelmed by a turmoil of emotions. It's a combination of relief, gladness and, at the same time, a feeling of horror mingled with some element of surprise, knowing that the man I once pledged to marry was the same man who would have let me drown in the lake, the same man intent on destroying our lives now dead himself. Oh, Marcus, I was so frightened when I thought I was going to die.'

Marcus held her tighter. 'So was I. When Joe Ruskin told me that Adele had gone to the lake with a man, I soon worked out that it had to be none other than Thomas Waring and that you had gone after them. You have no idea how my thoughts tormented me. What I went through.' Sighing, he kissed the top of her head where it rested on his shoulder. 'When I saw you in the lake, when you disappeared beneath the surface, I went through hell. I should have listened to Waring when he threatened to avenge me for all he had suffered at my hands. If I had, none of this is would have happened. I should have foreseen what he would do.'

'It wasn't your fault, Marcus. Neither of us was to know he would go to such drastic lengths.'

'You are very generous, but I cannot be acquitted so lightly, my love.'

Juliet stirred against him, raising her head and meeting his fierce gaze, seeing how much he had suffered on her behalf. 'Yes, you can. I think that my marrying you sent him to the far reaches beyond his control. I saw him in the boat which was heading towards the weir. The current was strong and he had lost control. He was looking at me, watching me as I struggled to get to Adele. There was madness in his eyes. He looked like a man possessed of the devil.'

'I would have had no compunction about killing him had I lost you.'

Juliet drew back and looked up at him, shuddering slightly on observing his taut features and the steely gleam in his eyes, knowing he spoke the truth. 'You would have done that for me?'

'I would do anything for you, Juliet,' he said achingly, unable to restrain himself, pulling her back into his arms. 'Never doubt it. I love you and cannot imagine my life without you. I adore you, Juliet.'

Juliet sighed, content to wallow in his doting gaze, having no doubts that he loved her—genuinely loved her. 'And I you, Marcus. I have come to love you dearly, and I cannot bear to think of my world without you in it.'

Marcus knew that the love between them would grow with time and supplant everything else in importance. He could see that in her eyes, and it made him ecstatically happy.

Epilogue

Richard's marriage to Amelia Fortesque, the Earl of Bainbridge's daughter, in the spring of the following year at the Palladian Fortesque House, was a truly grand affair. Adele was so excited she could hardly contain herself as she accompanied the other brides-maids in the wake of the bride. Juliet was relieved that her brother had turned his life around and that after all the years of neglect, the Endcliffe estate was showing signs of recovery.

Juliet was a vision of loveliness in a lavender gown, not quite as slender as she was for her own wedding to Marcus, due to the baby she was to bear two months hence. Her husband looked extremely hand-some in a midnight-blue jacket, beneath which he wore an ivory satin waistcoat, his dark hair brushed smoothly back from his brow.

The ceremony was followed by a wedding break-fast, where the atmosphere was light-hearted, and Juliet would catch her husband's eye and a smile would move across his lean face, his eyes becoming more vividly blue over the rim of his champagne glass, silently informing her of his impatience for them to be alone later. The love they felt for each other was plain to see; in fact, it was difficult to believe they were the same two people who had faced each other with so much rancour on their wedding day.

'Richard has done well for himself,' he told her softly when he managed to get her to himself for a brief moment. 'Things couldn't have turned out better.'

'And it is all down to you, Marcus. We would not be here now if you had not been there to guide and advise him. I'm thrilled for him. I have never seen him look more content, although I think Amelia has much to do with that. She's a truly delightful young woman, and it makes me happy to know she will be close enough for me to call on her and vice versa. She makes a beautiful bride, don't you agree, Marcus? Although I suppose all brides look radiant on their wedding day.'

'I only had eyes for the one,' he replied, his eyes caressing her upturned face. 'You were the most captivating young woman I had ever seen, and totally unaware of the effect you had on me.'

'And now?'

'Now that you are to bear our child, you look even more beautiful than you did that day.'

She smiled. 'I think you flatter me to tempt me, Marcus,' she teased.

'You are quite right,' he murmured, his eyes glowing with love and adoration as he gazed down at her. 'Are you complaining, Countess?'

'Not when I have such a passionate, attentive husband. But am I to believe you love me for my beauty alone?' she teased gently.

His features became solemn. 'No. I am not so stupid that I would have let your beauty alone make me love you. You have a multitude of other assets I admire and love. You are a rare being, Juliet. You are everything I dreamed a woman, a wife and a soon-to-be mother could be—and more.'

Juliet tilted her head up to his and could see he was perfectly serious. 'That is a compliment indeed, Marcus. Thank you.'

It was the greatest day Mulberry Hall had known for several decades when Marcus and Juliet's son was born, beginning a round of festivities suited to such an occasion. Happiness reigned over the great house, celebrating the new heir.

Marcus sat on the bed with his arm around Juliet, who was gazing at Adele looking adoringly down at her new brother sleeping in his crib beside the bed. He thought how changed she was. Happiness suited her. With the birth of their son her beauty bloomed with a new contentment and maturity as never before.

'What are you thinking?' she murmured.

'How lucky I am to have two wonderful children and such a beautiful wife—and how amiable you have become,' he teased gently. 'There is scarcely a trace of the contrary young woman I came to know in the early days of our acquaintance.'

'Do not be deceived, for she is still there, lurking somewhere in the background.' Juliet smiled softly, stirring within his arms, sighing and lifting her brilliant eyes to his, letting them feast on his handsome features. She adored this man, her husband, and everything about him, and she had come to know him like no other. 'She has not vanished. She is just waiting to be resurrected.'

'And you do love me, don't you, Juliet?'

'Absolutely. Have I not convinced you of it many times? When I have recovered from the birth of our son, I will show you how much.'

And she did, revealing the sweet anticipation of the rest of their lives to come.

* * * * *

COMING SOON!

We really hope you enjoyed reading this book.
If you're looking for more romance
be sure to head to the shops when
new books are available on

Thursday 24th October

To see which titles are coming soon, please visit

millsandboon.co.uk/nextmonth

MILLS & BOON

MILLS & BOON ®

Coming next month

ONE NIGHT WITH THE DUCHESS
Maggie Weston

'And you're here because…'

She exhaled a deep breath. 'I've come because…'

'Yes?' It was a single word, a simple word, but it left Matthew's lips weighted with anticipation.

'May I ask a favour?'

'You may ask,' he countered, 'but I will most probably refuse.'

'I would like you to bed me.'

Having become somewhat used to people expecting such behaviour from him, Matthew smiled grimly. But, in spite of that, when he said, 'No,' the word left his lips tasting bitter.

*

Isabelle was startled at the abrupt answer, issued from Lord Ashworth with no hint of doubt. 'You're not even going to *think* about it?'

The giant man standing in front of her grinned, his white teeth flashing wolfishly. He ran one large hand through his unstylishly shaggy hair.

'There's no need. I don't *bed* virgins. I don't ruin reputations—'

'That is not what I heard.'

Matthew ignored her comment. 'And I certainly will not be led by the nose into a situation where you could hold any sort of power over me. I'm not the man you're looking for, *Duchess*.'

Isabelle couldn't help the slightly hysterical giggle that worked its way up her throat. 'You… You think that I would trick you into *marriage*?' she asked, somewhat stunned by the notion. 'Have you not been listening to anything I've said?' She waved both hands down towards her heavy black dress. 'I'm in *mourning*. I will be for *years*!' she practically shouted. 'And even if I wasn't, marriage to you is the *last* thing I'd want!'

Because she felt hot and flustered by his looming presence and the entirely inappropriate conversation they were having, she started to pace.

She lowered her voice. 'I'm a *duchess*. I don't need your title. And marrying again before my mourning period is over would cause a scandal that would be completely antagonistic to my main goal—helping Luke.' When he only raised his eyebrows, she continued, 'Moreover, I have no *desire* to get married again.'

'But you're not a duchess—technically. And am I just supposed to trust whatever you say?'

Isabelle turned abruptly to find that he'd closed the space between them, and that instead of looking at his face she was staring at a patch of tanned skin where his collar lay open. She slowly craned her neck back, shifting her eyes away from his chest to his steel gaze.

'Do you honestly believe that I'd be here with any other motive? That I'd want to lose my—' she lowered her voice '—my *maidenhead* to a stranger whose name I picked off a list?'

Lord Ashworth did not try to fight his grin. 'You have a list?'

Continue reading
ONE NIGHT WITH THE DUCHESS
Maggie Weston

Available next month
millsandboon.co.uk

FOUR BRAND NEW STORIES FROM
MILLS & BOON MODERN

The same great stories you love,
a stylish new look!

OUT NOW

MILLS & BOON